INCOGNITO

What Reviewers Say About VK Powell's Work

Take Your Time

"The last book in the Pine Cone Romance series was excellent, and I reckon VK Powell wrote the perfect book to round up the series. …If these are the sex scenes VK Powell can write, then I have been missing out and I will definitely be checking out more because WOW! All in all… Fantastic! 5 stars"—*Les Reveur*

Captain's Choice

"VK Powell is the mistress of police romances and this one is another classic 'will she won't she' story of lost loves reunited by chance. Well written, lots of great sex and excellent sexual tension, great character building and use of the setting, this was a thoroughly enjoyable read."—*Lesbian Reading Room*

Deception

"In *Deception* VK Powell takes some difficult social issues and portrays them with intelligence and empathy. …Well-written, enjoyable storyline, excellent use of location to add colour to the background, and extremely well drawn characters. VK Powell has created a great sense of life on the streets in an excellent crime/mystery with a turbulent but charming romance."—*Lesbian Reading Room*

Side Effects

"[A] touching contemporary tale of two wounded souls hoping to find lasting love and redemption together. ...Powell ably plots a plausible and suspenseful story, leading readers to fall in love with the characters she's created."—*Publishers Weekly*

About Face

"Powell excels at depicting complex, emotionally vulnerable characters who connect in a believable fashion and enjoy some genuinely hot erotic moments."—*Publishers Weekly*

Exit Wounds

"Powell's prose is no-nonsense and all business. It gets in and gets the job done, a few well-placed phrases sparkling in your memory and some trenchant observations about life in general and a cop's life in particular sticking to your psyche long after they've gone. After five books, Powell knows what her audience wants, and she delivers those goods with solid assurance. But be careful you don't get hooked. You only get six hits, then the supply's gone, and you'll be jonesin' for the next installment. It never pays to be at the mercy of a cop."—*Out in Print*

"Fascinating and complicated characters materialize, morph, and sometimes disappear testing the passionate yet nascent love of the book's focal pair. I was so totally glued to and amazed by the intricate layers that continued to materialize like an active volcano... dangerous and deadly until the last mystery is revealed. This book goes into my super special category. Please don't miss it."—*Rainbow Book Reviews*

Justifiable Risk

"This story takes some unusual twists and at one point, I was convinced that I knew 'who did it' only to find out that I was wrong. VK Powell knows crime drama, she kept me guessing until the end, and I was not disappointed at the outcome. And that's not to slight VK Powell's knack for romance. ...Readers who appreciate mysteries with a touch of drama and intense erotic moments will enjoy *Justifiable Risk*."
—*Queer Magazine*

"*Justifiable Risk* is an exciting, seat of your pants read. It also has some very hot sex scenes. Powell really shines, however, in showing the inner growth of Greer and Eva as they each deal with their personal issues. This is a very strong, multifaceted book."—*Just About Write*

Fever

"VK Powell has given her fans an exciting read. The plot of *Fever* is filled with twists, turns, and 'seat of your pants' danger. ...*Fever* gives readers both great characters and erotic scenes along with insight into life in the African bush."—*Just About Write*

Suspect Passions

"From the first chapter of *Suspect Passions* Powell builds erotic scenes which sear the page. She definitely takes her readers for a walk on the wild side! Her characters, however, are also women we care about. They are bright, witty, and strong. The combination of great sex and great characters make *Suspect Passions* a must read."—*Just About Write*

To Protect and Serve

"If you like cop novels, or even television cop shows with women as full partners with male officers…this is the book for you. It's got drama, excitement, conflict, and even some fairly hot lesbian sex. The writer is a retired cop, so she really writes from a place of authenticity. As a result, you have a realistic quality to the writing that puts me in mind of early Joseph Wambaugh."—Teresa DeCrescenzo, *Lesbian News*

"*To Protect and Serve* drew me in from the very first page with characters that captivated in their complexity. Powell writes with authority using the lingo and capturing the thoughts of the law enforcers who make the ultimate sacrifice in the fight against crime. What's more impressive is the command this debut author has of portraying a full gamut of emotion, from angst to elation, through dialogue and narrative. The images are vivid, the action is believable, and the police procedurals are authentic. …VK Powell had me invested in the story of these women, heart, mind, body and soul. Along with danger and tension, Powell's well-developed erotic scenes sizzle and sate."—*Story Circle Book Reviews*

"*To Protect and Serve* drew me in from the very first page with characters that captivated in their complexity. Powell writes with authority using the lingo and capturing the thoughts of the law enforcers who make the ultimate sacrifice in the fight against crime."—*Just About Write*

Visit us at www.boldstrokesbooks.com

By the Author

INCOGNITO

by

VK Powell

2019

INCOGNITO

ISBN 13: 978-1-63555-389-5

This Trade Paperback Original Is Published By
Bold Strokes Books, Inc.
P.O. Box 249
Valley Falls, NY 12185

First Edition: July 2019

CREDITS
EDITOR: CINDY CRESAP
PRODUCTION DESIGN: SUSAN RAMUNDO
COVER DESIGN BY TAMMY SEIDICK

Acknowledgments

First, to Len Barot, Sandy Lowe, and all the other talented and insightful folks at Bold Strokes Books, thank you for allowing me to parlay my law enforcement career into stories of survival, the struggle to balance love and livelihood, and the fight between good and evil. I am grateful for the opportunities you afford me and for the guidance you continually provide through each project.

To Dennis and David for offering the perfect setting in which to write this story. Thanks for letting me house sit in your beautiful home—light and airy, near public transport for research trips and recreation, and close to more amenities than a girl could possibly enjoy in only three months' time.

Karen, thank you for the excellent tour around Port Botany, the explanation of the operation, and your patience with my never-ending questions. If any of the details in my account are incorrect, I accept full responsibility.

Cindy Cresap, many thanks for your time and attention on this project. Your fresh perspective and insights were invaluable. The steady doses of humor didn't hurt either. Hopefully, I learn something new with each project.

To my beta readers—D. Jackson Leigh, Jenny Harmon, and Mary Margret Daughtridge—you guys are the best! This book is better for your efforts, and I am truly grateful.

And last, but never least, to all the readers who support and encourage my writing, thank you for buying my books, sending emails, giving shout-outs on social media, and showing up for events. Let's keep doing this!

Dedication

To my beloved Aussie mate
for your time and the excursions around Sydney
to get everything just right. AIRTIC, still.

Prologue

US Marshal Evan Spears gathered the members of her team around her in the shadows of a loading dock near the runway used by private aircraft at Piedmont Triad International Airport. For over a year, her squad of four had assisted DEA in bringing down a large drug operation. She was proud of them. But the big guys, the brains behind everything, and the one responsible for orchestrating a murder, had persistently eluded capture. Tonight, their luck would run out.

Her informant said the three major players would be at the airport, attempting to flee the country on a chartered plane. The Embraer Phenom 100 light jet was already on the tarmac, fuel hose running to the right wing. As she watched, the hoses were disconnected, and the pilot conducted his exterior check of the plane in preparation for takeoff.

In a few minutes, the three criminals would be out in the open. There was no other way for them to board the plane. It was the perfect bottleneck. *Too perfect?* No. Evan pushed the nagging doubt away. Even the smartest criminals were stupid sometimes. And her source assured her they did not know their exit plan was compromised.

"Okay, guys." Evan didn't have to make eye contact with her agents to make sure they were listening, but she did anyway. As expected, their focus was absolute. "Just to review. Hank, you're covering the north side, Todd south, Maddie's got east, and Aaron will cover the west from the shadows here, in case they try to double back into the building." She pointed to the side of the loading dock. "Who has the warrants?"

"Here." Hank slapped the front of his vest.

"Good. Any questions?" Evan waited, but no one spoke. "Okay, let's get these guys. Take your posts and be careful."

She watched the team spread out across the tarmac, uncomfortable with just the five of them to arrest three fugitives, but this was a large coordinated operation and all the agencies were spread thin. Her guys knew what to do, and she trusted her informant, but a twinge of uncertainty shot through her. Just her overly cautious nature and adrenaline. Nothing more.

Her life was right on track—supervising agent, renovating the home of her dreams, exhilarating love life—and if this operation went well, she'd be top candidate to replace her boss when he retired in a couple of years. She'd be living the dream with an interesting woman, taking home a comfortable salary, and doing the work she loved, but first, she had to pull this arrest off without a hitch.

She glanced around the target area trying to spot her agents. If she could see them, the suspects probably could, but the guys had positioned themselves well in the shadows. She'd chosen not to use the airport staff's yellowish-green reflective vests because too many people on the tarmac this late at night would raise red flags.

"I've got movement on the south side," Todd whispered into the com unit. "Lone male."

"Hold," she replied. "Wait for the other two. We don't want to spook them." Evan watched the man walking toward the plane. Her pulse hammered, and sweat gathered under the heavy ballistic vest. Seconds ticked slowly past, and the man got closer to the plane. Where were the other suspects?

Her phone buzzed in the side of her vest and she started to ignore it, but her informant might have more information. Maybe there'd been a change of plans. "Spears."

"I fucked up."

The heat building under her vest turned to chills. "What do you mean you fucked up? Where are the other two?"

"They're not coming. I fucked up."

The informant's tone was harsh, almost trance-like. Evan's stomach tightened into a sick knot and she felt lightheaded. She tried to focus on the words but only caught a few.

"Not coming…escaped…warned them."

"*What?*" The line went dead, and the tarmac exploded with activity. A utility vehicle beeped at her from behind and breeched the target area. The jet engines whirred to life, drowning out other sounds.

"Evan, should we take him down?" Hank asked. "He's almost at the plane? Evan?"

She was still processing the phone call, and the grayish luggage train kept barreling forward. "Behind you, Aaron." He'd moved too close to the plane and couldn't hear over the engines. The driver swerved the vehicle suddenly, plowed into Aaron, and knocked him to the ground. "Take the suspect, Hank. You have command."

Evan dialed 911 as she ran toward Aaron. "This is US Marshal Evan Spears. I need an ambulance on the tarmac at PTI. Officer down." How had this happened? What had she done? As she knelt over Aaron and checked his pulse, she heard the answer as clearly as if someone screamed it. *You trusted the wrong person.*

CHAPTER ONE

A month later

Frankie Strong lay in bed and drew an imaginary connect-the-dots line through ceiling stains that resembled high-velocity impact blood spatter but could've been red wine. Still groggy from sleep, she took in the beige walls, beige carpet, and beige curtains of another hotel room, but where? Six years of DEA undercover had her changing legends and locations so often that every place felt the same—cold and lonely. She glanced at the notepad by the bed. Marriott Downtown. Greensboro.

"Damn." She jumped out of bed. Her boss was meeting her in the lobby in thirty minutes. She grabbed her clothes and thought about her last assignment shadowing another agent during a drug operation in the homeless community. She'd miss some of the colorful characters she'd encountered while posing as a mentally challenged street urchin. In some ways the homeless community had been more like family than her own. The lifestyle had a degree of predictability, an understanding that survival came first and treating everybody with respect was a given. She'd never felt she had to prove anything, but just like with her family and every other assignment, she'd never quite belonged because she was an imposter.

She wet her fingers and ran them through her hair to fluff the flattened parts and looked at herself in the mirror. But she'd also shot and killed a man during that operation, something she never imagined herself capable of. What came next, she had no idea. Maybe that was why Ted Curtis wanted to talk to her. She exited the elevator and spotted him in the lobby, and he waved her toward the restaurant.

"You didn't think I'd pass up a free meal? The agency is paying your tab, and I'm getting in on that action." Ted patted his abs and gave her a grin than colored his face all the way to the top of his bald head. "I don't run every day for nothing. I hear they have a great breakfast buffet for under twenty bucks. Have you tried it?"

"I'm not really a foodie or a morning person."

"You seriously need to eat more. You're looking a little twiggy."

Frankie trailed him through the buffet line and ended up with a small bowl of cottage cheese, some fruit, and coffee. Her stomach growled at the prospect as they settled at a table.

Ted scooped a forkful of omelet into his mouth and followed it with a slice of crispy bacon. "So, what happens now?"

She'd once dreamed of following in her parents' footsteps and traveling the world, but the experience had been spoiled. DEA briefly provided her with a feeling of stability and camaraderie until she landed in covert ops, which felt like being a drifter again. She'd enjoyed the freedom and results of undercover work, but since her last assignment, that too was tainted.

"I'm not sure." What she really wanted was a steady day job and a place to put down roots to test what normal might be like. She'd hoped to transition slowly, maybe start with a semi-permanent living space, but Ted was only concerned about her next assignment.

"You still don't know…because of the shooting," Ted said. "I get that, but you've got to move on." His green eyes sparkled a certain way when he was about to deliver what he considered a great idea. He already had something in mind.

"Just tell me the job, Ted."

"This is an opportunity to get back to work without going under again so soon." He waved a piece of bacon at her. "We don't have enough manpower to keep looking for Matthew Winston and Grady Tyndall from our drug diversion operation, so we're turning it over to the Marshals' Violent Fugitive Task Force. I thought you'd be an asset as a liaison. You can opt out of any operational stuff and won't need to be armed, if you're still uncomfortable with it."

"And who exactly would I *liaise* with?"

"The Marshals, of course. It's just a buzzword, for the record. Admin term."

Frankie stirred the multicolored fruit and lumpy white cottage cheese together in the bowl and felt sick. She hadn't realized until this moment how much she needed a break, a long one. "I don't know, Ted."

"As an incentive, while you're gone, I'll keep digging into that other matter you're so interested in. I can also ask the supervisor at the Marshals office to cut you some slack, if you work on the side. I've heard the task force leader is a real ballbuster and probably wouldn't appreciate you pulling double duty."

"What makes you think the Marshals will take me on?"

"You surveilled Winston's crew long before our other agent, Colby Vincent, went undercover with them. You know everything about the guy and how he operates. They'd be crazy to turn you down. Besides, helping to clear this case could do wonders for your career. It got Colby promoted to supervisor. And you'll still be on active status and have time to get over the shooting and adjust from being undercover. A smooth transition into a routine operation and casework, if that's what you want. What do you say?"

Maybe the new assignment was a good compromise, for the time being. And if she could kill two birds with one stone, all the better. She'd considered quitting after the incident, but it wasn't entirely the shooting that had thrown her off kilter. Just before the drug diversion operation started, she'd been wrapping up a human trafficking case in New York and seen a homeless man on the street who'd reminded her of the past, a past she'd sooner forget. The chance encounter had propelled her on a search for justice and redemption that was ongoing. "When do you need to know?"

"Before close of business today. You'd report to the Marshals office in the morning."

The offer didn't sound bad, and a task force meant more regular hours, a close-quarters supervisor, and rules—things she hadn't had in years and wasn't sure she could handle. Time and distance from the shooting and other memories of the assignment sounded good. If she had time, she'd surveil her potential boss, but Ted wasn't giving her much of a window.

Anyway, surveillance was detached—observations, times, dates—which left room for interpretation, nothing personal, no connection. She relied more on her senses, reading people's eyes, expressions, behaviors, and then tailoring her approach. Rule number one in swindling and undercover—know your mark. She'd have to go in blind on this one. "Fine. I'll do it."

Evan leaned against the iron railing of her loft bedroom drinking a lunchtime coffee and taking in her warehouse residence. She and her brother, Eli, had converted a portion of the upstairs into her master suite and added an industrial catwalk that encircled what would eventually be the living area downstairs. She loved the new windows set into exposed brick walls that let in light at all times of the day. Eventually, the space would feel more like a home than a construction zone. She envisioned retro furniture dotting the polished concrete floors, several comfy sofas and recliners for lounging, and plush rugs for the times when she wanted to roll around like a kid. Homey it was not, not yet.

But for now, the bleakness and solitude were what she needed, most of the time. However, today she wanted someone to confirm she was doing the right thing by keeping her team of US Marshals sidelined, that she wasn't being overprotective or paranoid. She squeezed the railing, feeling the dimpled texture bite into her palm and drawing strength from the rough reclaimed material. She got paid to make the tough decisions, and taking her team off active status had been one of the hardest.

At the bottom of the floating staircase, she placed her coffee cup on a rolling cabinet that served as a temporary kitchen island and glanced longingly at black wiring coiled against the walls like serpents. She'd much rather stay here and install outlets. The deadline she and Eli had set for that particular task had come and gone. She gave herself a pep talk on the drive back to her office at the federal courthouse, but it lacked conviction.

Evan aligned the case file in the center of her desk and glanced up at the three current members of her Violent Fugitive Task Force as they came in from an afternoon break. Today was the first time they'd all been together since Aaron's injury, and she'd wanted to say something…what? Inspiring, apologetic, sincere? But morning had slipped into afternoon and she'd said nothing. She tried to pretend this was like any other day. The guys were getting on with their work, minus some of their usual levity. She'd left them to reestablish their routine again, but the air felt heavy with tension or possibly her own guilt. "How's it going?"

"We're finishing the paperwork from yesterday, but with all due respect, we'd be more productive chasing fugitives." Hank, her second-in-command toed the line between hard-nosed marine and politician but usually erred on the side of politics. She appreciated his tact because she often leaned more toward the hardline.

She'd heard the argument before and didn't answer. After Aaron's injury and Madeline's transfer, Evan was left with only a functional two-man team and herself, which presented an unacceptable risk in the field, a risk she wasn't willing to take, especially after the last botched arrest. So, at her request, the team was managing background, research, and tech support for other active operations.

"Yeah, you've got to get us off this desk surfing gig before we start gnawing off our fingers," Todd added in a distinctive Southern drawl. Diplomacy was a dirty word to him. He always said exactly what he meant, but he was a hell of an agent. She'd gladly take a whole team like him, even if she had to spend more time doing cleanup with the brass.

Aaron stuck his head between the two large computer screens that served as his workstation, took off his round Harry Potter glasses, and shrugged. "Sorry, guys, if I could walk, you know I'd be just as eager to take a case." He shouldered more than his share of the blame for the team being sidelined.

Evan was the reason he couldn't walk now, possibly ever, and she'd never forgive herself. She met his gaze and tried to convey her apologies for the millionth time, but it didn't make her feel any better and doubted it helped him either. Her carelessness cost Aaron his mobility and what she thought would be her happily ever after. The only thing left in her life was work and the burden to prove once again that she could handle the job.

She couldn't face these men every day and have them think she was a spineless supervisor who couldn't accept responsibility for her mistakes. She took a deep breath and summoned her courage. "Hey, guys, it's Aaron's first day back, and I need to say something."

Hank and Todd placed their papers on their desks, and Aaron rolled his wheelchair from behind his computer. Everyone focused on her.

"It's my fault things went wrong on the arrest, and I can't fix what happened. If you want to transfer or ask for another supervisor, now's your chance. No hard feelings. I'll give you good recommendations." The room was quiet for several seconds, and Evan held her breath.

"Fuck that," Todd said. "Shit happens. I'm staying put. We're a team."

Aaron inclined his head toward Todd. "What he said. You've apologized like a thousand times. Stop already. It's getting embarrassing."

She could've kissed him. Aaron was not only smart but he also had a huge heart and sometimes too much compassion.

Hank was usually the last to answer any question, cautious and discreet to a fault. "We've been through a lot, and we all share responsibility for what happened that day. Someone we thought was a friend wasn't, so stop trying to be some kind of martyr. Nobody's transferring or asking for another supervisor. You're stuck with us and vice versa."

Evan's throat tightened, and she fought back the tears clouding her vision. "Thank you, guys. You're the best US Marsh—" Her phone rang, saving her from making a complete ass of herself. "Hello?"

"Evan, come to my office," her boss said.

She rose from her desk and pointed to the ceiling, the group sign for orders from above. "Call it a day, guys. See you in the morning." She took the stairs of the Preyer Federal Courthouse to Michael English's office, and his receptionist waved her in.

"Ah, you're here. Good." Michael rose and offered his hand. She liked working for him because he'd made his way up through the ranks, not been handed his position by some politician, and he was honest and dedicated to his agents.

"Afternoon, sir." She stood at attention, affording him the respect of his former military rank of colonel.

He gave her a careful visual once-over. "Still not sleeping?"

"Some better, not much, but I'm managing."

"And you're FFD?"

"Of course, I'm fit for duty, sir. And Aaron's back with us. It's all good." She told herself that every morning while staring in the mirror and willing her mind and body to comply. She'd messed up, gotten an agent hurt, and would wear the scar the rest of her life.

He motioned to a leather chair in front of his desk and sat back down. "Excellent, because I have good news and bad. Which do you want first?" Michael flipped his head and a shock of blond hair shifted sideways across his forehead and back into place, a tell she recognized as nerves.

"The good."

"I'm returning your team to field duty. I need you to find Matthew Winston and his associate, Grady Tyndall, from that DEA drug diversion operation."

Evan's knees trembled, and she lowered herself into the chair. The guys would be ecstatic, but she was having trouble seeing past the complications. "Aaron is still on light duty."

"And he can do his techie thing from his wheelchair. He'll continue to provide the same excellent support he always has."

"That still leaves us an agent short for field operations."

Michael picked up a file but didn't make eye contact, and Evan prepared for the rest. "Which brings me to the bad news. You're sort of getting a new team member—"

"But—"

"Let me finish, Evan. You're getting a new team member as a liaison for this case, not permanently. A DEA agent with extensive knowledge of Winston, his associates, and operation. This is a gift-wrapped bonus for us."

Evan shook her head. "I don't have time to teach a DEA agent our protocols. He'll need to bond with the guys before we work together as a team. And seriously, boss, DEA and the Marshals operate on different wavelengths. You know how it is."

Michael flipped his head twice. "About that...it's not a *he*."

Evan felt the blood rush from her face and her body chilled. "Sir, please."

"It's a done deal. We need the intel she has."

The team could be further fragmented by the introduction of some random agent so soon after Aaron's injury and Madeline's transfer. And she damn sure wasn't ready to trust another outsider, agent or not. "Can't we just debrief her and move on with our guys?"

"No, we can't. She'll be here in the morning. Here's her file."

She didn't reach for the folder Michael held, not ready to accept the inevitable. "Full personnel jacket? Background and everything?" Evan wasn't leaving anything to chance.

"Her work file, which is all that's relevant at this stage. Her childhood, psyche eval, blah, blah, blah won't tell you anything about how she operates. Look at her past performance."

Evan continued to stare at the folder with its curled and brown edges. Someone had reviewed this file, often. "I'd like a complete picture of who I'm being stuck with, if you don't mind, sir."

"And I'm saying it's not relevant. The important part for you is that she's been unsupervised for a while, but you can handle that. Like I said, she's a liaison, not really your direct report. Think of her as your equal, so no supervisory headaches. Read her file before you go and leave it on my desk. You can use the conference room. Winston has a three week jump on us because the locals and DEA have been chasing leads in the States, not thinking he'd left the country."

"Are we sure he has?" Evan was grasping at anything to keep this roller coaster from barreling over her, but Michael's expression said she couldn't refuse the case.

"Not definitely, but he's a man with extensive international resources, and the trail has gone cold here." He placed the case file on the edge of his desk and tapped the cover. "Can you handle this, Evan?"

She stood, finally took the personnel file from his hand, and met his gaze, trying to convey confidence she didn't feel. "Yes, sir, but I still want to see her complete personnel file at some point." What else could she say? She'd worked too long as a US Marshal to admit that a single mistake in judgment had her questioning every decision. "Is there anything else?"

"Just one more thing. I've given her leeway to tie up loose ends on an old case."

"So, she won't be totally focused on this assignment?" The thought sent a shiver down Evan's spine. Distractions led to mistakes, which resulted in bigger problems. She shook her head. "I have to take on a rogue DEA agent whose attention will be divided between our fugitive case and whatever else she's working on."

"She won't be actively pursuing another case, just searching for information. I granted her a degree of flexibility as a favor to DEA in exchange for her expertise on Winston."

"That doesn't exactly reassure me, sir. Flexibility to an agent who's been undercover so long can mean anything."

"I trust you to handle the situation as you see fit."

Evan couldn't help digging for more. "Do her loose ends have anything to do with Madeline's case?" Madeline's case, which had everything to do with Evan's latest mistake and would definitely spill over to this operation.

"No, it's nothing that will affect your pursuit of these fugitives."

Maybe not, but worrying when the new agent's agenda would jump up and bite her in the ass would certainly be distracting. Command was a double-edged sword, sometimes a blessing, others a curse. Today definitely felt like the latter. She gave Michael her best blank-faced smile. Mental or emotional preoccupation could be just as dangerous as a physical liability, and she was betting the new agent came with plenty of both.

CHAPTER TWO

Frankie stood on tiptoes and peeked through the square window in the office door to get a lay of the land before going inside. A typical government office—open rectangular space with conference room and a hallway leading farther back, probably to interview areas. Three old wooden desks, two occupied and one covered with papers, a more modern setup with computer stack, also occupied, and a sleek metal and glass desk off to the side completely clean. She balanced the biscuit bag on top of the donut box with one hand and opened the door with the other. "Somebody order room service?" She shouldered the door wider and smiled.

The three men gave her skeptical stares until a guy with a military haircut moved forward, blocking her path. "We seldom turn down food, but are you sure you're in the right place?"

"Violent Fugitive Task Force?"

"Damn right." A guy with sandy red hair and a light mustache, resembling a young Ron Howard, rose from his desk. "Let her in, Hank. She had to have ID to get past security." He turned to Frankie. "We'll gladly unburden you."

When marine guy stepped aside, Frankie headed straight for the vacant desk and spread the food out on top. The guys gawked, but she put it down to her spiked hair and eclectic clothes and offered her hand. "I'm Frankie Strong, DEA, assigned to your task force temporarily as a liaison on the Winston case."

"Todd Dean." The red-mustached man spoke first. "Welcome aboard. What's in the bag?"

"Biscuitville biscuits, half ham and egg, half bacon and egg."

"Sweet." Todd took two donuts from the box and slid them on his thumb like rings and pulled two biscuits from the bag. He walked to the third man in the room who sat in a wheelchair behind two huge computer screens and deposited half his bounty on the desk. "And this is Aaron Isley, aka Harry Potter." Todd drew circles around his eyes and pointed to Aaron's black, round-rimmed glasses. "Potter's our tech genius."

"Hi, Aaron, nice to meet you." Aaron pushed the glasses up on his nose, and Frankie could've sworn he blushed. She wondered how he'd ended up in a metal chariot, but a first meeting wasn't the time to ask no matter how many biscuits and donuts she brought. "Please tell me you have coffee."

"Always," Aaron said, pointing to a corner cabinet with a Keurig on top.

Frankie waited for the military man to introduce himself, but he was still evaluating her. There was always one who required more work, but she'd learned the fine art of wooing and winning friends at an early age. "Have I screwed up already?"

He finally offered his hand but kept looking to where she'd deposited her bribes. "Hank Korley. Thanks for this."

"Is something wrong, Hank?"

He turned to Aaron and pointed at the food-strewn desk. The three men shared a laugh, and Hank added, "I'll let you find out for yourself. Experience is sometimes the best teacher."

Frankie made a cup of coffee, perched on the edge of the desk beside the food, and grabbed a chocolate glazed custard filled donut. She chewed for a bit and let the silence settle while the others enjoyed the treats. When the time felt right, she said, "Wish I had a dollar for each stale donut I've fished out of dumpsters."

"I was so hungry on a stakeout one time..." Todd said, his tale was drowned out by boos and hisses from the other guys.

"Not that tired old story again," Aaron said.

Pretty soon everyone was sharing war stories, the yarns growing bigger and the laughs louder. When the laughter died, they all migrated toward the coffee pot again, and Frankie got down to business.

"So, who's the boss of this crowd? If I had to guess, I'd say Hank." She already knew the answer from her late-night intelligence gathering, but stroking the reluctant one sometimes produced results, and a few minutes alone with the troops went a long way toward bonding.

"Nope," Hank said. A cautious man or a political one. She wasn't sure yet.

"Evangeline Spears," Todd said, "Evan when she's nice. Spears when she's not and stabs you with those black eyes."

"Is she a ball breaker?"

Hank stuffed the remainder of a donut in his mouth to keep from answering, and Aaron chose that moment to adjust the arms of his wheelchair but finally looked up and said, "She's a good supervisor."

"She could stand to loosen up a bit," Todd added. "Too by the book sometimes, but she has her reasons." He glanced at Aaron.

Hank and Todd seemed particularly attentive to Aaron, and neither of them was telling Frankie everything, but she understood their reluctance. She was the new kid who had to prove her loyalty and reliability, but she tried once more. "What reasons?"

Hank cleared his throat. "I'm not sure we should talk about this right now."

"Why not?" Todd asked, flicking donut sugar from his moustache. "Everybody knows what happened." His tone was a cross between sadness and anger, but Frankie couldn't tell which was dominant or to whom his anger was directed.

"Not now," Hank said. "Leave it."

"Okay, no problem, guys," Frankie said. "Guess I better be ready for anyth—"

The office door swung open, and Evan Spears stood framed in the doorway. She was taller than Frankie had imagined, and the ankle-length black coat gave off a Gestapo vibe. The guys straightened a little as she passed. When she briefly focused on Frankie, a feeling shot through her as intense and fleeting as Evan's dark gaze.

"What's going on?" Evan's tone was cool, matter-of-fact, and her presence filled the room with confidence and the protectiveness of a mother bear for her cubs. "Who are you, and what can we do for you?"

"Boss, this is—"

She stuck out her hand. "Thank you, Hank, but I asked *her*."

Frankie imagined the mental ticks as Evan visually assessed her—small stature, weird hair, eccentric vibe, and shabby clothes, which now seemed a poor statement choice. Frankie looked like a vagabond off the street compared to Evan's tailored shirt, trousers, and dapper tweed jacket that screamed money, style, and control—three things Frankie couldn't claim.

Without her usual surveillance to fall back on, she had no idea what Evan was like, so she kowtowed, offering her hand and infusing her tone with deference. "DEA agent Francesca Strong, reporting for duty, but you can call me Frankie. You must be Evan Spears. Pleased to meet you, ma'am."

Evan didn't shake her hand. "I am, and it's customary to report to the agent in charge on a new assignment."

"But you weren't here—"

"I'm not sure how DEA operates, but in the Marshals Service we follow protocol."

The line was clearly drawn—hard-ass supervisor, by the book operation. Nothing to do but play along and try to win her over. "I apologize, ma'am. I meant no disrespect. I brought a goodwill gesture." She motioned toward where she'd left the food. All that remained were the empty biscuit bag, donut box, and the crumbs and powdered sugar that coated the glass surface of the desk.

Evan's face paled. Shit. The boss's desk. From her horrified expression, Frankie guessed Evan was a control freak. The learning experience Hank mentioned. She was off to a terrific start.

Evan bit her lip to keep from saying something she'd regret. Michael had refused her final appeal this morning, and she'd returned to the office in a foul mood. She'd watched from the hallway as Frankie, with the blond spikes of an eighties rocker and ill-fitting thrift store clothes, threw the room and her agents into chaos. Evan's desk had become a health hazard while the guys swapped war stories and scattered biscuit crumbs instead of work. But Frankie also laughed and bonded with the guys easily, something Evan envied. She wasn't sure she'd managed that after three years with them.

"Let me clean this up," Frankie said. "Sorry. I didn't realize this was your desk and you were so—"

"So what?" Evan snapped.

"Tidy."

The guys snickered behind her, and Evan whirled and waved the case file at them. "Get back to work, if you're not in a carb coma."

"Right, boss. On it, boss," Todd answered, grinning like a drunken fool.

When she turned around, Frankie was bent over the desk, working furiously at the mess, her butt swaying side to side. Her cropped top had crept up, revealing the pale skin of her back and a prominent spine and ribs—the embodiment of the street urchin, Sing Song, she'd portrayed in her last undercover job. Had she starved herself for the role or had the assignment and subsequent shooting taken its toll like Evan's last case? She shook her head. As long as Frankie could physically perform the job, it was none of Evan's concern.

"Again, I'm sorry for this." Frankie rubbed the powdered sugar with her hands, smeared it, and wiped the residue down the legs of her black tights.

"You're just making it worse." Evan shooed Frankie away and took a pen from her inside jacket pocket to push the box and bag off the desk into the trash can beside it. "Go to the bathroom down the hall, get some wet paper towels, and take care of this. I'll wait for you in the conference room." She nodded toward a small glassed-in space.

When Frankie disappeared down the hall, Evan turned back to her team. "Quick. What do you think? We could be stuck with her temporarily."

"She fits nicely in our gang of misfit toys," Todd said. "I like her."

"You like anybody who feeds you, Todd. What about you, Aaron?" He often sensed nuances the rest of them missed, and his opinion mattered most.

"She's nice."

"That's all? *She's nice?*" Somebody besides her had to see the problem with Frankie.

Hank sat at his desk clicking his favorite Marines logo pen on the surface and catching it as it sprang in the air. "Hank, care to weigh in?"

"She's friendly and seems to fit in..."

Evan had chosen the perfect team to supplement her deficits—Todd was personable and completely open; Aaron's emotional intelligence and tech skills were invaluable; and Hank kept her politically informed, but he was holding back. "I'm sensing a but, Hank. Hurry. She'll be back any minute."

"The two of you'll clash, big time. Oil and water. But if you can handle the pressure, we'll be fine with her. Your call, boss."

Hank nailed it. According to her file, every assignment Frankie had worked at DEA in her six-year career had been long-term undercover, basically unsupervised. Reintroducing an agent with that kind of experience to a team with defined protocols would be a supervisor's nightmare, regardless of Michael's reassurance that she'd have no direct supervisory responsibility.

She started toward the conference room and remembered her other news. "By the way, we've got a new case. In the field. I'll brief you as soon as I finish her orientation." The guys cheered as she closed the door behind her. If they were as happy a week from now, she'd be astonished. Francesca Strong was trouble.

A few minutes later, Frankie tapped on the door and came in without waiting for an answer. "I think your desk is as clean as before, but I didn't know where to put your stuff."

"Fine." Evan waved her to a chair on the opposite side of the table. First order of business, maintain distance and keep things professional. "Tell me about the Winston case."

Frankie pinned her with blue eyes so wide that she looked almost frightened, but in their depths, Evan detected only determination and curiosity. She quickly glanced away. Staring into someone's eyes was a gift that conveyed respect, interest, or sexual curiosity, none of which she was about to afford Frankie Strong.

"The Winston case, a prescription drug diversion operation utilizing homeless vets as the distribution ring. I was undercover as a homeless, mentally ill woman and conducted extensive surveillance on the boss and the group's MO before agent Colby Vincent infiltrated the gang."

"The homeless are basically invisible to the world, but a mentally challenged individual is even more so. People avoid you like three-day-old fish left in the sun. I got close, really close." Her voice dropped to a suggestive timbre on the last two words, and Evan shifted uncomfortably.

Frankie swiped a hand through her hair, and Evan noticed a hole under the arm of her beige linen shirt. The fabric was so worn Frankie's nipples stood out prominently. She obviously didn't wear a bra but really didn't need one, a distinction Evan shouldn't have noticed as a supervisor but found hard to ignore as a woman. She looked back at the open folder in front of her. In her experience, an agent who didn't take pride in her appearance probably let other things slide as well. Her reservations about Agent Strong increased by the minute.

"Do you have other questions, Agent Spears?"

Frankie smiled, revealing slightly crooked top teeth, compatible with the rest of her eccentric appearance, which gave Evan a sense of appreciation for the uniformity. After reading Frankie's file, even one degree of consistency was appreciated.

"Your record in undercover assignments is impressive. Weapons smuggling operation with a group of skinheads, human trafficking in the Asian community, and back-to-back drug cases, one involving a motorcycle gang, the other in the homeless community. You're apparently quite resourceful."

"And that worries you."

Frankie picked up on her tone and accurately interpreted its meaning, which didn't surprise Evan, because Frankie survived dangerous situations by reading people's emotions and the subtleties of their behavior. But Evan was usually better at hiding her own feelings, and would be again. "My concern is the amount of time you've spent undercover, which can lead to isolation, temptations of the criminal lifestyle, and problems readjusting to the real world."

Frankie nervously twirled a black and silver ring on her left thumb with her index finger before meeting Evan's gaze. "I'm afraid you have me at a disadvantage. You've obviously read my file. Personal history too or just the work parts?"

"Why? Is there something in your background I need to know? Something relevant?" Frankie shook her head, and Evan added, "Work history only."

"Care to share your assignments, Agent Spears?"

Frankie had courage for someone in what amounted to an employment interview, and Evan admired that, but asserting it so early was also another warning sign, an indication of her years without supervision and lack of command etiquette. "This meeting is about whether you can adapt to working with other agents."

"Let's be honest, Evan."

"Agent Spears."

"Fine, Agent Spears. This meeting is about sizing me up. I'm on the team whether you like it or not, and my guess is you don't. Not sure why, but the vibe is clear." Frankie lowered her gaze and let out a long breath before continuing in a softer, more conciliatory tone. "All I ask is that you judge me by results, not words on a page."

Evan bit back a retort about ends not always justifying the means and turned to the other issue. "I hate to bring it up, but are you still having problems from the shooting? PTSD?" Frankie didn't move, her expression blank, and her eyes focused on something in the distance—a trained response Evan also used to portray calm and control while covering her emotions.

"An occasional bad dream, but I'm managing."

Evan had told Michael she was managing as well. Everybody had the right to handle their emotional issues as they saw fit until it interfered with the job. She'd have to afford Frankie the same courtesy. "Medication?"

"Never."

"That's good." Evan jotted a few notes and tried to get a read on Frankie, but her expressions were as impassive as the roles she'd played in the field were varied.

"Is there something else you want to ask, Agent Spears?" Frankie slouched in the chair, stretched her legs out under the table, touched Evan's foot, and didn't pull back.

Evan's muscles tightened at the contact, but she forced herself not to react. Was the touch inadvertent or was Frankie testing her, pushing for a reaction, hoping to throw Evan off kilter? Men in positions of authority had tested her in the past, and she'd managed them with ease. Whatever Frankie's game, it further proved her recklessness, and Evan wasn't playing. After a few seconds passed to acknowledge the contact and show she wasn't bothered by it, Evan pulled her feet up under her chair and took a deep breath. "How do you feel about working with a team under supervision?"

Frankie glanced up at Evan through thick black lashes that contrasted with her blond hair. "Honestly, I get along with most people. Guess that's why I'm your liaison, which doesn't really make you my boss, Agent Spears."

"So Michael tells me, but every team has a leader. Since we're being honest, I'm not comfortable having you work on something that distracts your attention from this case. Care to share what that's all about?"

"I'll be tracking down some information on a cold case. Nothing to do with Winston, and I assure you, I won't be distracted, even if you try to play boss."

Was Frankie trying to irritate her or was she flirting? Evan tamped down her snarky comeback and kept it professional. "The Marshals have strict policies and procedures that must be followed to assure our cases are legally sound. If you work with us, in whatever capacity, you have to follow the guidelines, and it's my job to see that you do. Can you understand that?"

"I understand policies and procedures, but I don't agree with always following them to the letter. You have heard of the spirit of the law and officer discretion?" Frankie grinned and brushed the edge of her top teeth with her tongue.

The action was as provocative as Frankie's comment, but Evan would not be provoked or distracted, not again. "Maybe that approach works in undercover work, but not here. If that's your attitude, this arrangement isn't going to work. I'd appreciate any intelligence you have about Winston's activities, but we don't need you." She gathered the file and stood to leave. Convincing Michael that Frankie was unsuitable would be a problem, but she'd damn sure try again. "I'll brief my supervisor, and he'll contact yours. Thank you for coming in."

"Evan…Agent Spears, wait." Before Evan got to the door, Frankie was at her side. She held her palms up and all flippancy vanished. "Wait." Her tone was almost pleading.

Evan wavered at the sad tone and its underlying urgency. Why did Frankie want this so much? What wasn't she saying? An image of another eager face masking deceit flashed through Evan's mind and her resolve returned. "I can't risk the safety of my team on someone who can't take direction. I won't."

Frankie reached out and almost touched Evan's arm before pulling back. "Give me a chance? You don't have to trust me yet. I know I have to earn that. Just let me work."

"Why should I take a chance on you?"

Frankie fiddled with her ring again before answering. "Because Matthew Winston is responsible for the death of a good man and the betrayal of honorable veterans. I was almost sexually assaulted on this case, starved myself for months, killed a man, and came face-to-face with part of my past I never knew existed. The bastard owes me. We want the same thing. I promise I'll make this work."

Evan held Frankie's gaze and felt her anger, pain, and frustration. And damn it, she believed her. She prayed her instincts got this one right. "Let's brief the team."

"Should we hug it out first?" Frankie opened her arms and moved toward Evan with a roguish grin, her energy once again playful. Whether she was being purposely unprofessional, stupid, or just risky, it was hard to tell.

"Don't push it." When Evan opened the door and waved at Frankie, the guys cheered.

"Guess we have a new squad member, right?" Todd asked.

"Looks like you're stuck with me." Frankie gave Todd and Aaron a fist bump before glancing at Evan. "For now."

"Let's get you guys back in the field before I end up in an insane asylum." Evan slid four stapled packets of information from a folder and distributed them. "This is what we have on the drug diversion case and Winston's possible connection to the murder of Franklin Weber. Read it tonight and let's discuss recommendations for how to locate Winston and Tyndall. We've had a nationwide alert out for the past three weeks with no results, and international inquires have turned up nothing. He might have left the country, but we're not sure."

"What can the new kid tell us?" Hank asked, nodding at Frankie.

"Let's hold off on that until tomorrow," Evan said. "I'd like fresh eyes on the details before we hear from Agent Strong." She looked at the clock and decided the guys deserved a break, and she needed time to process her impressions of Frankie and make one more appeal for access to her full personnel file. "Let's make an early day of it. You've got reading to do. See you tomorrow, and be ready to hit the ground running."

"Lunch is on me at Stumble Stilskins," Frankie said, to another round of cheers. Hank led the way, and Todd helped push Aaron out, but Frankie stopped in front of Evan's desk. "Are you joining us?"

"No, but thanks for asking."

"And thank you for giving me a chance."

Without looking up, Evan replied, "Don't make me sorry." Anger, pain, and frustration like she'd seen in Frankie's eyes motivated good agents, but it could also make them careless. She watched Frankie walk away and already regretted her decision.

CHAPTER THREE

Frankie lay in bed and stared at the dubious red ceiling stains, waving her finger back and forth in different patterns. She needed a home with her own stains and permanent neighbors. Her whole life felt temporary, full of false identities and misleading information instead of her own history and experiences. But today was a new beginning. She'd show Evan Spears that she was valuable to the team and could be trusted to do the job. After a quick shower, she packed a bag with everything she'd need and headed to the front door.

She ran down ten flights of stairs, dumped her green straw bag on the running board of her old Vespa scooter, cranked the engine with a single try for once, and coasted down the garage exit ramp. Scooting around town on her orange baby, whizzing in and out of traffic worked for her.

She flashed her credentials to courthouse security, surrendered her bag for X-ray, and a few minutes later, walked into the squad office. "Greetings, US Marshals. No need for applause. I'll be in the area all day. Feeling all right, Aaron? How's it hanging, Todd?" She saluted in Hank's direction, but no one returned her greeting. So much for yesterday's donut and biscuit goodwill. She was back on the new girl list.

Evan drilled her with a stare and made a point of checking her watch.

"What's up?"

"You're late," Evan said, her tone somewhere in the subzero vicinity.

"It's only nine."

Todd snickered and quickly covered it with a cough.

"Exactly. We start work at eight o'clock. Sharp."

Frankie dropped her bag on the old wooden desk that yesterday had been stacked with papers, assuming it was now hers, and turned to Evan. "Seriously?" Evan pursed her usually pouty lips into a tight line. "I didn't get *that* memo. Did you mention work hours yesterday?"

Evan swapped the position of a pen holder and stapler on her desk and then switched them back, probably realizing she hadn't mentioned the schedule. "For future reference. Eight. Be on time. And I need your cell number and address. Ted Curtis didn't have either."

"He should have my address since DEA is paying the tab and he's enjoyed the free breakfast buffet a couple of times already. Marriott Downtown, room 1110."

Aaron grinned at her and nodded.

"I like the view. And I don't have a cell."

"What?" Todd piped up from his corner desk. "Are you one of those Lutherans?"

Hank shook his head. "Don't you mean Luddites, country boy?"

"Whatever, she knows what I mean. Well, are you?"

"No. Technology and I just don't mesh. I had one, but it got broken or something." She sat down, leaned back, and the chair kept going. Flailing her arms, she reached for the desk, but the chair stopped just before she tipped over. "Shit."

Everybody laughed, including Evan.

"New girl initiation?" Frankie asked, bending over to readjust the seat tension.

"My bad," Todd said, "but I didn't take the bolt completely out."

"Thanks for that," Evan said. "I'm not sure the government could afford the lawsuit. Now back to business. I'll have a phone for you by the end of the day." She came around the front of her desk and tapped on her tablet.

Frankie settled in her chair without acknowledging, determined Evan wouldn't wear her down with petty details, but she had to admit Evan was totally hot when she got bossy. Evan cocked a jeans-clad leg on the corner of her desk, and Frankie flashed on an image of her dressed in only her long black coat, unbuttoned, stalking toward her in the bedroom. Frankie shivered and licked her lips.

But Evan didn't get where she was on her looks or by being timid. Frankie knew from experience women didn't fight those battles without collecting scars. Evan had risen in a male-dominated profession by sheer tenacity and hard work, but what had it cost her?

"I assume everybody read the brief?" Evan asked. "We have drug charges on both Winston and Tyndall, but only suspicion about their connection to Franklin Weber's murder. So, what do we know, how do we find out more, and how do we locate them?"

"Maybe we should reinterview Robert Griffin, the guy we arrested at the airport." Hank said. "He's been in jail three weeks, and nobody has made a second pass at him. Incarceration sometimes loosens the tongue."

Exactly what Frankie thought, but she waited to see if anyone else brought it up first. She didn't want to seem like the new kid trying to impress the teacher. She noticed, irrelevantly, how Evan's eyes darkened almost to black as she glanced at her tablet and considered all the angles. She had to think it over? It was a no-brainer. A leader who had a hard time with easy decisions would be difficult to trust when the shit hit the fan and she had to make hard decisions fast. Tension slowly squeezed the muscles in Frankie's neck. This was why she preferred to work solo.

"Good idea, Hank. Take Todd with you," Evan said.

"Would anyone mind if I went instead?" Frankie asked.

"Why?"

"Because I've worked the case and know these people. I'm sure Hank and Todd are excellent agents, but I know how Grif thinks. He's a gay man who likes strong butch men, like Hank, but he's in a hostile environment and probably feeling the pressure."

"Thanks, I think." Hank said, scrubbing his hand over his short dark hair.

"A little harmless flirting can't hurt," Evan said. "Remember the old saying about catching more flies with honey than vinegar."

"No disrespect, Evan, I mean Agent Spears, but I'm not sure flirting is what Grif needs right now. He's probably trying to avoid the tough guys in lockup who want a turn at him just to prove they can. I have a different approach in mind, and Hank would be the perfect foil."

Frankie sensed Evan's discomfort with the potential change of plan and her struggle for a plausible excuse to keep her sidelined. Evan didn't like not being in control. "Nothing illegal?"

Frankie slapped a hand to her chest. "You cut me deep, boss. Of course, it'll be legal."

"You can go with Hank, but he does the interview."

"But—"

"Hank takes the lead, or you don't go. Interviewing for evidentiary and court purposes is very different from trolling for information on the streets."

"I'm aware." Frankie chose not to be insulted by Evan's comment. "As you wish." Easier to get forgiveness than permission. Evan would be grateful when she returned with a solid lead.

Evan checked her tablet again. "Todd, crosscheck Winston's and Tyndall's passports, including facial recognition, with every exit point in the country. Aaron, would you work your computer magic and make sure we haven't missed anything in financials, phone records, wire transfers, or credit cards?"

Evan hadn't asked Hank or Todd if they *would* do anything. She'd simply barked orders. Why the deference to Aaron and why did it seem to pain Evan to look at him? Maybe she was one of those people uncomfortable with handicaps. Frankie hoped not. She wouldn't be able to stand working for her.

"And get CCTV footage around the airports, train and bus terminals, ports, and from highway border crossings. I'll start double-checking friend and family contacts. This has probably been done, but everything needs to be triple-checked before an international manhunt." Evan marked items off a list as she talked. "If you complete your task, get another lead, or change location, let me know. Now, let's review what we're doing. Hank, go."

"I've got it, boss," Hank replied.

"Humor me, please." Evan gripped the edges of her tablet, the corners of her mouth in a tight line, and Frankie felt the tension from across the room.

She picked up her bag and waited by the door while Hank obligingly regurgitated his assignment. Not playing this game. She'd been on her own too long and seen too many controlling supervisors blow an operation by being overly cautious. Hank finished his recitation and joined her.

"Frankie, your assignment?" Evan met Frankie's gaze, and for an instant, she detected a flicker of insecurity behind the confident façade. If not for the impatient scowl on her face, Evan would've been the most appealing woman Frankie had ever seen—a contrast of power and vulnerability wrapped in a snazzy outfit.

"I understand my assignment. Everybody understands their assignment. We can be trusted to play in the sandbox unsupervised. P.S., you're not my boss. That's Ted Curtis's job. I'm a liaison. Look it up." She hefted her bag onto her shoulder and followed Hank out.

As the door closed behind them, she heard Evan say, "*Excuse me?*"

Hank gave her a stunned look and shook his head. "You're going to pay for that."

Frankie took another step, determined not to be micromanaged, but then stopped and turned back. "Damn it." She'd told Evan she would make this work. She opened the door, and said, "I'm sorry, Agent Spears. I'll be at the jail with Hank. If we complete our task, get another lead, or change location, we'll let you know." She purposely repeated the instructions verbatim, but her assurance earned her only a steely glare from Evan.

On the short walk to the county jail, Frankie pumped Hank about Evan's obsession with details and her Velcro-style supervision, but he clammed up like a good soldier. A question about what had happened to Aaron would probably meet the same fate. Apparently, she had more schmoozing to do before she won his trust.

She stepped into the lobby restroom at the jail and changed into her costume for the day's performance. When she came out, Hank gawked.

"What the hell? Frankie?"

"I prefer Francesca. You like?" She waved her hand down the front of her outfit to the red three-inch heels.

"You'll have every guy in the room drooling."

"That's the idea." He sounded a bit awestruck, which worked in her favor. Maybe he'd see her as a viable member of the team if she added something different to the mix.

"You want to see him in the visitors' area or should we get an interview room?"

"The more public the better. It's part of the plan to get Grif to talk." Hank started to walk away, but she touched his arm. "I need to question him. Can you trust me to do that?"

"I don't have a problem letting an agent with more knowledge of the facts and more experience with the suspect take the lead, but in this case Evan will."

"Why is she so inflexible? I've been here less than a day, but it doesn't seem like she trusts you guys to do anything on your own."

Hank scratched his beard stubble and seemed to struggle with the question. "She didn't use to be that way. Try not to give her such a hard time. She'll come around." She started to ask another question, but he walked toward the check-in area.

They showed ID and signed in at security where she left her bag, depending on Hank to take notes while she wove her magic. "So, we're on the same page, right?" Hank nodded, and she added, "I'll handle the fallout with Evan."

"Damn right you will."

They waited in the crowded visitors' area that consisted of small square tables, straight-backed chairs, and an old vending machine until deputies escorted Robert Griffin to their table. Grif had the physique of a bodybuilder but looked like someone had used him as a punching bag. His face sported two black eyes and a swollen lip, and purple handprints marred his beefy forearms. The orange inmates' coverall made him look even more forlorn and out of place. Several of the inmates eyeballed her as he got closer. She had their attention.

Frankie grabbed Grif in a hug, kissed his cheeks before planting a long one on his lips, and then slipped into her best Southern accent. "Oh my God, darling, what have they done to you? Who did this? I'll complain all the way to the top." She noted Grif's shocked expression and whispered, "Call me Francesca and play along if you want to get out of here."

He hesitated only briefly before falling into character. "Francesca, I've missed you, babe." He hugged her waist and bumped his hips against hers, rocking a little for added effect.

"Stop that," the guard bellowed.

Frankie gave Grif's ass a quick squeeze and guided him to a chair that groaned under his weight. "Love you, honey. The kids are absolutely frantic to see you. Are you sure you're okay?"

Grif cleared his throat and said, "Slipped in the shower." With added effort, he'd made his voice sound deeper and gruffer than normal.

Frankie motioned to Hank and said loud enough for everyone to hear, "I brought my brother. He's in training with the Carolina Panthers for next season. If these assholes give you any more trouble..." She let her voice trail off hoping the implied threat would stop some of the violence against Grif.

He leaned closer and whispered, "Who *are* you?"

She channeled Sing Song, her UC persona, and lowered her voice. "This man is not my brother, but I could be your fairy godmother."

Grif's eyes grew wide. "You're that weird homeless woman. Whiny, no, Sing Song."

"DEA Agent Frankie Strong. I'm guessing the past three weeks haven't been pleasant for you in here."

"You think?" He started to push away, but Frankie captured his hands.

"I'm hoping this little show will deter some of your macho friends, but you have to keep up the act. Maintain eye contact, keep smiling, and let me do the talking."

He nodded and edged his chair closer to the table.

"I need information about where Winston and Tyndall have gone."

Grif snorted. "You can bet wherever they are, Winston is puffing on an expensive Cuban. Torpedoes. He's addicted to the damn things. And Tyndall will be fucking an overpriced stripper. Guaranteed."

"I need real information, actual intelligence I can use."

Grif started to say something Frankie was certain would be a lie, and she shook her head. "Don't. You were part of the inner circle. If you ever want to choose your own sex partners again, you'll tell me everything you know. Otherwise, you can take your chances in prison with the sadistic homophobes who want a free pass to get off with a handsome guy like you."

Grif looked around the room and swallowed hard. "I want immunity."

"I can't promise anything until I hear what you have to offer."

"I've got everything to offer. International drug connections, transport lines, money laundering locations, and Winston's escape plan. And the cherry on top, the guy that was murdered behind the Daytime Resource Center."

"What do you know about that?" Hank asked.

Grif grinned at Hank and licked his lips. "Wouldn't you like to know, handsome?"

"Hey," Frankie said, "Eyes on me. We already know who killed Franklin Weber." She bluffed, hoping Grif would let something slip.

"Yeah, but you don't know who ordered the hit, do you?"

"Tell me."

"Immunity," Grif said. He stood, leaned over the table, and kissed Frankie on the mouth before heading toward the guard. "See you soon, babe."

On the walk back to the office, Frankie shoulder bumped Hank. "We nailed it. Won't the boss be impressed?"

"You've got a different approach, I'll give you that, but she'll never go for the deal."

"Of course, she will. He's only charged with assault on an officer and drugs. We make those kinds of deals every day to work our way up the distribution chain."

"I'll let you break the good news, but I'm telling you, she won't sanction immunity."

Evan spent most of the day tracking down and reinterviewing the list of Winston's and Tyndall's friends and family and discovered nothing new. Now for the paperwork and talking to Frankie about her unprofessional conduct this morning. She was determined to keep her cool and not be goaded into a sparring match. Frankie was a firebrand who'd been basically unsupervised for six years. What did Evan expect, instant conformity?

She finished her report, settled back at her desk with a bottle of water, and took a big gulp as Hank and Frankie walked in. She sucked in a breath when she saw Frankie again. Gasping and swallowing at once didn't work. She choked and coughed, and water spurted all over her desk.

"Damn, girl, you look hot," Todd said. "Next time I'm going out with you."

Aaron gave a catcall from behind his computer screen, and Frankie grinned weakly.

She wore the same clothes she'd had on earlier but looked totally different. The loose gray silk blouse now fit tightly across her chest, and two unfastened buttons revealed a glimpse of cleavage that wasn't there earlier. The black skirt had crept up her thighs, and dangerously high heels accented lean calves. A wig of wavy blond hair that stopped just above her breasts replaced her spiked locks and made her blue eyes pop. Evan's coughing spell slowed, and she mopped at the spill to avoid staring any longer. She'd seen enough, actually too much.

This morning Frankie had been more modestly dressed, enthusiastic and upbeat, transforming the mundane office environment into something livelier and more vibrant. She'd even challenged the way Evan ran her team, which she had to address, but now, Frankie not only looked different, but her energy had shifted as well. Her eyes lacked some of their sparkle, and the corners of her mouth weren't quite as perky. What had caused such a marked change?

"Any progress?" She squeezed her water bottle to control the nervous energy of anticipation and curiosity. She looked to Hank for an answer, but he inclined his head at Frankie. "You didn't question him?" Again, he nodded toward Frankie who stood at her desk pulling her blouse out of her skirt. She slid her hands discreetly underneath, unfastened her bra, and slid it off her arms. "What are you doing?"

"I was trying to get comfortable without making a scene." Frankie dropped the padded push-up bra into her bag and kicked off the heels. "Thanks for making that impossible." She ripped the wig off and scrubbed her fingers through damp, matted down hair. "That's better."

"Can I talk to you for a second?"

"Sure."

"In private." Evan pulled a cell phone from her desk drawer and started walking.

Frankie followed her into the conference room, closed the door, and leaned against it as if she needed support. "Yes?"

The resigned attitude wasn't what Evan expected, but she should be relieved. Did she want Frankie to act out so she could throw her off the team? "This morning—"

"I know. Sorry for mouthing off in front of the guys. Wasn't very professional. Won't happen again."

"Thanks for that." The way she spouted the apology made Evan think she was eager to leave. "And what were you doing out there just now?"

"I can only breathe so long with my boobs pushed up under my throat. Not a cleavage type girl. And if grown men haven't seen a woman shed a bra before, they need an education."

"I realize you've worked alone for a long time, and you seem quite uninhibited, but I'd prefer you not be the one to educate my agents." That sounded like she had some kind of claim or interest in Frankie, which was totally wrong. "I meant not in the office, in public."

"Southern Baptist state. Got it."

"It's just unprofessional and not the way we do business." Evan was being picky, but proper protocol kept things running smoothly, her in charge, and her agents safe. "And why did you question Robert Griffin when my instructions were clear?"

"I improvised. He'd taken quite a beating and chatting with a hunk like Hank in a room full of thugs wasn't going to help him or us."

The muscles in her jaw tightened. "Improvisation gets people hurt and can have procedural and legal ramifications. I can't believe you just conducted a spontaneous interview. No list of questions. No prep. Nothing." She admired agents who operated so effortlessly off the cuff, when they also followed protocol, but she didn't know or trust Frankie to do so.

"It's all up here, boss." Frankie tapped her forehead with her finger, obviously not taking Evan's concerns seriously.

"Is everything funny to you?"

"Not at all, but a little levity never hurts."

"Frankie, did it occur to you that I might have reasons for asking you to do things a certain way?" Why did she have to explain everything to Frankie? She should be the one justifying her actions.

"I'm sure you have reasons for everything, but flexibility, delegation, and trust in your agents isn't a bad thing."

"You haven't been supervised in six years and you've been here less than a day. I hardly think you're in a position to judge anyone's supervisory style. Besides, as you so colorfully pointed out earlier, I'm not your boss." Having Frankie question her was beyond annoying, but Evan kept her expression neutral and her tone even.

"Could've fooled me."

"What was that?" Evan asked.

"Nothing. I'm not trying to be disrespectful or difficult, but as an outsider, I see things," Frankie said. "All I'm saying is loosen the reins a little. Try it." Frankie's voice softened and she settled into a chair as if her body ached.

Evan started to fire off a comment about insubordination, but something in Frankie's expression stopped her. "Are you all right? You look...like you're in pain. Did something happen that I need to know?"

"Depends. Have you finished with my litany of sins?" Frankie grinned and her eyes sparked before she let out a long sigh.

Evan sounded like a harpy, but she had to maintain order or things would get out of hand, and she had a feeling things could get out of hand quickly around Frankie. "Yes, I'm finished, except for this." She handed Frankie a cell phone. "Keep it on you at all times. Our numbers are programmed in. All you have to do is hit the number assigned to each of us. I'm number one, Hank two, Todd three, and Aaron four. And before you make a smart comment, we're listed by seniority." She waved to give Frankie the floor.

"Grif agreed to talk to us—"

"Oh." Evan had been expecting Frankie to address why she looked so drained and wasn't sure she'd heard correctly. "What? Well, maybe I was too quick to judge. Good job."

"In exchange for immunity."

Evan's chest constricted with the familiar ache, and she took a few seconds to slow her breathing and force calm into her voice. "No."

"What?"

"That's not going to work." She had her reasons. Hank, of course, knew what they were, but telling them to an outsider—and that's exactly what Frankie was—would reveal too much. She'd consider another incentive for the suspect's cooperation, but not this.

"I don't understand. This man is willing to give us everything. The total drug operation, including transport, associates, money laundering, and Winston's escape plan. He's got it all. The only thing you have to do is sign off on—"

Evan stood so quickly her chair banged against the wall. "I said no. End of subject."

"Actually, it's not. I'm not technically your subordinate, so I could go to your boss with the offer. We have an understanding of sorts."

Frankie's voice was not as fiery as earlier today and when she made eye contact, her expression was more fatigued, but the challenge was real. How had she managed in such a short time to question Evan's authority and supervision and to pinpoint her Achilles' heel?

"I don't want to go over your head, but if it means closing the case, I will."

"And I'll fight the request." Frankie was exhausting with her ideas and challenges, and Michael allowing her to work two cases irritated Evan even more. "I run my team, and I say we'll find another way to get the information. Maybe three more weeks in jail will help."

"Three more weeks for Winston to get ahead of us and burrow deeper underground? Can we really afford another delay? Isn't it time to end this?"

"Good night, Frankie." She forced herself to walk slowly through the office toward the front door that suddenly felt miles away. Frankie had a point. It was long past time to close the Winston case. She and her team couldn't move forward until all parties involved were arrested and convicted, but making agreements with criminals wasn't the way she wanted to do it.

"Are we doing the deal?" Hank asked.

He'd obviously shared the details of their interview with the rest of the squad because Todd added, "Let's do it, boss." The only person who didn't offer an opinion was Aaron, even when Hank and Todd looked his way.

"We're not giving him immunity."

Evan blocked out her walk to the garage and the drive home until she parked in front of the warehouse and held the door key in her hand. She sprinted through the open downstairs, climbed the metal steps to the loft bedroom two at a time, and stripped off her work clothes. She needed to sweat out this stress.

A few minutes later, she tore at old plywood on the lower section of the walls with a long crowbar and ripped it away in pieces to expose the brick. She and Eli had started the process the weekend before, so it was now easily a one-person job. She surrendered to the steady rhythm of sliding the tool under the wood, prying it up, and peeling it back. Nails screeched and screamed as she ripped them loose. The tightness in her shoulders and chest slowly evaporated, but Frankie's subdued state this afternoon and her proposal to offer Robert Griffin immunity churned over and over in her mind.

She worked quickly and attacked another section. Did Frankie think she could make such a request without considering all the facts and consequences? What kind of agent operated in an information vacuum? *You didn't give her all the facts.* Evan ignored the thought and continued her mental rant. And what kind of person worked only undercover assignments, assumed other identities, and surrounded herself with strangers with no potential for personal connections? How isolated and unbalanced she must feel.

Slide. Rip. Peel. Evan worked from the back, tossing the shredded discards toward the door until her eyes burned with sweat and her lungs screamed for air. She stopped, took a long drink of water, and wiped her face on the tail of her ripped T-shirt. Was her life that different from Frankie's? She chose a demanding career, compartmentalized her feelings, and while she worked with the same people every day, avoided becoming personally involved. Which was worse? "I'm nothing like her."

"I knew sooner or later you'd crack." Eli stood with a crowbar in one hand and a six-pack in the other. His tanned arms and legs, muscled by years of construction work, bunched under tight faded jeans and a white T-shirt, and his collar-length black hair swept back in a style similar to her own. People often asked if they were twins, but he was five years older, to the day.

"You're a lifesaver, big brother."

He nodded at the wall. "Somebody must've really pissed you off."

"I'm trying to forget." But the only thing she'd thought about was the situation with Frankie and the decision she had to make before tomorrow.

"Take a break?" Six-pack in hand, Eli led the way to a couple of metal stools they'd rescued from the side of the road and handed her a beer. "Remember what Dad used to say about trying too hard?"

"You don't need a sledgehammer to crack a nut," they said together.

She shook her head. "I never figured out exactly what that meant."

Eli nudged her with his elbow. "Because you're a sledgehammer-type girl. Learn the rules. Follow the rules. Live by the rules. Force everybody else to do the same. Some folks might need a gentler approach."

"You have no idea what I'm dealing with." She pressed the frosty beer can to her forehead and rolled it back and forth, enjoying the cool against her heated skin.

"No. I'm explaining the adage, but the principle applies in any situation." He took a hefty gulp of beer and stretched his legs. He knew her too well to push.

Did she want to talk about Frankie, to admit she was bothered by her cavalier attitude, spontaneous decisions, unsolicited advice, and flirty behavior? Bothered in a strictly professional sense. "Michael put a DEA agent on the team temporarily, and she's not the rule-following kind. She's been working undercover for six years with little supervision."

"Uh-oh, not good for either of you. Do you have to keep her?"

She nodded. "She's got the inside track on our fugitives."

He studied her for a few seconds, but she didn't make eye contact. "What else?"

"Isn't that enough?"

"Supervising problem agents has never been an issue for you. I recall you winning Marine Hank over in record time. What's so different about this one?"

"She's a *liaison*." Evan made air quotes around the term Frankie used regularly. "Which basically means I have no real authority over her."

"Is she hot?"

"I…Eli, really?" She almost admitted that Frankie was appealing in a bizarre sort of way, personable, and probably damaged or at the very least adrift. And Evan had responded to Frankie's footsies game. Totally an automatic reflex, not intentional. But none of that had anything to do with the job. "She's a rule breaker, which means trouble for me and increases risk for the team. I can't let that happen, not after—"

"First, that wasn't your fault. Lose the guilt for your sake and everyone else's. Shit like that happens in your line of work too often for you to take it so personally. Second, would you whip a puppy for peeing on the floor on his first day of potty training?"

She stared into Eli's eyes, the same onyx color as hers and her father's, and saw a kindness she'd never seen in her dad's. "How did we get on the subject of potty training puppies?"

"Stick with me. I do have a point. I'm a builder and start from the foundation. This new agent is probably trying to do the same thing. She's been operating her own way, relying on her instincts, and surviving situations you've never faced. You have no idea what years of isolation from friends and family and second-guessing every move has done to her. Give her credit for what she's been through and provide the support she needs to get back on her feet. You might make a difference in the rest of her professional career if you handle her properly."

Maybe Eli was right, and she'd been too tough on Frankie the first day. Her dull expression and lethargic apology this afternoon returned, and Evan wondered again what had caused the dramatic change in her mood and behavior. Maybe she was trying too hard. "I swear, you should've been gay. You're entirely too sensitive for a straight man."

"Don't tell my girlfriend. She'll expect it all the time. Let's get back to work so I can be home when she gets there tonight."

Evan finished her beer, picked up the crowbar, and they fell easily into a steady rhythm. She'd purposely withheld the immunity argument from him, but with the other feelings racing through her, Evan didn't want to talk about it. Griffin was the only suspect they'd caught the day Aaron was injured, and she wasn't letting him walk away when Aaron couldn't. Eli might have another perspective. He might even try to change her mind, and she wasn't ready to hear it.

But she was lucky to have him as a confidante and sounding board. She couldn't imagine living like Frankie, bouncing from one assignment to the next without any stability. Who did she trust, talk to about her case, her life, or socialize with? Even in the past few weeks of her own self-imposed isolation, Evan would've been lost without Eli. But she didn't really know anything about Frankie. Maybe she had a support system. Evan hoped so.

Frankie closed her hotel room door and changed into a pair of threadbare flannel pants and a sweatshirt. She snuggled into the softness and collapsed in the chair by the window. Bit by bit, as she had role-played with Grif and sparred with Evan, her energy had drained, and now she was exhausted. Since the shooting, slipping into another persona took more of a physical and emotional toll and she remembered less of her true self. Was it because of the shooting, the PTSD, or had she simply reached her saturation point as a changeling?

Maybe it was time to stop pretending and find out who she really was, but that required facing some hard truths, settling down, and letting people in. The possibility terrified her. Emotions were simply weaknesses to be exploited for profit, or so her parents warned. She shook her head and refocused. One problem at a time.

She opened the mini bar and pulled out a shot-sized bottle of vodka, poured it into a glass, and filled the remainder with Diet Coke. Everything she'd done today irritated Evan, even though she'd found a way to locate Winston.

Something was going on with Evan, but what? Underneath her rigid, by the book insistence on order, Frankie sensed turbulence. Anger? Fear? Sadness? She didn't know what it was, but it was almost as if for Evan something about the Winston case was personal.

That was it. Some feeling deep in her gut told her she was right. Instinctive leaps had saved her skin in too many dark alleys for her to have any doubt—something about the Winston case was deeply, personally disturbing to Evan.

But intuition, no matter how accurate, was no substitute for facts, so Frankie sipped her drink and thumbed through the case file in her lap. Had she missed something in the brief? Had Grif played a more significant role in the drug ring or facilitated Winston and Tyndall's escape? Was that why Evan wouldn't consider immunity? The answer had to be in the reports or an agent's notes. She pulled the folder onto her lap and started reading.

Two hours later, she'd finished the vodka and was no closer to an answer. She started to close the file, but a name caught her eye again. Madeline Gallagher arresting officer. Frankie flipped through the documents but didn't find her follow-up. The alphabet agencies were sticklers for details so where was Gallagher's report? She pulled the phone cord, sliding the landline closer, and dialed Ted Curtis's number.

"What?" He sounded grumpy-sleepy, and she glanced at the clock.

"Shit. I'm sorry, boss. I didn't realize it was so late. Guess you were sleeping?"

"Trying. Are you okay?"

She skipped over the question and got straight to the point. "Where's Marshal Gallagher's follow-up report?"

"What are you talking about, Frankie?"

"The Marshals, ATF, and local police assisted on our drug roundup in the Winston case. Marshal Madeline Gallagher arrested Robert Griffin at the airport, but her follow-up report isn't in the file." Ted grunted, and she heard shuffling as she imagined him getting out of bed and going into another room.

"Hold on." The phone clunked on a hard surface, and Frankie waited while Ted pounded the keys on his computer. "Classified. Order came from division."

"Why?" Classified files weren't unusual, in fact they were pretty common in government, but the reasons were limited. The only one that might apply in this case was the protection of an intelligence source or agent.

"Did I get promoted while I was sleeping? I have no fucking idea, Frankie."

"One more question." Needing to ask about the distasteful subject brought the vodka back up her throat, and she swallowed hard. "Do you have any leads on those other people I'm looking for?"

Ted scoffed. "'Those other people?' They're not strangers. They're your parents, Frankie. But no, I don't have anything yet. One of my nerds is running a facial recognition check, but that could take a while. We're talking about an international search across multiple databases for people you haven't seen in ages."

"I know and I appreciate your help, but I've been looking for over a year." The homeless man she'd seen in New York had brought back too many memories and too much guilt about her pre law enforcement life and ignited a search she hoped would vindicate her in some small way. But the constant lack of results and roadblocks was frustrating and draining.

"Did you consider they might not want to be found?"

"Oh, I'm sure of it. Anyway, thanks for letting Michael English know I might need some leeway to search for leads." Ever since deciding to locate her folks, Frankie had wondered if she was doing the right thing. Could she go through with what she had planned? She'd feel guilty if she did and guilty if she didn't.

"Can I go back to bed now?" A door closed, and Ted shuffled again. "By the way, how's the new assignment?"

"As much fun as making out with a skinhead."

"Sorry, kid, but at least Spears is easy on the eyes. Am I right?"

"Good night, Ted." Evan Spears was damn sexy with her androgynous looks and take-charge attitude, a particularly appealing combination. Freeing uptight women with control issues was Frankie's favorite leisure activity, on the rare occasion she had any. But Evan had ignored Frankie's inadvertent game of footsies under the table that first day. She hadn't meant to touch Evan, but found it hard to pull away when she did, and that was a new feeling for her.

She needed to stay focused on the job, not come off as some creeper who disrespected personal and work boundaries. She propped her feet in the chair, wrapped her arms around her knees, and glanced at the clock. Only two more hours before the impress-the-boss charade started again. She was actually looking forward to seeing Evan and working with her, but she'd need to up her game because Evan Spears wasn't easy to impress.

CHAPTER FOUR

E van dropped her inside-out umbrella in the trash on her way into the office and swept her fingers through her soaked hair, pushing it off her face. Cold water rolled down her neck as she closed the door. "Morning. Freaking monsoon weather." She hung up her coat and plopped her soggy briefcase beside her desk. She'd gone back and forth about Griffin's immunity deal most of the night but wasn't close to a decision—and the team would be expecting one.

She scanned the room and stopped at Frankie, shocked at yet another transformation. Today she looked like a human matchstick—beige skinny jeans, a tight matching T-shirt, and bright red hair. Why the need to constantly change her appearance? Disconcerting to say the least, but Eli was right. Evan knew nothing about Frankie's childhood or how her many undercover assignments had affected her. Her current outfit did confirm Evan's initial assessment that she was underweight, bordering on unhealthy. Hank cleared his throat, drawing Evan's attention back to the squad.

He and Todd stood near the coffee pot with grim expressions, and Aaron was sitting in the conference room doorway gripping the arms of his wheelchair. "What's up, guys? We out of coffee again?" Everyone looked toward Aaron.

"Can I have a minute, boss?" he asked and then rolled backward toward the rectangular conference table.

She hated surprises and the guys knew it. Her first instinct was always to expect the worst, and Aaron's situation could certainly deliver that. "Of course." She followed him in and closed the door. "Are you all right? Something new from the doctors?"

"No, nothing like that. Sorry. I didn't mean to scare you." He took off his glasses and wiped them on the tail of his red flannel shirt. Whatever he had to say wasn't going to be easy because he couldn't look at her.

"Just tell me, Aaron. I'd rather know, whatever it is."

"I want you to submit Griffin's immunity request to the US Attorney. We can't—"

"No." Evan cringed and looked away. A knot settled in her gut as that horrible day flashed through her mind again. Everything she believed, felt was true, and all her preparations had vanished in seconds leaving injuries and scars that would probably never heal.

Aaron held up his hand. "Let me finish, please?"

Evan choked back a visceral reaction and settled beside him. "I'm listening."

He clutched the wheels of his chair and started again. "I want you to put his request forward. The USA might not approve it anyway. This case needs to be closed. *We* need to close it for all our sakes. It's not an ideal outcome, but if Griffin's information puts us closer to finding the others, we have to go for it."

Aaron had impressed her as a young, energetic marshal when he joined her team, but since the accident, he'd amazed her with his maturity and courage. He had come back to work in record time, refusing to let his inability to walk ruin his life, and his positive attitude more often than not kept the team's spirits high. She, on the other hand, remained mired in the minutiae of what went wrong, unable to forgive herself. How he could be so objective and benevolent escaped her. "I'm not sure I can do that, Aaron."

"I know you blame yourself for this." He slapped his legs. "But don't. We all trusted the wrong person. And what happened to me was just the luck of the draw. Let it go, Evan. It's not helping any of us, especially you."

"But somebody has to pay…and I have to make sure nothing like that happens again. I have to protect the team."

"And you do. Every day. Maybe a little too much protection. I don't know about the other guys, but I'm tired of being treated like a kindergartener and getting your pitying looks." He paused and his face flushed. "Sorry, guess I crossed the line. You are still my supervisor."

She shot him a grin. "Yeah, you did, rookie, but I needed to hear it. I'll work on the micromanaging, but I'm still not convinced about an immunity deal, maybe a reduction."

"Do it, please. Griffin gets a little less time but doesn't go free, and we catch the main players. Besides, it's not Griffin's fault some drunk airport employee ran me over with a luggage train." He pushed his glasses up on his nose. "And that's me, done." Aaron wheeled away from the table, opened the door, and returned to the safety of his computer cove.

If Aaron was willing to accept a reduction in sentence, she couldn't justify holding out. And as long as Griffin didn't get off completely, she could stomach the deal. She took a few minutes to settle with the idea before walking back into the squad room. "Update. I'm sending a request for a reduction in sentence for Griffin to the US Attorney. This doesn't mean the request will be approved, but I'll fill out the paperwork and walk it upstairs today."

The agents whistled and whooped until she motioned for them to quiet. Every man nodded enthusiastically when she made eye contact. "I can't justify total immunity. Griffin can take the reduction or leave it. In the meantime, we have holes to plug if…" She glanced at Frankie and got a sideways grin that sent a flash of heat through her, probably annoyance. "*If* Griffin's information points to an international manhunt."

"You got it, boss," Hank said.

"Where do we start?" Todd asked, playing with his reddish moustache like it had handlebars.

"Interpol Blue Notice," Aaron said, tapping furiously on his computer. "Right?"

"Precisely, Mr. Potter." She used Aaron's nickname in her best British accent. "Check it and see if anything has popped up recently."

Frankie lowered her feet from her desktop. "Blue notice?"

When Frankie's gaze settled on her, Evan felt a rare urge to be playful. Frankie was fully engaged, and her unbridled interest was attractive and exciting. Evan waved to give Aaron the floor. "Mr. Potter, if you please."

"A Blue Notice is issued when Interpol grants a member country's request for assistance with the location of someone connected with a criminal investigation, identifying someone connected with a criminal investigation, finding witnesses to a criminal act, or locating friends, relatives, or associates of offenders or suspected offenders." He rattled off the definition like he was reading from a cheat sheet. "In our case, several of these apply. We submitted requests based on drug charges and international business dealings on both Winston and Tyndall."

"Wow. Impressive," Frankie said. "And when was the notice issued?"

"Almost immediately. International flight was always a real possibility."

Evan collected her iPad from her desk. "Let me know if there's anything, Aaron. Hank and Frankie, go back to Griffin and get a signed statement containing everything he knows. And I do mean every single detail." Frankie raised her hand. Good girl. She was learning not to blurt and at least attempting to show some respect. "Yes, Frankie?"

"This time it might work better if the sheriff's department brought him to us. I've already established a cover with him. And," she pointed to her bright red hair color, "this shit is off the hook, but I can't exactly undo it here."

"Hold up," Todd cut in. "Why the hell did you do that anyway?"

"It's just organic food coloring. Washes out, but it takes a while. And because I can. I've been a sort of chameleon all my life, so why tinker with perfection. Right?"

"I had to look twice when you came in this morning," Hank said. "That's certainly different from your business suit yesterday and the seductress outfit at the jail. Anyone would have a hell of a time identifying you in a lineup."

"Or she'd stick out like a sore thumb," Todd added.

"Exactly," Frankie said.

Frankie's comment piqued Evan's curiosity again. Why was being unidentifiable a positive thing for Frankie? What if she did it because she liked it? Liked playing with people, keeping them off balance, never letting anyone know who she really was? What if from an early age she'd had to disguise herself and eventually embraced hiding in plain sight? Evan's heart contracted. No matter the reason, such anonymity would be a lonely way to live.

She wanted to know everything about the woman who'd slotted herself so quickly into position on the team and stirred Evan's interest. But she'd made the mistake of trusting too quickly before and couldn't let it happen again. She jotted a note on her iPad—review Frankie's full personnel file—and returned to the task at hand.

"Call the jail and get them to bring Griffin over. If he demands the agreement first, let me know. It'll probably take at least two days to fully debrief him and verify what he tells us. Aaron will monitor the Blue Notice, and we'll combine everything into a warrant and then—"

"Red Notice," Aaron interrupted. "Oh, let me school the new girl."

Evan stifled a laugh and nodded.

"An Interpol Red Notice empowers authorities to arrest and detain our suspects, not just provide information or their location."

"And once that's done?" Frankie stood, stretched, and walked toward the coffee pot, her lean body stressing every seam in her tight jeans and T-shirt. She glanced over her shoulder and caught Evan looking. "Anybody want anything?"

Evan realized she was fanning herself with her iPad and dropped it on her desk. "If Griffin's information indicates Winston has left the country, a warrant and the Red Notice will be issued and the team, or most of it, will gear up to travel."

"Most of the team?" Frankie asked.

Evan avoided eye contact, aware that Frankie had caught her staring once. "We don't usually travel with a full team. Fiscal restrictions and so on have to be approved." She pointed toward the ceiling. "We rely on local agencies and liaisons for support, but I'll make that determination when we know more."

"Hey, Frankie, would you set up the recorder in the interview room while I get the sheriff's department moving on transport?" Hank asked as he reached for the phone.

"On it," Frankie said, gathering a notebook and pen from her desk.

"Everybody knows what they need to do?" Evan asked. She started to request an individual recap but got a headshake from Frankie and changed her mind. "Let's wrap this tight."

❖

Frankie grinned at the flush of Evan's cheeks as she checked out her ass. She liked what she saw, and though Frankie had vowed to be professional, she wanted to explore that interest. She approached quietly from behind, cupped Evan's elbow, and guided her toward the small interview room away from the other agents. The heat of her skin coursed through Frankie and she leaned closer to Evan's side.

"What…what are you doing?" Evan tugged her arm from Frankie's grasp.

"Just a second of your time? In private." She couldn't resist the urge to be alone with Evan for just a few minutes and perhaps test her control.

"You could've asked." She looked momentarily panicked when Frankie closed the door behind them. "If this is about the case, everyone needs to hear."

"It's not really about that. Well, it is and it isn't." Watching Evan, usually so reserved and in charge, avoid eye contact and inch farther away told Frankie she'd been right. Evan was either attracted to her or afraid of her, possibly a little of both. "Your cheeks are pink. Are you okay?"

Evan wiped her face as if that would clear away the betraying evidence. Then she took a deep breath, squared her shoulders, and seemed to make a decision. In a few seconds, all signs of discomfort and vulnerability vanished. Impressive control.

When she spoke again, her eyes met Frankie's. "Yes, I'm fine."

"Anything I can help with? You look a little thirsty…or maybe hungry." Frankie stepped into Evan's body space and focused on her mouth.

"No thank you. Nothing I can't handle myself."

Frankie licked her lips, certain she was pushing the limits but unwilling to stop. "Well, that's unfortunate. I'm always free to lend a hand, especially to help my faux boss, if you're interested sometime. We can keep it on the DL." She was on shaky ground coming on so openly, but everything about Evan pushed and pulled her at the same time, and she was at a loss to understand why she was so drawn to her.

"Did you ask me in here so you could flirt without witnesses? Are you hoping for a sexual harassment claim or are you just that desperate for sex?"

Frankie chuckled. She hadn't expected Evan to be quite so candid or to call her out. "I have no intention of harassing, sexual or otherwise. And I'm sure sex with you would be many things, but never desperate. I'm pretty good at spotting interest and just wanted to let you know I'm available."

"Your time would be better spent fitting in more with the team instead of working so hard at being different...or whatever you call this." Evan waved at Frankie's clothes and settled her hip against the edge of the table, her eyes sparking. "Don't confuse interest with intention. And this," she wiggled her index finger between them, "is totally business."

"Touché. Sorry if I offended you."

"I'm not offended, but since we're being honest, I am curious, in a strictly academic sense about what makes you tick. And I will get to the heart of you, Francesca Strong. Knowing your teammates and your opposition is always a good strategy." She placed a finger under Frankie's chin and forced eye contact. "Don't test me like this again." She started to open the door but turned back. "Was there anything else?"

Frankie studied nonverbal clues and behavior like other people did their smartphones. The sparks in Evan's eyes, the slight uptick in her breathing, and the pulse at her throat were as good as a confession. Evan was attracted to her. Frankie scooted up on the table and leaned back on her hands. "Yes. The real reason I wanted to talk to you."

Folding her arms across her chest, Evan propped against the doorframe as if she needed support. "I'm intrigued."

Frankie was as well. Now Evan appeared unaffected, her facial expression blank like they'd just discussed the weather before moving on to more interesting subjects. But those dark eyes and the way she wrapped her arms around herself said it wasn't easy to shake off their closeness. And she hadn't yet expelled Frankie from the team. "I'd like to be part of the overseas search team."

Evan's left eyebrow arched slightly, the only indication that Frankie had surprised her. "I don't know what to say. I was certain you'd want to move on once you'd given us your intel. May I ask why?"

Frankie sat up straight, brought her hands together in her lap, and twirled the spinner ring on her left thumb with her forefinger. The nervous habit calmed her and reminded her that life was a circle, constantly in motion. She'd been going in circles most of her life. Would there ever be an end, a settling? If this trip brought closure, maybe then. "I can be useful, but I'd prefer not to carry a weapon at the moment...in case I froze and put the guys at risk."

The corners of Evan's mouth twitched slightly, and her shoulders relaxed. "I'm impressed and appreciative of your consideration for the team. It's always my first priority. How do you plan to be useful?"

"Like I said, I blend in well, which comes in handy for intelligence gathering, or I can stand out which serves as a nice distraction when necessary."

"Is that what the chameleon comment was about?" Evan asked.

"Guess you should've read my personnel file after all. It's a boring story, but let's just say I excel at being anyone but myself." She flinched at the unintentional admission and the sadness in her voice.

Evan studied her for several seconds, and the concern in her eyes tugged at Frankie like a tether. "Can I ask another question?"

"Sure, since we're being honest," Frankie parroted Evan's earlier comment.

"What happened yesterday when you interviewed Griffin at the jail? In the morning you were upbeat and annoyingly defiant, but when you came back, you looked exhausted."

Frankie twirled her ring again but couldn't look at Evan. The metal felt cold now, offering no comfort. The question went to the heart of who she used to be but wasn't sure she was anymore. Could she answer without revealing too much? Her life story wouldn't help secure a spot on the manhunt. She hedged. "Pretending to be someone else requires a lot of energy. I was drained."

"Then why do you do it?"

"Sometimes you have to make sacrifices to get the job done."

"You don't have to come with us, Frankie. We'll see this through. Do you want me to talk with Michael about having you reassigned?"

She should've anticipated the question, but Frankie wasn't ready for the loneliness that caught her off guard at the prospect of another assignment in another place. She was like a drug dealer with no buyers, so much to offer but no takers. "If it's okay, I'd really like to finish the job with you...with the team."

"I can't make promises, but I understand the need for closure. I'll find out about the budget before making my final decision. And thanks again for thinking about the guys."

Evan lightly touched Frankie's arm almost as an afterthought before reaching for the doorknob, and Frankie felt immediately calm and centered. She wanted to grab Evan with both hands and hold on. Her impulsive flirting suddenly felt like a shallow attempt to connect, a throwback to a time when she'd hidden from her feelings and used other people's to deceive. "Thank you."

When Frankie returned to the squad room, Evan went to the restroom at the end of the hall and locked the door. She turned on the cold water, gripped the sides of the cool porcelain sink, and forced her pulse and breathing to level. She felt like she'd been in an electrical storm, not knowing where the next bolt would strike, her body and senses on high alert. Holding her hands under the tap, she breathed slowly and then splashed her face with water.

Why did she touch Frankie, and *why* did she admit her interest? The answer was simple. Frankie would never have believed a mere denial. She was too intuitive, and besides, the room crackled with their chemistry. So, Evan admitted the obvious, established her boundaries, and kept repeating what she'd told Frankie. *Don't confuse interest with intention.*

But one brief touch confirmed what Evan guessed the first time she saw her—Frankie was vibrant, free-spirited, and dangerous—and Evan was struggling to control her reactions to her. The team was already charmed by Frankie, but she couldn't afford to follow that path. Frankie's concern for the guys, and her comment about making sacrifices for the job had shown Evan another side, and now she wanted to know the rest, but she couldn't afford to drop her guard even a little.

Evan looked at her reflection in the mirror. "Haven't you learned your lesson?" But Frankie wasn't like anyone she'd ever met, and Evan wasn't going to ignore her instincts this time. She had no intention of being distracted by or succumbing to the temptations of Frankie Strong.

CHAPTER FIVE

Frankie drummed her purple ballpoint on the tabletop in the small interview room while she and Hank waited for the deputies to deliver Robert Griffin. She shook her leg in time with the drumming, her insides still jittery from her encounter with Evan. She'd been touched by women before, but a grateful press of Evan's hand had her searching for a memory that came close to its intensity and tenderness and coming up short. What was *that* about?

Before things got out of hand with Evan, Frankie needed to nail this interview and close the case. Though Evan wasn't technically her supervisor, those boundaries seemed important to her, and Frankie was trying to honor them. But it wasn't easy. Words like intensity and tenderness weren't familiar to her, and she'd never been this attracted to anyone, certainly not this quickly.

"What's up with you?" Hank asked.

"Huh? What? Oh, nothing. I'm good."

Hank glared at her. "You're wired. Did something happen with the boss?"

Frankie lost her grip on the pen, and it flew across the table. "No, of course not."

"You were in there alone for a while. Evan is usually open about everything but hasn't mentioned your chat. You got a problem with her?" Hank's protectiveness was evident as he leaned back in the chair and crossed his arms over his broad chest.

"Not at all. Besides, I'm sure she can take care of herself." Now if Frankie could do the same they might get through this case without her combusting.

"Looks can be deceiving, and what you don't know *can* hurt you, Frankie."

"What does that mean? Why don't you just tell me what all of you are keeping from me? I don't like working without all the facts either."

Hank raked his hand across his buzzed hair and gave her a hard stare. "Fair point, but you have to promise—"

"Finally." A deputy flung open the door and guided Robert Griffin to the chair on the opposite side of the table. "Took forever to check him out. Visiting hours at the jail. Want us to wait, come back, or will you return him when you're done?"

Frankie was so annoyed by the timing of the interruption that she threw her hands in the air. "Whatever, man."

"We'll take him back," Hank said. "This could take a while. Thanks."

The deputy grunted, gave Frankie a narrowed stare, and closed the door as he left.

"Boy, you look different," Grif said to her. "I prefer this redheaded edgy look to the Dolly Parton impersonation at the jail, but it worked. The heteros took me in, so thanks."

"Glad it helped. Looks like your bruises have faded."

"Some, but this costume," he pulled at the oversized orange jumpsuit, "doesn't complement the purple splotches or my ivory complexion."

"I see that." She nodded to her right. "You remember Marshal Hank Korley." Grif gave him a wide smile. "We're going to ask you questions about your association with Matthew Winston and Grady Tyndall and their involvement in criminal activities. If you answer our questions honestly and fully, we're prepared to ask the US Attorney to reduce your charges."

"Full immunity, like I walk today, or no deal."

"That's not happening, sport," Hank said.

Grif bristled and pushed back in his seat. "Then this meeting is a waste of time."

"Grif, listen." Frankie leaned forward. "We can't just let you walk away without serving any time, but maybe we can swing a sentence reduction, if you cooperate. We have a lot of questions which will take several hours, possibly days, depending on your answers. And when the interview is over, we have to verify as much as possible or we can't use it in court. So, your release won't happen today, but I assure you, we're not trying to trick you." She tried to make it sound like he had some power in the situation.

Grif exhaled a deep breath and rubbed his hands back and forth on the table. "Okay. Let's get started."

Frankie nodded for Hank to begin. Her mind was still on the unsettled feelings Evan raised, and on what Hank hadn't gotten to say. Besides, Grif was more attentive to Hank, which could prove useful in the long run.

Four hours later, a light tap sounded on the door and Todd stuck his head in. "The boss ordered dinner. Is this a good time for a break?"

"I'm starving," Grif said. "Anything but vegetarian. Will you join me, Hank?"

"You got it." Hank rose and stretched his back. "I'll make a bathroom run and bring the food. You all right until I get back, Frankie?"

She nodded.

"He's a really nice guy," Grif said. "Too bad he's not gay."

"He's probably heard that a time or two. You doing okay with all these questions, Grif?"

"Yeah." He twisted a chewing gum wrapper in his fingers and glanced up at her. "Do you think I'll get my money back?"

"Not unless you can prove you earned it legally. Otherwise, it's considered proceeds of illegal activity."

"But I had a suitcase full of cash when they stopped me at the airport."

"Exactly. Maybe you should've made that request part of your agreement."

"Is it too late?" Grif's face lost some of its enthusiasm.

"Why don't you ask your new best friend? Maybe he can put in a word with the boss. I'm new here and don't carry a lot of weight."

He nodded. "I'll do that over dinner."

Frankie edged closer to the table and lowered her voice. With Gallagher's report missing, and the guys not talking, Grif was her next best option to find out about his arrest. "Hey, while we're waiting, tell me about the day you were arrested."

"Man, wasn't that a clusterfuck? I mean seriously. The whole—"

"Dinner is served." Hank opened the door with his foot, carrying two delivery boxes.

"Grif was just about to tell me the story of his arrest."

Hank narrowed his eyes at her like she'd done something wrong. "We don't need to go there right now. I'm hungry. Come back in thirty."

She started to object, but showing dissention in front of a suspect was a no-no. Frankie stepped outside the interview room and stretched toward the ceiling. The cramped space and Grif's insistence on giving every detail from the day he met Matthew Winston and Grady Tyndall were wearing on her. And his comment that something went wrong on the day of his arrest confirmed the team was holding back.

When she entered the squad room, Todd, Aaron, and Evan gave her expectant looks. She slumped into her chair and stared at the takeout container in the center of her desk, trying to decide if she was too tired and annoyed to bother.

"Well?" Todd came up behind her and reached toward her shoulders. "Back rub?"

"I'd pay major bucks," she said.

Evan cleared her throat, shook her head at Todd, and said, "No."

He backed away and raised his hands. "Just thought she could use a little stress relief, boss. They've been at it for hours."

Was Evan's intervention strictly professional or more about what happened between them earlier? Frankie chose to interpret Evan's behavior as protectiveness, and she liked the way it felt. No one had ever shielded her from anything in her life. But she was also being excluded from part of the truth, and that didn't feel so great.

When Evan cleared her throat again, Frankie realized everybody was waiting for her to say something. "Oh…he's talking, but everything so far we already know or don't need. Hank is letting him ramble, developing rapport, but we'll nail him down on specifics soon."

Evan stepped in front of Frankie's desk and looked down at her, an unreadable expression on her face. "You look…I don't know, weird."

"I'm not good with tight spaces. I'd never make it in prison." She needed to keep her mind on work instead of what Evan was thinking or feeling every time she looked at her. She'd already breeched workplace etiquette, not to mention ethics, too many times with Evan.

"Is Hank staying in there?" When Frankie nodded, Evan said, "Grab your dinner and follow me."

Frankie tried to maintain eye contact, but Evan's gaze was intense and Frankie was distracted by what was possibly behind it. She was usually better at interpreting emotions, but right now Evan had her stumped. "Okay."

"Hold down the fort, Todd. Call if anything breaks."

Evan led the way to the stairs, and Frankie followed up three flights to a door at the top. Evan ran her fingers along the upper frame, removed a key, and unlocked the door, standing aside for Frankie to enter the attic.

She gaped at the large, empty space and expanse of windows and felt drawn to the last orangish rays of daylight pouring in. The morning rainstorm had given way to a clear afternoon and a fiery sunset. "This is fantastic. Do the windows op—"

"Wait for it." Evan placed their food on a dusty card table, threw several locking bolts on the windows, and pushed the panels open.

"This is better than fantastic." Frankie stuck her head out into the fresh air and breathed deeply. The orange, red, and purple colors of the sunset captivated her, and she imagined for a second that she and Evan were on vacation somewhere exotic. Evan's chuckle drew her attention back to the room, and she had a look Frankie couldn't quite decipher. "What?"

"You're like a dog with her head hanging out the car window. No one can accuse you of not experiencing life to the fullest."

"Sorry. I just love fresh air and sunshine." And apparently, fantasies that involved Evan.

"Don't apologize. It's nice to see someone who hasn't been jaded by life and still enjoys the simple things."

"And what about you?" Frankie couldn't resist since Evan had opened the door.

The smile on Evan's face vanished, replaced by her professional façade. "I brought you up here to relax for a few minutes and have dinner, not to engage in another intense conversation." She pulled two old wooden chairs from under a drop cloth, unfolded them, and waved for Frankie to sit.

"I like intense conversations with you." Frankie grinned as she joined her at the table.

"That was inappropriate this morning."

"Talking honestly is inappropriate? I prefer it to meaningless small talk." Frankie took a bite of her club sandwich and hummed in appreciation.

"So do I, but I try to keep my personal and professional lives separate. I'm not always successful..." Evan pressed her lips into a tight line as if realizing she'd revealed too much. She picked at her sandwich but didn't actually eat any of it.

Frankie tried for humor. "You don't bring all the guys up here?" She wanted to know how Evan felt, because their conversation had seemed intimate to her. The thought was a jolt of reality. She didn't do intimate, partly because of time and circumstances, but she'd also been taught that emotions were tools, and she didn't get attached to her tools. Why did that feel wrong with Evan? She circled back to the question. "So, our chat *was* personal?"

"Don't do this, Frankie." Evan finally looked at her, and a combination of sadness and pain darkened her features. "Eat your dinner and enjoy the fresh air before we go back to work."

Frankie flinched as she imagined the door slamming between them. "Okay. So, am I allowed to ask a business question?"

"Sure." Her tone sounded anything but.

"Why are you and the other guys so protective of Aaron, other than the obvious?" She immediately regretted the question because Evan's face paled and her eyes turned black. "I'm not trying to be insensitive. He seems like he can handle himself."

"He's had a rough time lately, and we're looking out for him."

"But what—"

"Let it go." The simple sentence closed the subject.

"Okay, then tell me about Robert Griffin's arrest."

Evan dropped her sandwich on the table. Her jaw tightened, and she spoke through clenched teeth. "You don't give up, do you?"

"Not when the whole team is keeping things from me. Are the two connected somehow? What is it, Evan?"

Evan wrapped her arms around herself and seemed to withdraw. She stared at the floor so long Frankie wasn't sure she was going to answer. "If I asked you to please drop this, would you?" Her expression said this secret caused her considerable pain, and Frankie didn't want that.

"If you told me it doesn't impact finding our fugitives, yes, I'd drop it. For you."

Evan nodded. "Then please do."

Frankie studied Evan a few seconds longer, unconvinced that she was being honest because she looked everywhere in the room except at her. But she'd agreed to move on, so she retreated to a safer subject. "What is this space used for?"

Evan released a long breath and some of the tension in her body eased. "Nothing at the moment. I'm surprised they don't use it for storage, but it would be a shame to close off these views, not to mention my secret hiding place. I sneak up here sometimes when I need a break."

"Seriously." They ate in silence, exchanging glances that felt more intimate than words. Why was Evan so determined to keep their relationship professional? She had to feel the chemistry between them. What was the rest of the story behind this case? And who or what had hurt her so badly that distance was her first defense? Frankie wanted to know all of it but had no right to ask.

"Okay, if that was dinner, I've done it." Evan balled the remainder of her sandwich up in the paper and stuffed it back in the bag. "You ready?"

"Yeah, Hank is probably getting antsy." Evan started to fold the chairs, but Frankie clasped her hand, and felt Evan tense before briefly relaxing. The comfortable, calming connection Frankie had felt earlier returned, but the warmth in Evan's eyes vanished as she pulled away. "Thank you for this. I really needed it."

Evan hesitated a second longer. "You're welcome. It's part of my job to keep my agents healthy and functioning at full capacity." She waved toward the door. "Shall we? You and Hank wrap this up in the next couple of hours. We'll start fresh in the morning."

After a quick trip to the bathroom and a scolding to refocus, Frankie eased the interview room door open and returned to her chair. Hank finished writing something and passed her a sheet of paper with several banks in the United States and abroad along with some individuals' names and countries of origin. "What's this?"

"Winston's money laundering locations and drug contacts abroad." He gave her a grin and nodded toward Grif. "The man knows everything." Grif sat up straighter and smiled broadly. Hank had established a solid connection with him, and Frankie was happy to let him lead.

"That's excellent. Now, do you mind if we jump forward to the incident behind the Daytime Resource Center?" Frankie avoided using the term murder because it sometimes put suspects off and she wanted to keep him talking.

"Sheriff killed Mr. Weber," Grif said, looking at the floor.

"Sheriff whose real name was Dennis Lowell?" Hank asked for clarification.

"Yeah." Grif nodded toward Frankie. "The one she shot and killed." Frankie started to respond, but he continued. "Not that he didn't need killing. He was one nasty piece of work. Scared me just being around the dude."

"Did Sheriff make the decision to kill Weber?"

Grif's laugh sounded harsh and acidic. "Ha! The only decisions Sheriff ever made were…" He put a finger beside his nose and snorted and then lowered his hand to his crotch and pumped in an up and down motion.

"So, who gave the order?" Frankie asked.

"Who do you think?"

Hank rolled his hand at Grif. "We need you to tell us."

"Matthew Winston told Sheriff to handle Weber because he'd been snooping around his drug business."

"And you were present when this conversation took place?" Grif nodded, and Hank scooted his chair to the opposite side of the table. "Can you remember any more details?"

"Like it was yesterday. Me, Grady Tyndall, who we call Ty, Ty's girlfriend, Winston, and Sheriff were in Winston's den at his home having our weekly business meeting. He was puffing on one of those stinky Cuban cigars he loves so much, making my stomach queasy as fuck. When Ty said Mr. Weber was asking questions at the DRC and checking prescription numbers, Winston slapped his hand on the desk, jumped up, and pointed his cigar at Sheriff and said, 'Take care of that motherfucker, and I mean permanently.'"

Frankie shot Hank a questioning look, but he wouldn't make eye contact. "What girl?" She got a chill, certain this was important.

"That's good, Grif," Hank said as if she hadn't spoken. "You've done really well today, and we appreciate it. Unfortunately, we have to start again tomorrow. I don't know about you, but I'm beat."

"Tomorrow? You mean I have to spend another night in jail?" Grif shook his head. "Isn't there something you can do? I'm not going to try to escape. Can't you treat me like a protected witness? Get me a hotel room? Anything. Please?"

"*What girl?*" Frankie asked again, but Hank seemed determined to ignore her. "Is she the reason you're all being so secretive?"

Hank didn't look at Frankie before saying, "I'll talk to the boss, Grif, but no guarantees." He gathered his notes, bolted for the door with Frankie behind, and didn't stop until he reached Evan's desk.

Frankie didn't give him a chance to brief Evan. "Who the hell is Grady Tyndall's girlfriend and why isn't she in any of the reports?"

Evan's face blanched.

"How is she connected to the case? Is this what everybody's been hiding from me?" She tried to make eye contact, but none of the guys would look at her. Even Evan studied her tablet like it held some magic answer.

"It's not like that, Frankie," Hank said.

She ignored him and stared directly at Evan. "What else aren't you telling me?"

"Frank—" Evan's voice cracked.

"You said your little secret had nothing to do with this case. You lied to me." That knowledge alone made Frankie feel sick. She thought she'd crossed a barrier with Evan, but at the very least, she should be able to tell when she was lying. Maybe those warm, fuzzy feelings were clouding her judgment.

"No, I said it wouldn't impact finding our fugitives," Evan fired back.

"Semantics. What else are you hiding?"

"Frankie...we...I—"

"Never mind. I'll ask someone I trust. Thanks for the vote of confidence." Pressure pounded behind her eyes. She grabbed her bag and started out but turned back. "I didn't expect a lot from this assignment, but I hoped we could at least be honest with each other since we want the same thing." A cold, empty feeling settled in her chest, and she walked out of the office, ignoring Hank's and Evan's calls to stop.

Chapter Six

While the grass was still wet with dew the next morning, Frankie coasted her scooter into Colby Vincent's driveway and briefly reconsidered intruding, but she needed answers the team wasn't providing, and they'd had chances. During her sleepless night, the cell had rung twice, once from Evan and once from Hank, but she'd ignored the calls. When she talked to them, she'd do it face-to-face to gauge the truth of what they said. The fact that Evan had kept something vital from her was an especially bitter truth. They weren't friends, but she thought they'd reached an understanding. Frankie took a deep breath and rang the doorbell.

Colby, her reddish-blond hair only slightly longer than her shaved undercover look, opened the door. "Hey, girl, long time no see. Damn, can you say obvi? I'd tag you as a spy for sure in that outfit. What's with the getup?"

"I was snooping at the DRC and didn't want anybody to recognize me as Sing Song."

"Is everything all right down there? No trouble, I hope." Colby waved her inside.

"No trouble. I was looking for someone. Besides, you know me, constantly reinventing my look." It was probably more about not feeling totally comfortable in her own skin some days or needing a mask to hide behind. "Thanks for agreeing to see me so early."

"You're always welcome." She gripped Frankie's shoulder and guided her toward the kitchen. "I'm having a second cup of coffee. Can I tempt you?"

"Definitely."

"Light and two sugars if I recall?"

"Yes, please. If you have espresso, I'll take a double." Frankie pulled her fedora and sunglasses off and placed them on the table. "I feel like being somebody else today." She'd been hurt when the Marshals boxed her out, especially Evan.

"Ouch. New assignment not going well?" When Frankie gave her a sideways look, Colby added, "You shadowed me for weeks undercover. I learned a few things about you."

Frankie shook her head unable to find a simple or witty comeback. She'd thought she was making progress with the guys. They'd been out to lunch and even had drinks after work, and Evan was thawing too, but she'd apparently misread the whole situation. Was it all a ruse to keep her in the dark? Could she have totally missed the signs?

Colby motioned her toward a pale yellow upholstered banquette overlooking the backyard, placed Frankie's brew on the table, and slid in beside her. "Still trying to find Winston?"

Frankie took a sip and looked around for Colby's partner. "Adena isn't here?"

Colby shook her head. "She got called in early on a pro bono case by one of her pals at the DA's office. Tell me what's going on, Frankie. I'll share it with her when she gets home."

Frankie nodded. "I didn't relish telling her the latest news. Looks like Winston might've fled the country. And…he's the one who ordered Franklin Weber's execution."

"Damn. That'll be hard for Adena to take. He was once a family friend."

"Sorry to be the bearer of bad news," Frankie said.

"It is what it is, but we have to find this guy. None of us will rest until Winston is brought to justice."

"You have my word. No matter what it takes." Frankie looked up at Colby. "I need your help."

"Well, you know that's happening. Anything." When Frankie didn't answer immediately, Colby nudged her. "What's up, pal? Are the Marshals not playing nice with DEA?"

Frankie stared into her coffee cup for several seconds, wondering if she was making the right decision, but she had to know. "During your investigation, did you hear anyone mention Grady Tyndall's girlfriend?"

Colby sipped her coffee and finally said, "He was a total cock hound, but I wasn't aware he had a steady girlfriend. On the other hand, I wasn't asked to socialize with the bosses, so anything's possible. Why?"

"It came up in the interview with our witness, and my new team members didn't seem surprised. They've been holding out on me, and I don't know why. I asked around the DRC this morning, and nobody knows anything about a girlfriend. And there's something else. Our witness, Robert Griffin, alluded to his arrest going wrong somehow. The agent who arrested him at the airport made a report, but it isn't included in the case file. It's been classified. And she's been transferred."

"The only reason to restrict access to a report in a case like this is to protect a witness's or an agent's identity."

"That's what I thought. Can you get hold of the report? The marshal's name is Madeline Gallagher. My boss said it was classified at division level, which leaves me out."

Colby finished her coffee and reached for her cell phone. "Making supervisor has its privileges. Watch this." She punched a number and when the other party picked up, she said, "It's Colby Vincent. I need a favor. The Matthew Winston case. I'm missing a classified report from Marshall Gallagher on the arrest of defendant Robert Griffin. Can you email that to me? Thanks, I owe you."

"Damn, wish I had connections like that. How long will it take?"

"Matter of minutes usually. Another shot while we wait?"

Frankie drained her cup and handed it to Colby. "That's damn good coffee."

"I have it blended and shipped from my favorite shop in Seattle."

Frankie watched Colby prepare their coffees and grinned at the domesticity of it. Would she ever feel as comfortable sharing a home with another woman? Would she even find a woman she wanted to pledge her life to and who felt the same about her? The ring of her cell phone startled her, and she glanced at the display. A surge of emotions tumbled through her, and she switched the phone off. When Colby gave her a look, she said, "My new boss."

"Evan Spears?"

Frankie nodded.

Colby placed their coffees on the table and sat. "Tall, dark, mysterious, and sexy as fuck?"

"You know her?"

"I've seen her a few times on cases, but I don't know her, just her reputation." She winked. "She could be your type."

"Seriously? She can't stand me. I'm too much of a rebel."

"Well, you do have an impulsive streak, which makes you a kick-ass agent. She'll warm to you if you let her think you're following the rules. You might be good for her...and maybe vice versa. Aren't you ready to settle down?"

"Stop trying to play matchmaker. You suck at it." Frankie touched her cup to the side of Colby's. "Here's to finding Winston and putting him away for life."

"Roger that."

Colby stretched back in her seat and grinned at Frankie. "So... what's the real story with you and Marshal Spears? Those blue eyes of yours go all shimmery when we talk about her."

Frankie took another sip of coffee to cover any expression. "Shimmery? Really, Vincent? Domesticity has softened your brain."

"I don't thin—" Colby's phone pinged and she held up a finger. "Hold that thought while I print this off." She came back a few seconds later waving a single sheet of paper in her hand. "This isn't going to help much."

"Why?" Colby placed the page on the table, and Frankie stared at it. "Really? Redacted? What the hell is going on with this case?"

"I'm not sure why an arrest report would need to be classified and redacted. Let's see what we have." She sat down beside Frankie again.

"Madeline Gallagher and other marshals, all named here, arrested Robert Griffin at Piedmont Triad International Airport," Frankie continued reading. "Two other suspects who were supposed to be there didn't show. An entire paragraph is blacked out."

Colby took over. "Matthew Winston and Grady Tyndall escaped, obviously. The identity of the other marshals isn't a big deal, so the secret is in the paragraph we can't read."

"Now you see my concern. How am I supposed to trust and work with people who aren't honest with me?"

"This doesn't match what I've heard about Evan. She's usually by the book. We have to be missing something. Why don't you leave this with me and I'll find out what's going on?"

Frankie checked her watch. "I don't like facing the team again without all the facts."

"I get that, but let me handle it. I'll contact you as soon as possible."

"Okay. If I don't leave now, I'll be late again and face the wrath of Spears." She gulped the last of her coffee and gave Colby a quick hug at the door. "Thanks for this. And please tell Adena that I'm sorry again for the bad news."

"You got it, pal. Talk soon."

Evan glanced at the wall clock as Frankie burst into the office at exactly eight. Today she sported a long brunette wig, black fedora pulled low on her forehead, tortoise shell sunglasses, and a baggy army fatigue jacket. Was she hiding after her angry exit yesterday or just trying to push Evan's buttons again? She stifled comments about cutting it close and not answering her cell because any reference to rules or protocol would probably send Frankie over the edge. "Right. Let's pick up where we left off. Aaron, anything new from our Blue Notice?"

He pushed his glasses up on his nose and without looking away from the computer said, "No, ma'am."

Evan turned her attention to Hank. "Is our guest ready to continue this morning? I hope he got a good night's sleep at the Marriott."

"What?" Frankie glared at Hank over the top of her glasses.

He rose from behind his desk and started toward the interview room. "Tried to call you and tell you we were putting him in a hotel overnight. You ready for round two?"

"No. Not really."

Hank stopped, Todd dropped his copy of *Sports Illustrated*, and Aaron rolled from behind his computer screens, ready for the show. Evan clasped her hands in her lap. *Here we go.*

"What's up?" Hank asked.

Frankie stood beside her desk, arms stiff at her sides, fists clenched, and her face flushed. She was outraged and absolutely gorgeous. The garb that made her look like a poorly cast TV spy was both sexy and humorous, but didn't begin to cover her anger, righteous anger. Evan's wayward thoughts vanished when Frankie finally spoke again.

"Are all of you seriously going to pretend yesterday didn't happen? Who the hell is Grady Tyndall's girlfriend, how does she fit into this case, and what happened during Griffin's arrest? Why does he think it was a total clusterfuck?"

Evan felt Frankie's frustration mingle with her own fear that she was putting the pieces together. She considered explaining everything, answering all Frankie's questions, but the case had to come first. They had a cooperative witness, and the clock was ticking. As soon as she had all the facts, she'd consider the pros and cons of filling Frankie in. "Why don't you take it down a notch?"

"And you…" Frankie, a five-feet-five mass of vibrating emotion, stalked toward Evan. "For all your sermons about protocol, accountability, and trust, how can—"

"Come with me. Now." Hank grabbed Frankie's arm and ushered her down the hallway.

"But I'm not finished."

"Yeah, you are. We have a job to do and it's not soothing your hurt pride. Either help or get out of the way." Hank released Frankie's arm and waited. Her face transformed from barely contained rage to irritation and finally to complete calm.

Frankie glanced back at Evan and when she spoke, her words were clipped and ice cold. "Sorry. This isn't over." Then she followed Hank into the interview room.

"Damn. I wouldn't want to piss her off in a dark alley," Todd said. "She be small but she be mighty."

"We should've told her," Aaron mumbled and retreated to his computers.

Evan rested her elbows on top of her desk, and her insides roiled. Frankie was right. She hadn't lived up to her standards of honesty and transparency, having purposely left vital information out of Frankie's briefing. She had every right to be upset.

The rest of the day, Evan reviewed the case file and the agents' reports, and located her checklist for overseas operations. She prayed Griffin's information led to a search close to home, but her gut said she wouldn't be so lucky. Handling such an operation on foreign soil was always challenging, but with Frankie along, it could be a nightmare.

She pulled Maddie Gallagher's arrest report, coffee-stained and crumpled, from the folder and read it again, filling in the blacked-out paragraph she'd memorized. A shiver of pain and disgust lanced through her as the scene replayed in her mind. How could she explain such a catastrophic fuckup to Frankie? How had she been so careless, so trusting? She was running through another version of possible speeches when footsteps sounded in the hallway.

"Well, guys, saddle up. We're going to Australia," Hank said.

Frankie went straight to her desk without speaking, Todd did a cowboy yee-haw, and Aaron spun his wheelchair in a circle in the middle of the floor. The tense wait-and-see atmosphere morphed into a more expectant one.

"Let's not get ahead of ourselves," Evan said. "Details, please?"

"Winston's escape plan was a cargo ship out of Miami to Sydney. He kept a container at PortMiami for the past six months and filled it with personal items, and of course, money. He started draining his US accounts after Franklin Weber's murder, figuring things were taking a bad turn. He and Tyndall flew to Miami the same day we arrested Griffin. The only things we don't know are which ship they were on and the names they were traveling under. I believe Griffin has given us everything he knows." He looked to Frankie for confirmation.

She nodded in agreement but didn't say anything. Frankie didn't seem like the pouting type, so Evan guessed she was still annoyed at being shut out. But even in her silence, Frankie was a presence in the room. The guys waited for her input, already considering her part of the team.

"Where does that leave us?" Evan regarded her agents one by one but avoided Frankie, her discomfort a combination of guilt, liking her, and having kept her in the dark.

"PortMiami is the busiest cruise and passenger port in the world, the largest container port in the state of Florida, and ninth in the United States. We've got our work cut out for us trying to find out which ship they're on," Aaron said.

Todd shook his head, his red curls shifting side to side. "How the hell do you keep all that crap in your head?"

Aaron pointed both thumbs at himself and said, "This guy is legit."

"Get your legit behind on cameras, passengers, and cargo manifests out of PortMiami ASAP," Evan said. "Todd, have pictures of Winston and Tyndall, complete with facial hair mock-ups, compared to every passport out of Miami and into Sydney in the past month. And I mean a thorough search. I want everything Griffin told us verified as much as possible before we spend the taxpayers' money flying overseas."

Evan had gotten so involved in passing out assignments, she almost missed Frankie heading for the door. "Going somewhere, Agent Strong?"

"You obviously don't need me anymore. I'm out."

"Frankie, wait…" What could she say? Frankie probably wouldn't be approved to go to Australia since she was junior and not a marshal, so she didn't need to be briefed on the mission. And anything else she might've said was irrelevant to the case. Each of the guys in turn glanced between her and Frankie with the same question in his eyes.

"Anything else, Agent Spears?"

"No. Thanks for your help with the interview."

When the door closed behind Frankie, Evan turned back to her team. "Before any of you ask, no, I didn't tell her about the arrest, Aaron's injury, or the mole. She probably won't be going with us abroad, so she didn't need to know…any of that. End of story." She checked the wall clock. "Let's get to a stopping point and call it. Good job today."

Hank and Todd started packing up, but Aaron met her gaze and shook his head. He didn't have to say anything. She knew exactly what he was thinking—coward—and he was right. But now she wouldn't have to retell her heartbreaking story one more time. It was probably best for everyone. She continued her mental justification of the unjustifiable. Frankie wouldn't see what a fraud she was. The guys would be safer working with the team they knew. And Evan wouldn't cross another line with Frankie Strong.

CHAPTER SEVEN

E van stuffed her reports and the tape of Griffin's interview into her bag and made her way to the parking deck, second-guessing her decision about how she'd treated Frankie. Had withholding information affected her contribution to the team or her interview with Griffin? If so, Evan saw no evidence of it. She'd made the right decision. She took a few more steps and then faltered. Who was she kidding? She didn't *want* Frankie to know the whole story. Add withholding witness information and her inability to admit she'd made a mistake, and Evan felt even more inadequate.

She started to drive home but instead kept north on Elm and pulled into the parking lot of one of her favorite pubs. Frankie, the case, and another international manhunt spun through her mind and she wanted to talk it through, to hear the words aloud. It was harder to mislead herself when someone else was listening. She fished her cell out of her pocket and dialed Eli. "Hey, big brother, got time for a quick bite at Fishers?"

"Sure. Just finishing up for the day. See you in fifteen."

The restaurant was filling up quickly for the live music set due to begin at six. Evan hurried to the back booth, ordered two beers, and waited. She was grateful for the soft jazz band because she and Eli would be able to talk over the music. When he came through the door, she waved to get his attention.

He grinned and sauntered toward her. "This is a nice midweek surprise." He settled across from her and his smile vanished. "What's wrong?"

"I just needed to talk something through with you. I might've fucked up big time."

He cupped her hand on the table. "I doubt that. Tell me." He took a sip of his beer and stretched out across the bench seat while she retold her story about keeping Frankie in the dark. When she finished, he drained the bottle and motioned for two more beers. "You made a judgment call. It could've gone either way."

"But it went the wrong way. She found out I was hiding information. I don't blame her for being pissed. If that happened to me, I'd—"

"You'd have somebody's head on a platter." Eli thanked the waitress for the beers and slid one in front of Evan.

"Yeah. I would." She buried her head in her hands. "What a hypocrite."

"It's called being a supervisor and making decisions. You can't get them all right. Give yourself a break." When she didn't respond, Eli asked, "Is this only about the decision or is there more to it? Are you worried about how it affected Frankie?"

Evan jerked upright. "What? Of course not. I can't consider agents' feelings every time I make a decision." But Eli's eyes were so much like hers it felt like lying to herself in a mirror. "I don't know. Maybe. Possibly." His gaze didn't waver, and their connection demanded the truth. She felt like she was somehow admitting defeat. "Yes."

"Then you need to talk to her."

"It's too late. She's pretty much finished her work with us, and I failed, again, to maintain professional boundaries. What's left to say?"

The band's song ended with the low strum of a guitar, and Evan heard laughter from the booth behind Eli, familiar laughter. Frankie. Eli started to say something, but she held up her hand and strained to hear more.

"After the day I've had, a vodka tonic sounds perfect."

"On the way," another woman's deeper voice said. "We might need several before this night is over."

Eavesdropping was a low Evan didn't aspire to, and she started to get up, but Frankie's next comment stopped her.

"I really appreciate you looking into this missing report for me, Colby."

"You're not going to understand it any better, but read it first and we'll talk."

Evan peeked around the side of the booth as Colby handed a folded paper to Frankie. Frankie spread the document on the table and stared at it for several seconds before looking back up at Colby.

"The only thing this tells me that I didn't know this morning is that Aaron also assisted with the arrest. That explains the assault charge and why the guys are so protective, but doesn't answer the other questions."

"What isn't on the arrest report is the full account of the take-down and why it went wrong. I talked to some folks off the record and filled in the blanks. Gallagher filed another report that didn't go into the Winston file." She reached into her back pocket again and offered another page to Frankie.

Evan couldn't stand it any longer. "I have to take care of something, Eli. Sorry about dinner. Can I call you later?"

"Sure. Just be honest with her." He waved away Evan's offer of money, stopped to pay their tab, and headed to the exit.

She pulled in a deep breath to steady her nerves. She'd dreaded this moment since Frankie joined the team but knew it would happen eventually. Grabbing her beer, she slid from her seat and stood beside Frankie's booth. "Don't do this, Frankie." Both women stared at her, but Frankie's expression was pained.

"What are you doing here? Did you follow me?"

"Of course not. I'm pretty sure I was here first with my brother." She'd been so focused on their conversation that she hadn't seen Frankie and Colby come in.

Frankie nodded but didn't break eye contact. "So, why are you here? Now? We're finished, as far as the case is concerned. You got what you wanted so just walk away."

Why was she here? She could've, actually should've, left when she heard Frankie's voice. Maybe she wanted to confess, to be open with Frankie, but why? What was the point now? "I…I needed to talk to someone. And if I'm honest, I have no idea about the rest." Frankie held her gaze until Evan's insides tightened.

"Bad day at work maybe?" Frankie's mouth quirked into a partial grin, and Evan let out a long breath at the hint of levity.

"You could definitely say that. What about you?"

"Same." Frankie hoisted her glass. "Nothing a vodka tonic and that report in Colby's hand won't solve."

"I really wish you wouldn't read that."

"Because it will tell me everything you didn't?"

Evan finally looked away and regretted it. Frankie could blank her facial expressions like a pro, but her eyes were a direct line to her feelings, and Evan needed the connection to continue. "Because it reports something in clinical terms that was anything but."

"Then tell me, Evan, please."

"And that's my cue," Colby said, rising from her seat and offering it to Evan. "You two obviously need to talk." She squeezed Frankie's shoulder. "Call if you need me."

Frankie took Evan's hand and guided her into the booth, and for the first time Evan didn't resist her touch. Didn't want to resist. She clung to her as if she could somehow mitigate what was about to happen.

"Just talk to me, Evan. I deserve the truth. I've given too much to leave with questions."

"You're right."

Frankie placed the report Colby had given her on the table between them and stared at it. "You really don't trust me?"

"It's not about that." Frankie gave her a skeptical look. "Okay, maybe it's a little bit of that, but it's more complicated."

"And I'm incapable of understanding complicated?"

Frankie's voice was husky with emotion, and Evan wanted to help her understand, but she'd have to open up for that to happen. Was she ready for the pain, for Frankie to know what she'd done? She wrapped her hands around her cold beer bottle and grew very still, forcing her emotions down. If she was going to tell this story, she had to keep it together long enough to make it to the end.

"It's not about you, Frankie. Really. I made mistakes. People I cared about were hurt. How can I explain to someone I—" Someone she, what? Found exciting, cared about, wanted to sleep with? How did she feel about Frankie? Part of her wanted to leave now and have nothing further to do with the reckless, unpredictable agent. But she couldn't stop thinking about Frankie, wanting to be swept away in her passion and revitalized by her enthusiasm for life, but their circumstances and the potential complications paralyzed her.

"We all make mistakes, Evan." Frankie leaned across the table. "Just tell me."

Once she heard the whole story, Frankie would regard her with disgust and pity. Evan looked away and began. "You've already figured out that Aaron was injured during Robert Griffin's arrest. It's the reason he's in a wheelchair and may never walk again." The words gushed out, and her stomach churned at hearing them aloud for the first time.

"And the reason you were opposed to the plea agreement?"

"Yes, I let him and the team down, and someone needed to pay," Evan said.

"How was his injury your fault?"

"The agent covering one of the escape routes at the airport was distracted, and the op went sideways. An intoxicated employee driving a utility vehicle rammed through the target zone and hit Aaron from behind. It was dark, and none of the agents were wearing reflective vests."

"Shit," Frankie said. "I had no idea. That night must've been horrible for all of you."

Evan threaded her fingers together and squeezed until they ached. "Is there more?"

"I...I was the agent covering that escape route." She choked down the vile taste that accompanied her admission.

"Oh my God, Evan. How awful." Frankie reached for her hands, but Evan pulled back.

"Don't. When you know all of it, you'll never want to see me again."

"You blame yourself for not planning enough, not executing properly, not having the guys wear reflective vests, which by the way would've been stupid for a UC arrest. The list goes on in your mind I'm sure, but that still doesn't make it your fault."

She wanted to take comfort from Frankie's words, but she didn't know everything yet. "But it was my fault. Read that report, and then I'll fill in the blanks."

"Are you sure? A few minutes ago, you were trying to stop me."

"I guess I really am a coward. Just read it." Evan took a sip of her beer for courage to face what came next but had difficulty swallowing. How could she harp on rules and procedures every day when she hadn't followed them herself? She searched Frankie's face for a reaction or an emotion of any kind as she read the report, but found none. What was Frankie thinking? What would she think of her?

Frankie scanned the document several times before she looked up again. Her face was impassive, and her gaze settled somewhere over Evan's shoulder. "So, Agent Gallagher interviewed a witness, Judith Earl, later about Winston's escape and supposedly turned her as an informant."

Evan felt the blood drain from her face and she shivered at the name. "Judith Earl was...my lover."

Frankie gasped. "Fuck." She stared at Evan until her expression changed from disbelief to understanding and then something else Evan couldn't identify. "But I'm still lost."

"Jude, Judith was also Grady Tyndall's girlfriend at the time of Griffin's arrest."

Frankie's mouth dropped open. "Wait. What?"

"Yeah. I had no clue what she was doing, which makes me an even bigger fool." She'd since put the pieces together—their first meeting, times Jude was supposed to be with her but wasn't, incidences where Winston seemed two steps ahead of the hunt, and finally, all the money she flaunted with no obvious source of income.

"What exactly *was* she doing?"

"Sleeping with me for information about the case to pass to Tyndall and Winston." Frankie looked like she'd been sucker punched, and Evan felt like it.

"Jeez, Evan. I can't imagine. That explains a lot. And I'm guessing this woman was the distraction the night of the arrest?"

Evan nodded. "She called Tyndall and warned him about the arrests."

"And you?"

Evan felt another wave of nausea followed by anger. "Judith called me and said she'd fucked up, that she was in love with Tyndall.

Her call came at the same time the team noticed Griffin heading for Winston's plane and moved in for the arrest. I was distracted for only a second, but that's all it took. In the aftermath of Aaron being hit, Winston and Tyndall got another jet and flew to Miami. She played me exactly right."

"That's cold. I'm so sorry." She reached for Evan, but she leaned away.

"I can't. Not right now." Evan couldn't let Frankie near her. She didn't deserve comfort. She'd lied, withheld, and jeopardized any relationship she and Frankie might have professionally and possibly personally as well. She still had to get through everything. The worst was over, the rest merely details.

"What happened to her?"

"Tyndall left her behind for some reason, and she briefly went to ground. Maybe he thought she was a liability, maybe she was supposed to meet up with him later. When we located her, Michael English transferred Madeline Gallagher to another team and let her run Judith as an asset, but it fell through. Jude pulled the same scam on Maddie, coming on to her while still maintaining contact with Ty and Winston and keeping tabs on the manhunt. In the end, Jude couldn't resist the temptations of money, exotic places, and excitement, even if she was on the run. Last track we had on her, she was on a flight to Hong Kong. She could be with them now or already in Australia."

"So, the report was classified to protect Judith as an informant." Evan nodded. "And this Judith, your ex, is also charged in the case?"

Evan nodded again. "I'm sorry I kept this from you, but I needed to know I could trust you. Then I thought you'd only be with us a few days and move on to another assignment." She dug deep for the courage to continue. "And, if I'm totally honest, I was embarrassed about how stupid I'd been. Not exactly a glowing recommendation for a supervisor…or anything else."

"I'm sorry she betrayed you, Evan. I can't imagine how hard it's been for you."

"Don't." The tenderness in Frankie's voice was a balm of relief she hadn't earned.

"Don't what? Try to understand?"

"Try to make me feel better. I got Aaron hurt, let three suspects escape, and the cherry on top, was deceived by my girlfriend for a drug dealer. I should've seen the signs. And then I kept the details from a member of my team to cover my professional and personal embarrassment."

Frankie reached for her again, but Evan shook her head. If she let Frankie touch her right now, she'd lose it. Repeating this story had been painful enough, but falling apart in front of a woman she hardly knew and was crossing boundaries with could break her. Emotions and faulty instincts had gotten her in this mess in the first place.

"Please, let me touch you."

"Can't." She turned away, unable to meet Frankie's gaze. Why had she told her? She could've left it alone, and Frankie would probably be out of her life by tomorrow.

"So, how did you meet this Judith person? Fellow agent?"

Evan scoffed. "That might've been easier to swallow. I literally bumped into her at a bakery and spilled coffee on her. Should've seen that as a setup. She was already sleeping with Tyndall and—"

"And you were the mark," Frankie added. "Evan, you don't have to feel guilty or ashamed. Things happen in life that we have no control over."

"But I *should've* had control. I should've sensed a setup, but I fell for her too quickly without any idea who she really was. I'll always feel responsible for Aaron's injury and letting them escape." She took a steadying breath, and the burden of hiding her secret from Frankie lifted but was replaced by more shame and guilt. At least she'd cleared the air. No more secrets.

When Frankie didn't have an immediate comeback, Evan glanced over at her. She was staring at her empty glass and seemed miles away. "So now you understand why you and I can't happen. I'm afraid it would destroy me, not to mention my career."

"If it's about you supervising me, we've already established that isn't the case."

Evan shook her head. "It's not necessarily that. The whole job mixed with relationship doesn't work for me. I have to keep them separate. Both are just too intense."

"I see."

When Frankie looked at her again, Evan saw more hurt than shock or disgust. Was Frankie also having feelings she couldn't easily dismiss? "Are you all right? TMI perhaps?"

"Fine, just processing. How about you?"

"I would've been glad to never say those words aloud again, but you were right, you deserved to know." She drained her beer and glanced toward the bar as the band started another set. "What do we have to do to get a refill around here? I feel like I could use another." She had to get off this subject before she broke down completely. She'd shed enough tears for her mistakes.

"I'm really sorry for your pain," Frankie said. She paused and her eyes got a mischievous glint. "At least now I understand why you're so shut down. That long black coat you wear is like a shield against feeling anything, and even when you take it off, you're still untouchable."

"What? I am *not* shut down and untouchable. If I were, I wouldn't be here. With you. Spilling my guts." Frankie chuckled, and Evan glared at her. "You baited me."

"We were drowning in funk. But you have to admit, you are a little distant, especially with me. I'm hurt that you didn't trust me, but I get why." They briefly made eye contact, and Frankie winked. "But now you realize I *have* to go with the team to Australia."

"Why?" Evan's neck and shoulders tightened again.

"I have to make sure this ex of yours pays for her crimes and for what she did to you. It's only right. You have to get me on the away team."

Evan's heart stuttered. Frankie cared about her, wanted justice for her, but if she went on the hunt, they'd be together even more. Could she handle that? Did she want to? "No, Frankie. I can't afford for anything like that to happen again. Ever. I might not be strong enough yet to...it could be a problem." Evan fisted her hands in her lap. The possibility of spending more time with Frankie was both exciting and distressing, but Evan didn't want to battle her attraction to Frankie while searching for the woman who betrayed her.

"You care about me?"

"Let's not have this discussion, Frankie. Please."

"Just answer that one question, because I'm struggling where you're concerned."

Evan felt like running. She'd bared half her soul already and wasn't sure she could rip open the other side so soon. "The scary part is, you already know the answer. You're annoyingly intuitive, and I'm not very good at hiding my feelings. But having them and acting on them are different things."

"That's nice to hear, because I like you, and it confuses the hell out of me." Frankie traced a small trench cut into the table with her forefinger and then stopped. "Are you afraid I'll pull some lone ranger stunt and get someone hurt if I go on the trip?"

"That and...other stuff." She glanced at Frankie wondering if she felt the energy roiling between them like a growing thing.

"Yeah, other stuff. I feel it too." She trailed her fingers up Evan's arm, leaving goose bumps and heat.

"That right there, and the fact that I like it so much, says this is not a good idea. Please let me do my job and then we'll see." Frankie pulled her hand back and the void made Evan wince.

"You can trust me, Evan. The truth and I can be strangers when necessary on the job, but I'm loyal and dependable. I'm not your ex."

The pleading look in Frankie's eyes tugged at Evan. She wanted Frankie with her, but the possibility of a repeat Judith situation terrified her. The feelings between them were already too strong. She should say no, absolutely not. "If you promise to work with the team..." Frankie broke into a wide smile. "And listen and follow directions. *And* no more of the...other stuff until the case is over. Deal?"

"Not even touching, just a little?"

Evan gave her a hard stare.

"Aye aye, ma'am." Frankie mock saluted. "Yes, ma'am. When do we start?"

"I have to arrange transport, finalize a few details, mostly logistics. We could be on our way tomorrow evening."

"Thank you, Evan. I won't let you down."

Since she'd accepted Frankie on the team, life had been a roller coaster of highs and lows but never boring. Frankie had blasted through the wall around her emotions like it didn't exist, gotten her to talk about her greatest fear and reveal her worst nightmare. Evan prayed she wasn't making another huge mistake. "I should probably go."

"Yeah, me too."

Evan waited by the door until Frankie paid her bill and then walked her to the parking lot and stopped beside her scooter. "Interesting choice."

"It does the trick, and I like feeling the wind in my face."

Evan shook her head. She could imagine Frankie weaving in and out of traffic on the orange death trap, tempting fate and reveling in the adrenaline rush. "Don't be late tomorrow, rookie."

Frankie started toward her, eyes focused on Evan's lips, but stopped short. "Right. No other stuff."

CHAPTER EIGHT

Frankie tugged her seat belt tighter as the diplomatic transport jet they'd hitched a ride on began its descent into Sydney, but her mind was on the conversation she and Evan had at Fishers Grille two days ago, specifically the personal parts. She'd replayed them over in her mind and come up with the same conclusions— Evan was willing to let her see the case through in spite of her better judgment. She was attracted to her and determined nothing could happen between them. Her admissions only made Frankie admire and want her more, because now she understood and wanted to prove she wasn't like Judith.

Evan had trusted Judith and been trampled personally, professionally, and rather publicly. She didn't have the option of grieving in private because her team, supervisors, and anyone else who read the reports knew she'd trusted Judith. Cops could be brutal about betrayal because they somehow imagined themselves above it all. And facing Aaron daily had to remind Evan of her failure. Her caution, insistence on following the rules, and unapproachability made perfect sense. Frankie regretted pressing her to relive everything.

She glanced at Evan, flipping through a pile of neatly stacked papers, as the plane dipped lower and Frankie's ears popped. She reached into her bag for gum and passed it around. Even in profile, the worry line across Evan's forehead and tightness at the corner of her mouth were evident. And something else. A deeper sense of vulnerability Frankie hadn't recognized before their talk. She felt a connection to Evan—like protectiveness and an unfamiliar but persistent tug on her emotions—and she vowed to make this assignment easier for her.

Evan placed each paper back into the folder, neat and organized as ever, checked her phone, and motioned for the team. "Gather round, guys." She, Hank, Todd, and Evan sat at a small table more typical of a train setup with Aaron anchored at the end in his wheelchair. "We've caught a break. The ship Winston and Tyndall are on is scheduled to arrive about the time we land. Our local liaison has asked the port authorities to delay passengers from disembarking until we get there. He'll have transport waiting to take us directly to Port Botany where the ship will dock. Let's do another quick run-through of the plan before we land."

Frankie stifled a groan, but Todd wasn't so restrained. "Seriously, boss? We've been over the plan a zillion times already. We know what to do."

"Yes, and—"

"Please." Frankie raised her hand as a strained look crossed Evan's face. "Allow me." She turned to Todd. "I could use another run-through." The more they planned, the better the chance of a flawless operation and the sooner they'd get back home, which really excited her, because when the job was over, she hoped Evan might loosen up with her a little.

"Ha! You're one to talk about planning," Todd shot back, stroking his red moustache.

"I'm turning over a new leaf. Foreign countries aren't always as lenient with rogue agents." She winked at Evan and settled back in her seat.

Evan gave her a quick nod of thanks. "I've asked for a van that will accommodate Aaron's chariot. We'll use it as a mobile command post for daily operations if our stay is extended. Today, Mr. Potter will be our eyes and ears from inside Claymore Ports. They offered one of their conference rooms that overlooks the dock. I've forwarded the layout of the area to your phones along with the passport pictures and names Winston and Tyndall are using."

The message pinged on Frankie's phone, but she didn't bother pulling it up. She'd studied the new photos on the trip and would conduct onsite reconnaissance as they approached. If she needed to improvise, she wouldn't be staring at her phone to do it.

"Now," Evan continued, "I'm not sure how many additional agents we'll have to assist, but I want one of us at each major location. Hank, you've got the bow, Frankie stern, and Todd will accompany the customs officers on board. If we have enough guys, each of you will have an Aussie counterpart for backup and jurisdictional issues. No one is allowed to leave the ship until customs officers have checked all passengers and crew documents. Our Interpol contact will cover the entrance and exit near the middle of the ship, and I'll be on the observation deck with Aaron, coordinating and keeping an eye on the overall operation. We'll be provided with communication devices on arrival. Stay on the assigned frequency and keep in touch. Don't leave your post without approval. Got it?" She made eye contact with each agent and stopped at Frankie. "We're clear?"

"Absolutely," Frankie said. She was totally clear that Evan wanted everybody sharp and perfectly prepared for the arrest, but nothing was perfect. Frankie excelled at ad-libbing when plans went tits up, so she'd be ready for the worst even if Evan hadn't planned for it.

She glanced out the window as the plane glided over the sprawl of Sydney and the container port that was their destination. She'd been to Australia with her parents, but like now, always on business, never as a tourist. One day she'd return on her terms and explore the country. Had Evan traveled much for fun or had work consumed her life like it had Frankie's the past several years? She tried to shake Evan from her mind and focus on her job at the *stern* of the boat. Why didn't they just say the back?

When the jet's wheels bumped against the runway, Frankie dug her nails into the armrests until the plane skidded to a jarring halt. She hadn't slept at all during the flight, but adrenaline surged through her after the landing and she was wide awake, ready for the op. They'd gotten lucky with the ship's arrival time and could possibly be on the way home the same day. If everything went according to Evan's plan.

The plane taxied away from the main terminal and into a private hangar, the door opened, and a tall man with a ruddy complexion climbed aboard tugging a carry wheelchair with him. "G'day all. Who's Agent Spears?"

Evan rose. "I'm Spears. You must be Comer from Interpol?" The man nodded. "This is my team—"

"We'll get acquainted later. We're ready to move out. The ship is just coming into port." Comer positioned the carry wheelchair next to Aaron and waited until he was settled. "I'll bring his chair down if you guys can help him to the bottom of the steps."

Todd and Hank guided Aaron's chair toward the exit, and Frankie grabbed their backpacks and followed all-business Agent Comer and Evan off the plane. The two of them should get along great.

Three other agents waited in a van at the bottom of the steps, and a few minutes later, they were on a busy street leaving the airport. Except for the fact Comer was driving on the left side of the road, this could've been any other large city in the world. Traffic was bumper to bumper, horns were sounding, and no one was giving way. Frankie suddenly missed the relative calm of Greensboro and the fifteen-minute commute to any part of town.

Evan rode shotgun in the front with Comer, and the rest crammed into the windowless body of the van. The three Aussie agents sat on a bench on one side, and she, Hank, and Todd on the opposite side with their knees almost touching the others. Aaron's wheelchair was anchored near the front with the surveillance equipment. She stretched her hand across the narrow space. "Frankie Strong."

In turn, each of the light-haired, rugged men responded. "Smith. Jones. Brown. G'day, Strong." Not much for conversation, but easy names to remember, if she could just find a way to differentiate which was which once they got out of the van.

"How long?" Evan asked Comer, who blew the horn at a slow driver.

"Less than fifteen minutes to the terminal, if this dickhead will move on." He honked again, swerved around a small yellow car, and cut in front of a blue van to make a right turn.

"Damn, dude." Todd grabbed the bench seat. "You must've grown up around here."

"Nope," Comer said. "In the outback dodging roos and wombats in a ute."

Frankie tried not to laugh at Todd's confused look. "A utility vehicle," she whispered.

"A Claymore rep is waiting to take us to the security check-in. Have your IDs ready." Comer glanced at one of his men in the rearview and added, "Pass out the com devices and do a check."

Smith handed Frankie a Secret Service style earpiece, and she tucked it in place. "How do we talk through this thing?"

He grinned at her and showed his cell to Aaron.

"It syncs wirelessly with your phone through their secure app," Aaron said. "This technology is seriously dope."

"All I heard was blah, blah, blah." Frankie offered Aaron her phone. "Hook me up?"

He clicked on the screen a few times and gave it back. "We're all connected now. When you want to talk, just tap the red button. To anyone watching, it looks like you're making a call. Simple."

"That's easy for you to say. Technology and I don't get along." When she reached to take her phone back, Comer whipped between several cars and flung her sideways. She clutched an overhead grab handle and held on, sucking in a breath every time they narrowly missed sideswiping another vehicle. He finally slammed the van to a stop, and Frankie overcompensated and tumbled forward into Aaron's lap. "Sorry."

Without missing a beat, he said, "Any time." His boyish face blushed bright red.

Hank and Todd chuckled, bailed out of the van, and rolled out the ramp for Aaron to follow. The Australian guys hurried toward the security office and the gorgeous brunette waiting.

Frankie turned in a circle taking in her surroundings. A huge container ship dwarfed the people and vehicles rushing toward it like a termite mound being invaded by picnic ants. How would they find two people in that maze of stacked cargo and frenetic bodies?

A massive crane on rails slowly moved sideways closer to the ship, and tall machines on stalk legs queued nearby. When all the equipment went into action, the guys would be lucky not to get run down, forget trying to spot their suspects. She'd never seen anything like it and fought the urge to stand and gawk at the whole process.

When Evan stepped out of the van, Frankie lightly brushed the back of her hand. "Don't worry. We've got this." Evan's expression was completely calm and confident, but her eyes darkened, and Frankie sensed her anxiety spiking. "Really. We're good." She jerked her thumb over her shoulder toward the docked ship. "I'll be at the stern, if you need me."

Frankie sauntered toward security, and Evan prayed she was as ready as she thought. The operation was complicated logistically, and Frankie was used to one-man ops in which she made every decision. All Evan could do now was hope Frankie understood the plan and followed it. At least she'd dressed appropriately, no spiked heels, outrageous wigs, or trench coats.

"She'll be fine," Aaron said from beside her.

She was so focused on Frankie that she didn't notice him wheeling up next to her. "Yeah." She needed to get *her* head in the game. Fourteen hours was a long time to pretend not to notice Frankie sitting across from her, trying to engage her, occasionally bumping knees and sending shivers through her. Now was the worst possible time to be preoccupied.

Sweat prickled the back of her neck as she and Aaron headed toward the building. The scene was too similar to the failed airport scenario—transport hub, open space, unpredictable people, and too many variables outside Evan's control. She produced her ID, signed in, and followed their female guide who led them into a conference room on the third floor. With windows on three sides, the space was perfect for observing the operation below, but the separation from the action amplified Evan's anxiety.

Aaron pulled one of the armrests of his chair up, unfolded a tray in front of him, and plopped his computer on top. A few seconds later, he said, "I've got the layout on screen, and the guys' locations are coming through the app nicely. We're good to go."

She keyed her mike. "Com center operational. Acknowledge." Each agent answered, and then Evan leaned against the large table to wait. At least Frankie knew how to operate the app and everyone was connected. As soon as the customs officers checked the passenger manifest and bill of lading, her team could retrieve their fugitives.

"This place is about to get really busy," their guide, Jemma, said.

"Would you walk us through what to expect?" Evan asked.

Jemma pointed to the left of the ship. "That red monstrosity lumbering its way along the side of the ship on rails is the gantry or key crane which spans the width of the ship. After the lashings that hold the cargo in place are released, the crane operator will start unloading the containers onto the dock. Once that happens, the army of blue straddles standing by over there," she pointed to the right, "will pick up the containers from the dock one at a time and move them onto the yard. If we're discharging and reloading the same ship, both processes can happen simultaneously."

Aaron stared at the attractive brunette, his eyes wide and attentive. "I assume the straddle system is automated and controlled onsite in a command center."

"Exactly."

"How many ships come in daily?"

"We average about three a day, ninety to a hundred a month, from five or six countries," Jemma said. "It takes between sixteen and twenty-two hours to unload, depending on ship size."

Aaron seemed enthralled, but Evan couldn't tell if it was the subject matter or the woman. "And how many employees handle the work?" Too many people running around was a nightmare when trying to identify suspects.

"One hundred fifty to one sixty full-time, plus casual or wharfies, like your unionized longshoremen."

Evan zoned out, leaving Aaron to his fascination. That was a lot of people to monitor and potentially interfere with the operation. As the machines moved into place and the activity on the dock intensified, she scanned for her agents. Todd had gone on board with the customs officers, Hank was at the bow with an Aussie agent, and Frankie was exactly where she was supposed to be with one of the Aussies. Evan breathed a little easier.

In hindsight, Frankie's addition to the team might not have been such a bad thing. She gelled with the guys, brought new vitality to the team, and had only gone off book once. And Evan had to admit, that time had turned out for the best—the plea agreement with Robert Griffin. On this trip, she'd helped Todd manage Aaron's wheelchair, made sure everybody had proper equipment, paid attention to the updates, and even supported Evan's insistence on additional briefings. Maybe she'd judged Frankie too harshly in the beginning. Or maybe she'd been compensating for her own duplicity. She wanted to believe in Frankie because she liked her…more than she should. *Stop it.*

She forced her attention back to the dock and the woman who occupied too many of her thoughts recently. Frankie wasn't at her post. Evan moved closer to the window and glared at the empty spot. Her backup was gone as well.

"Spears to Strong." No answer. "Agent Strong, what's your location?" She heard a burst of static, but no words. "Anybody have eyes on Strong?"

"Comer took her backup on board to help with the passengers and crew, but she was there a few minutes ago," Hank said. "Damn it."

Evan grabbed the windowsill to steady herself as a wave of fear made her weak. This was why work and emotions weren't good bedfellows. Had Frankie been knocked into the bay by one of the straddles or purposely left her post without checking in? Too many possibilities, most of them not good, ran through her mind. And just when she'd started to give her the benefit of the doubt. "Aaron, what is Frankie's location?"

"Sorry?" He reluctantly pulled his attention from Jemma.

"I don't see Frankie."

"Oh, crap." He wheeled his chair toward the windows and tapped a key on the computer. Evan looked over his shoulder as the dock plan opened with bright green dots for each agent currently signed on to the communication app. "I don't see her either. It's like she vanished."

"Keep looking. I'm going down there." She'd covered all the bases, double-checked her plan, and made sure everybody knew their assignments. Frankie had promised to follow the rules. Something was wrong. Her chest tightened, and she pulled for breath. *Please let her be okay.* Evan couldn't have another agent hurt or worse. Where the hell was she?

CHAPTER NINE

F rankie stood at the stern of the ship fascinated by the hypnotic movement of the machines. A massive crane unloaded cargo containers onto the dock as easily as assembling a Lego set. Star Wars looking tall boys then retrieved, moved, and stacked each piece in a neat line on the yard. Over and over, the process repeated, and the continuous warning beeps of the contraptions made hearing anything else impossible. She felt small and insignificant in the hubbub and unsure if she'd be able to spot their fugitives in the midst of it all. A horn sounded, and she moved closer to the edge as a truck passed. She glanced up the side of the ship that seemed to disappear into the gray morning sky.

A crewman leaned over and motioned to Frankie from the deck. She waved back. He motioned again, urging her on board. She glanced toward Hank's position at the front of the ship and tried to get his attention, but he was laughing with his Aussie mate. Comer had taken her counterpart to help inside so she was alone. She couldn't leave her post without notifying someone.

"Strong to Com Center." Static. She tried again. More static. "Hank, can you hear me?" Nothing. "Todd? Comer? Evan?" Time to improvise. She pressed the button on her phone. "If anybody can hear me, I'm going on board at the stern of the ship. One of the crew wants to talk." If this was a trap, she was on her own.

She tucked the phone in her back pocket and climbed the narrow salt-encrusted ladder toward the man who'd signaled to her. "What's going on?" Up close, the man was more boy, possibly a teenager,

Asian and terrified. "Is something wrong?" A recent undercover case came to mind. "Are you being held against your will?"

The young man stared at her with wide eyes and shook his head vigorously. "Come."

Frankie studied his demeanor and the scared look in his eyes. He was afraid but not dangerous. She tried her com device again and got more static.

The man motioned for her to follow and retreated to a dark alcove sheltered by an upper deck and concealed from view on three sides.

She followed him into the shadows. "You can trust me."

He hesitated and then pointed to himself. "Tai."

She did the same. "Frankie."

Tai glanced around to make sure no one was watching before continuing. "Tai, no trouble. Need job."

Frankie nodded. "I'll keep your name out of it. You have my word."

He stared at her for several seconds more. "You look for someone."

"Yes." She pulled the pictures of Winston and Tyndall from her jacket pocket. "Have you seen these men?"

Tai looked at the photos and nodded. "Big man have box on ship." He pointed to a container over their heads. "There."

"How do you know that's his container?"

He motioned with his hands. "Open at night, take things out."

Frankie felt a surge of adrenaline and shivered. This could be the piece of information they needed to catch Winston and Tyndall before they went ashore and were lost in Sydney's sea of humanity. "Do you know where they are?"

Tai nodded.

Almost an hour later, after getting all the information Tai could offer, Frankie descended the steep ladder at the stern of the boat.

"Do you have any idea what I—we've been going through looking for you?" Evan asked.

Frankie flinched at Evan's too-calm tone and pointed up. "One of the crewmen—"

"Was any part of my instruction to you unclear?"

"No, but—"

"So, why did you leave your post without letting anyone know where you were? That's how people get hurt or...We've spent valuable time looking for you when we should've been making arrests."

Evan's expression was as frightened as Tai's, but his was naked self-preservation and Evan's pulsed with concern and protectiveness for Frankie. Thank goodness the guys weren't close enough to see or hear their exchange.

"I thought—"

"Evan, if you'll let me explain."

"I don't want an explanation. I want you safe...and off this case."

Frankie hoped Evan was just lashing out because she was angry or scared, but her words felt personal and they shattered the tentative truce they'd formed. She pushed her feelings aside and delivered the news she'd learned. "They're not on the ship."

"I can't focus on these fugitives if I'm worried—what?"

"Winston and Tyndall aren't on the ship."

"She's right," Comer said as he and the other guys joined them. "We checked the passenger list and visually accounted for everyone as they came ashore. The two remaining passports are the fake ones our fugitives used."

Evan looked from Frankie to Comer and back. "But how?"

Comer motioned toward the office. "Let's take this inside before we're run down by bloody straddles."

Frankie followed Evan back to the conference room feeling like a delinquent going to the principal's office. Evan hadn't let her explain that she'd tried to follow her orders. Maybe she was grasping for any excuse to get rid of her now that they'd acknowledged their attraction. And that might be for the best because Frankie was conflicted about her feelings too.

"Could we have the room please?" Evan asked Jemma, who sat looking very comfortable at Aaron's side.

Jemma stood and said, "Of course, I'll have tea, coffee, and biscuits brought in. Let me know if you need anything else. The space is free the rest of the day."

"Where were you, Frankie?" Aaron asked.

Evan held up her hand. "We'll get to that later. Right now, we need to know about Winston and Tyndall." She turned her attention to Frankie. "Tell us."

Frankie tried to make eye contact with Evan, to reconnect, but she looked away. "They jumped ship near a place called Little Bay in scuba gear with their money."

"What?" Comer asked, his ruddy complexion turning redder. "Are you serious?"

"I talked to the crewman who was assigned to look after Winston. He saw them go overboard just before daybreak. He doesn't want to lose his job, so we can't burn him."

Evan squared her shoulders, and Frankie sensed the return of her control and focus. "Where is Little Bay, Comer?"

"Just north of Botany Bay. It has a semicircular beach that's enclosed by headlands to the south and north. The narrow entrance is sheltered, and it doesn't usually have a rip or undertow unless the sea is really stormy. Two strong swimmers could swim in easily and have somebody pick them up. It's only fifteen minutes from here by car."

"But they've got a head start on us and could be anywhere by now," Hank said.

"That's the problem for sure," Comer added. "We should search their cabin for a lead about where they're headed."

Frankie nodded to a woman who brought in a full serving cart, poured everyone a cup of coffee or tea, and passed out what looked like shortbread cookies. "My guy said both Winston and Tyndall spent a lot of time on the computer. Maybe their searches will turn up something we can use." She handed Evan a cup of coffee and stifled a yawn.

"Why don't you guys catch a few hours' sleep and let my team do some legwork?" Comer asked Evan. "We'll check the computer and any camera footage around the beach at Little Bay." When Evan started to object, he added, "I promise we won't make any moves until we're back together. And I'll call if we come up with anything."

"I'm not comfortable leaving everything with you, not that I don't trust you, I just—"

"You like to be in charge," Comer said. "I get it, but I'm not comfortable with sleep-deprived agents who could get my guys or themselves hurt."

Evan flinched. He'd nailed the only reason she'd relinquish control. "Point taken." She glanced at her watch. "It's only noon, but feels much later. Can you recommend a hotel close to your base of operations?"

"Taken care of. We'll drop you off on our way to Little Bay."

Frankie finished her coffee. "We also need to check Winston's trailer. It's blue container 530787."

Comer tapped the info into his phone. "You did have quite the chat up there, didn't you? Once we've given it a look, we'll leave it on the yard and have port authorities notify us if anyone comes to pick it up. Owners have three days to retrieve containers without a penalty. Afterward, they're moved to another location and start accruing charges. I'll be interested to see if Winston comes back for his."

After another wild ride, Comer stopped in front of the hotel and turned to Evan. "I've reserved two rooms. Budgets. You understand. I figured one for blokes and one for Sheilas."

"Two rooms?" Evan's voice rose an octave.

"That'll work," Hank said.

Evan glared at him over her shoulder. "Grab some sleep and regroup at six in the bar."

Frankie got out of the van and led the way to the registration desk. The last thing Evan probably wanted was to be confined in an Aussie-sized room with her. She was still steaming from Frankie's disappearing act. So Frankie made it easy. After they checked in and the guys headed to their room, she said to Evan, "I'm going out for a bit."

"You're what?"

She guided Evan to a seating area away from the busy check-in desk. "Look, I know you don't want to be around me right now, and I need some air."

"So, you're disappearing again, just walking out. You do that a lot, you know."

Evan's tone was a cross between pained and angry, and while Frankie understood both, Evan's lack of confidence stung. "Number one, I was never missing. The com device didn't work. Second, I'm going out and I don't need a lecture or a chaperone."

She took the stairs down and out into the chilling afternoon air. She'd probably made things worse and could've handled that better but just didn't have the energy for a fight. Besides, she was operating on nothing more than a hunch, something Grif had said during their first meeting at the jail.

She hailed a taxi and threw her backpack in the surprisingly clean seat beside her. "The most expensive cigar shop in Sydney, please." Tai had told her that Winston ran out of cigars three days before they docked and had gotten really grumpy. If Grif was right about Winston's addiction, he was jonesing and would be desperate for a fix the minute he hit land.

The driver gave her a skeptical look in the rearview mirror.

"My dad is an aficionado. If I don't bring him something special from Sydney, he'll never forgive me."

The man grinned. "I'm a fan too. It's a long ride from here though, and you're American. I mean you're a young woman and I'm a stranger. From what I've heard, you're not a trusting lot."

"Thanks, but I'm fine. My dad said I could trust a man who loves a good cigar." Winston would definitely be an exception. She settled back in the seat. Maybe by the time she returned to the hotel Evan would've cooled down and they could talk.

It wasn't like she'd purposely disobeyed Evan's orders. Well, she sort of had, but she'd tried to make contact. Still, Evan's reaction seemed over the top. The Judith thing and Aaron's injury were still haunting her. Or maybe her feelings went deeper than she'd admitted and that was affecting her. Frankie survived by interpreting behavior and divining motivation, but Evan was alternately transparent and obscure, defying a consistent reading. She was complicated and emotionally cautious, and while that frustrated Frankie, it also intrigued her.

"Here you go, miss," the taxi driver said as he stopped in front of a pedestrian mall. "Martin Place. Havana Express is on the right just down there."

"Thanks. Would you mind waiting…what's your name?"

"Rick."

"This won't take long, Rick. And I'm Frankie."

"Right-o. If I'm not here, I'll be back. Might have to circle the block."

Rick would've looked more natural riding a wave at Manly Beach with his blond hair and tan, but he was friendly and accommodating, and that worked for Frankie. Folks in the service professions were often excellent sources of intelligence so she made it a point to chat them up and tip well.

Frankie pulled a linen jacket from her bag and slid it on over her T-shirt as she walked toward the high-end shop. She opened the glass door and stepped inside the comfortably cool store with shiny black-and-white tile floors that smelled like the inside of a cigar box.

"May I be of assistance, madam?" the clerk asked.

She breathed deeply to lift her breasts just a touch and gave the man her best smile. "I'd like to order some cigars for my father, but I'm not sure if he's already made the purchase. Would you be able to tell me? They're for his birthday, so I want it to be a surprise." She pulled the cell from her back pocket and pretended to flip through photos. She'd missed two calls from Evan but she'd have to wait. "I'll find a nice picture. I'm sure you'd remember him. He'd go into the humidor room just to breathe in the air." She showed the man Winston's photo.

"Oh yes, he was in earlier today. He bought the Montecristo No. 2."

"Torpedoes."

"Your father has excellent taste. Unfortunately, he wanted ten boxes, and we only had five on hand. I'll call him when the rest come in, probably the next two days. I'm so sorry."

"Could I see the order, please?" She glanced at the form and memorized the phone number Winston had listed as a contact. Probably a burner, but worth checking. "Would you mind calling me when he picks up his cigars? Just in case there's a problem with delivery or whatever. I want to know he has them before I move on to a less desirable gift."

"Of course." He took her details and smiled. "Such a devoted daughter."

"I try. Thank you for your time." Her hunch was worth the trip. Winston definitely had more than a casual appreciation for good cigars because he'd dropped over three thousand dollars. He'd be back to pick up his order, and all she had to do was convince Evan they needed to stake out the place. Easier said than done?

Frankie found Rick's cab idling at the corner of George Street and Martin Place and slid into the back seat.

"No luck?"

"They have to order what I want."

"Where to now?"

"Back to the hotel, please." On the ride, she thought about Grif's tip about Ty. "You seem to know the city well. What would you say is the classiest gentlemen's club in Sydney?"

Rick gave her another of his questioning looks. "Your father again?"

She chuckled. "I can't lie. He always was a rogue, but don't tell my mother."

Rick laughed with her and flipped his long blond hair. "The Dollhouse Strip Club at Potts Point has the best reputation. Gorgeous women, clean, and the owners keep it tight. No riffraff, no touching the girls, and no drugs. It's less than ten minutes from here, but opens at nine."

"Perfect." Rick pulled in front of the hotel, and Frankie looked at the clock on the dash. She'd barely have time for a quick shower before meeting the team at six. "I might need you later, if you're available. Do you have a card or a number?"

Rick pushed a card through the payment slot, and she slid two hundred-dollar bills back.

"I don't have change."

"Keep it. You've been an excellent tour guide."

When she opened the door to her room, Evan was dressed, sitting at a small table by the window drinking coffee. "Where—"

"Hold that thought. I need a shower."

"Have you slept at all?"

"No." She tossed her bag on one side of the bed—two twins pushed together posing as a double—and closed the bathroom door behind her. The cool shower tingled her skin and brought her situation clearly into focus. She had a lead on Winston and she was alone in a hotel room with Evan, a very pissed off Evan, and only one bed. Exciting and troubling. She wrapped a towel around her and opened the door.

With her attention still on her phone, Evan asked, "Can we talk now?"

"Sure." Frankie dropped the towel and reached for her backpack. Evan finally looked up and froze like a buffering download. "Do you mind?"

"Not at all. Go ahead. I can multitask." The hungry look in Evan's eyes said she wasn't sure she could. All that concern and heat she'd felt from Evan earlier was definitely about more than work. "Don't tell me you have a problem with naked women."

"Not…not usually." Evan finally looked at Frankie and scanned the length of her body before returning to her face. "Why do you have to make everything so difficult?"

"I didn't realize I did. I'm dressing and getting my dressing down at the same time since we only have fifteen minutes before we meet the guys." She understood why Evan was so tense, but if she could get her to loosen up, blow off a little steam, or laugh, maybe they'd survive the assignment and sharing a bed. She pressed her luck and moved closer, her stare trained on Evan's mouth. "Maybe you're the one making things harder than they have to be."

Evan pushed her coffee cup aside, rose from the table, and stared at Frankie. Was Frankie right? Was Evan the one complicating things? She *had* panicked when Frankie went missing this morning. She'd been angry and afraid, afraid for Frankie because she cared for her. And now *she* stood in front of a naked Frankie, unable to deny she wanted to kiss her. "Maybe I am." The defeated tone of her voice made Evan cringe.

She watched, unable to move, while Frankie tugged on a pair of jeans and pulled a T-shirt over her head. "I just meant there might be an easier way than constantly fighting the flow."

"How?" Frankie stopped so close that Evan felt her heat and the energy pulsing between them. She gazed into Evan's eyes, and her body tingled. "Frankie, please."

"Please do or please don't?" Frankie's eyes flashed with mischief and desire.

Just one kiss. To diffuse the tension and confirm there was nothing compelling about Frankie, nothing she couldn't walk away from. One kiss couldn't hurt. "Don't?" The word came out as a question, and Frankie grinned, as unconvinced as Evan that she didn't want this. "We shouldn—"

"Shush." Frankie placed a finger over Evan's lips and slowly traced her mouth before covering Evan's lips with her own.

Evan tensed and started to pull away, but Frankie slid a hand behind her head and held the connection. Her lips were soft, wet, and so hungry that Evan surrendered. She had to. Frankie's taste exploded on her tongue. Kissing her was so much more intense and exciting than she expected. Evan ached everywhere. One kiss would never be enough. And then a sneering image of Judith invaded her thoughts.

"Jude. No." She backed away and pressed her hand over her mouth. Why had she thought about *her*? Was her subconscious warning her not to make the same mistake again, not to trust too quickly, jump too soon? And she'd said the words aloud. If she could disappear, she would.

"No way. Did you just call me Jude?"

The look on Frankie's face gouged at the damaged place inside Evan, and she backed farther away. "I'm so sorry. For all of this. I didn't actually call you Jude. I never would. I had a flash...a nasty reminder. But this...shouldn't have happened. At all. We made a deal."

Frankie trailed her retreat, one slow footstep at a time, eyes focused on hers, and arms outstretched. She read the desire in Frankie's eyes and her body language, and it was the sexiest thing Evan had ever seen.

"You liked it." Frankie was within touching distance, but didn't reach out. "Didn't you?"

The truth was supposed to be a good thing, but in this case, it would probably just make Evan more miserable. Why admit what was already obvious when it could do no good.

"Don't leave me hanging," Frankie said.

"You know I enjoyed it. The problem is, we shouldn't be kissing, at all. We agreed to keep things professional." The words tasted bitter, and Evan wanted to take them back immediately, but she had a job to do and being close to Frankie, or even thinking about her, was too distracting. "You have questions to answer about this morning, and then we have to get back to work."

Frankie grinned, gave a mock salute, and did a twirl. "You liked kissing me. That's a good thing because I *really* enjoyed kissing you, except for the Jude thing." She got a teasing look in her eyes and started toward Evan again.

"Stop." Evan stuck out her hand. "Focus, Strong. What happened this morning? You've got five minutes to explain."

"I'd rather talk about us…or not talk at all."

"Tell me."

"You're giving me whiplash, Spears."

Frankie made a good point. A few minutes earlier, they'd just been coworkers, but Evan had no name for the place they'd ended up after that kiss.

Frankie dropped on the edge of the bed and shook her head. "Oh, the pain of rejection." When Evan rolled her hand, she continued. "Like I said earlier, I tried to contact you, everyone, but all I got was static. I told you technology hates me. The crewman had information about our fugitives. What was I supposed to do, ignore him, or ask him to wait while I got a permission slip from the principal?"

Evan searched Frankie's face trying to decide if she believed her. She had heard some static at one point. "You have—" Eli's voice echoed in her head. "*You don't need a sledgehammer to crack a nut,*" and she started over. Maybe Frankie would respond more favorably to a gentler approach. It was worth a try. She didn't want to be the supervisor or coworker who browbeat her agents into submission but was never truly their leader. "I was really worried."

"I'm sorry. I know how important this assignment is to you and what you've been through to get here. I only want to help. Can you trust me?"

"You're asking a lot…and it's a process." Frankie gave her a sad puppy look, and Evan caved. "I'll try, if you'll keep me informed." Frankie nodded, and Evan asked, "Where were you this afternoon?"

"You have to promise not to get upset again."

Evan reached for her phone but stopped. Time to break out the sledgehammer again so soon? She kept her voice calm. "You weren't working the case? Without backup?"

"Not exactly. I had a hunch, nothing that rose to the level of actionable intelligence, so I just took a ride and asked a few questions. Something Grif said during our first chat at the jail stuck with me, and it panned out. I've got a lead."

Evan vacillated between lecturing Frankie and kissing her again. Damn it, she was frustrating, exciting, infuriating, and challenging, and Evan didn't have time for any of it. "Let's go. You can brief everyone at the same time. We're late."

When they reached the bar, both teams were gathered at a large table in the corner. She didn't waste time. "Do you have anything?" she asked Comer.

"We went through Winston's container but didn't find anything useful. We left it on the yard for pickup. And the cameras on Little Bay have been shut off while the council and public debate their audio capability. Government overreach versus right to privacy, you know the drill."

Evan waved toward Frankie, unable to look at her for fear one of the guys would detect something in her eyes or her expression. "Frankie might have something."

While Frankie relayed what she'd learned at the cigar shop, Evan took notes on her phone and tried not to stare at her too long, but it was so difficult. She was gorgeous, her skin flushed with excitement, her blue eyes sparked, and her mouth—*Stop it.* This preoccupation was why one kiss was so dangerous. She returned her attention to her phone but listened closely.

"Why would he risk going to a cigar shop? Why not just order online?" Comer asked.

"He'd need a credit card he might not have yet? And it leaves a trail." Frankie shrugged. "How do I know? Maybe he's like a porn addict, every now and then he just has to see, smell, and touch the real thing."

"Maybe," Comer agreed.

"And," Frankie continued, "I think Ty will show up at a strip club called the Dollhouse."

"At Kings Cross. I know the place," Comer said.

"I've heard it's the most exclusive gentlemen's club in Sydney, and Ty's been on a ship for three weeks with no women."

"Strewth," one of Comer's men said. "I'll volunteer for that assignment."

"That's a stretch, isn't it?" Evan asked.

"I think she may have something, boss," Hank said, tugging a Marines baseball cap lower on his forehead. "Grif told us about Winston's weakness for Cuban cigars and Ty's for beautiful women. Besides, we can't do anything about Winston until the shop opens tomorrow."

"And," Aaron added, "the computer in Tyndall's cabin was full of porn sites."

"And we've never been to an Australian strip club," Todd said and pulled at his moustache like a lecherous old man.

Evan shook her head. "I'm pretty sure they're all the same, but if we think it's worth a…" The guys talked over her, all agreeing that Frankie had a great idea. Evan wasn't convinced. Would Ty be careless enough to go straight to such a place? And why, if Judith was joining him? It seemed a long shot, but the team deserved a little joy on the trip. However, being trapped in a room full of nearly naked women, after what happened with Frankie, wasn't her idea of fun.

"Fine," she conceded. "Aaron and I will man the command post nearby."

Aaron's joyful expression vanished, but he quickly recovered. "Okay, I guess."

"No way," Frankie said. "Nobody leaves Potter in the van. He goes in." She grabbed his shoulder. "I don't mean to be insensitive, but you'll be a perfect cover."

Aaron's grin said it all. He wanted to be with the team, especially for this job, and Evan couldn't deny him. "Okay, I'll keep the van warm."

"And I'll keep you company," Frankie said. "Titty bars are not my thing."

Evan started to object, but the guys were already headed for the door.

Comer kept pace with Evan as they walked to the parking lot. "I've got something to dress up that boring van so you won't stand out like a sore thumb." He popped the trunk of his car, pulled out two magnetic Sydney Water signs, and slapped one on each side of the van before climbing behind the wheel. "My guys will follow in our cars in case we need to split up."

Thirty minutes later, she and Frankie were alone in the back of the van, and the guys were heading toward a Victorian terrace building on a leafy street that looked like a residence. Without the illuminated Dollhouse sign, the place wouldn't have stood out.

Evan settled into a chair in front of the surveillance monitor and turned down the volume as the guys entered and the noise engulfed them. She hated stakeouts, all the waiting, watching, and listening. She told herself this one was no different, except for Frankie hovering over her shoulder, breathing on Evan's neck and sending shivers down her body.

"Seriously, look at that kid," Frankie said. "She looks like a teenager."

"If you don't look below the neck."

Frankie nudged her. "So...you're a boob woman?"

"Not really." She pointed to the screen. "Pay attention."

"I'm just trying to pass the time. It could be a long night. Just you and me. Alone."

"Are you serious about anything, Strong?"

Frankie swept her hands across Evan's shoulders and massaged the tight knots that sent tension up the back of her neck. "I've been very serious the past twenty-four hours, gathering info about our fugitives and finding our first lead. And less than an hour ago, I demonstrated how thoughtful and restrained I can be by going for only one spectacular kiss. Don't you agree?"

In spite of her attempts to resist Frankie's charm, Evan relaxed slightly into her touch. "You did well today. And our one and only kiss was pretty fantastic, but you are an enigma."

"I think a little mystery would be good in your life, just enough to keep it interesting."

"No, thanks. You *have* heard the story of my last ex who kept secrets."

Frankie scrunched in next to her at the small observation screen, and her staccato breathing reminded Evan of their kiss and the telltale acceleration of her heartbeat. "Maybe we should take turns monitoring," Evan said. "The guys will be in there for hours. You didn't get any sleep, and I haven't done much better. Lie down, and I'll cover first watch." The image of Frankie sprawled across the long bench flashed through Evan's mind, and she stifled a moan.

"Only if you join me."

"Frankie, focus on what we're doing." *Pot, kettle.*

Frankie leaned against Evan's side. "What we're doing is avoiding another amazing kiss while watching a bad porn film."

Evan scooted sideways. "If we can't work together, I'll have to—"

"Fine." Frankie slid onto the bench and pulled a backpack under her head for support, her feet closer to Evan, her eyes never disengaging.

Just the intensity in Frankie's eyes was enough to make Evan forget where she was and what she was supposed to be doing. Very bad. "And stop looking at me like that."

"Got it. Don't look. Don't touch. Don't distract. Be invisible."

"As if," Evan muttered.

"What was that?"

Evan turned back to the screen and waved Frankie off.

"Oh, I almost forgot," Frankie said. "I have a phone number Winston left at the cigar shop. We should run it, though it's probably a burner." She rattled off the number, and Evan jotted it down. "Maybe we can track him, if he's careless. And if not, the shop owner said he'd call me when Winston comes to pick up his cigars."

"Good work, Agent Strong. You keep surprising me."

"So, surprise me, Marshal Spears. Tell me about your family."

Evan shot her what she hoped was a back-off look, but it didn't work. Few of her defenses did with Frankie. She simply twirled the spinner on her thumb and smiled innocently.

"You know how I feel about tight spaces," Frankie said. "If you don't distract me, I'll go crazy in this tin box with no windows. Please, Evan, it's your duty as a sister agent and my faux supervisor."

The topic was benign enough, so Evan stared at the monitor and started talking. "My father was an FBI agent and my mother a housewife who took care of me and my older brother. Dad quit the agency when Eli and I went out on our own, and he and Mom started a security company with some of Dad's FBI cronies. They do government and corporate contracts with all sorts, like utilities, chemical companies, financial institutions, construction conglomerates, hospitals, ports and airports, residential communities, retail and commercial real estate, and transit systems."

"Wow," Frankie said. "Now I understand the snazzy tailored clothes."

Evan spun around in the chair. "You like how I dress?"

"I like almost everything about you, Evan, except your intensity and that stubbornness when it comes to—never mind." Frankie adjusted the knapsack behind her head.

"I buy clothes I feel comfortable in, and it's part of the whole put-together agent image I try to maintain. Eli and I have never needed our parents' money. He owns his own construction company because, like you, he loves the outdoors, and I sort of followed in dad's footsteps, which pays a decent salary. And I live in a warehouse, not very glamorous."

"A warehouse? Really?"

"It was going to be torn down when I found it."

Frankie nudged Evan with her foot. "Look at me. I like to see your face when you're talking. It gives me a sense of how you feel about what you're saying."

Maybe that's why she preferred looking away, but she glanced briefly toward Frankie. "I have to keep my eyes on the prize." Why was it so easy to tell Frankie things she hadn't spoken about in years? Why did she want to? "What else do you want to know?"

"Were you and your family close?"

"Close in the sense that we got along, knew we were loved, had a roof over our heads, food on the table, and a good education, but not in the talk about our feelings way. Dad was strict but fair, and Mom more understanding, but never overruled anything my father said. Eli is by far the most sensitive, compassionate, and communicative one of the clan."

"Do you still see your folks?" Frankie asked.

"We only gather for Christmas now. They still travel for work. Eli and I see each other often, especially now. He's helping me renovate the warehouse."

"It's good you have each other."

Frankie's voice had a wistful tone, and Evan started to look at her, but something on the screen caught her attention. She studied the monitor and got a quick update from everyone before speaking to Frankie again. "And what about your family?"

"I'm an only child. We traveled a lot. They weren't very nice." The tone of Frankie's voice had changed from pensive to sad and a little angry.

"What do your parents do?"

She waited, not wanting to pressure Frankie. A few seconds later, Evan heard a light thump. She turned, and Frankie was fast asleep, her arm dangling off the side of the bench. How could anyone fall asleep so quickly? She rolled her chair over and eased Frankie's arm up beside her. She was a sleeping angel—no frenetic energy, no tantalizing touches, no mischievous grin or teasing stare—just a vulnerable woman with pale skin, dark lashes resting on her cheeks, and luscious, tempting lips. Evan was in so much trouble.

CHAPTER TEN

Frankie woke to the gurgling of a coffeemaker and Evan hunched over her suitcase, neatly folding her clothes and repacking. Her side of the bed looked barely touched. Had she been awake all night thinking about what happened between them? Evan had kissed her yesterday. And what a kiss. She'd replayed the softness of Evan's lips and the heat of her mouth over and over during the stakeout and dreamed about it when she fell asleep. Her body came alive again with the memory, and she craved more. Did Evan, or was she regretting it, chastising herself for crossing that line? She could ask, but the set of Evan's shoulders and her rigid, controlled movements were answer enough.

"How did I get here?" Frankie rose on her elbows and propped the pillows behind her. "The last thing I remember was lying on the bench in the van."

"You sleep like the dead." Evan slowly straightened and stared out the window for a few seconds as if gathering her composure. She then placed a tray with coffee, creamer, and sweetener on the nightstand beside Frankie. "A couple of the guys carried you from the parking lot, up the elevator, to bed, and you never opened your eyes or grunted. How is that possible?"

"When I reach a certain point, I just pass out."

"What I'd give for one night of sleep like that." Evan settled on the side of the bed, raked her fingers through Frankie's hair, and slid her forefinger down her jawline. "You look rested."

Frankie's body ached at the touch, and she leaned closer, staring into Evan's eyes. She stifled a moan when she saw her desire reflected back. If she didn't do something with her hands, she'd grab Evan and urge her into bed. She lifted the covers, surprised that she was still fully clothed. When she looked back up, Evan was shaking her head.

"I couldn't. It didn't seem right."

"But you've already seen me naked. No biggie."

"Looking isn't the same as touching, though it can be just as painful." Evan held Frankie's gaze briefly before reaching for her cup. "I'm glad you got some sleep."

"Did you?"

Evan shook her head and stood. "I'll be fine."

Boundary established. Evan was back on comfortable ground and in control, so Frankie shifted to a safer topic. "What happened at the club?" She stirred her coffee and took a sip.

"Tyndall didn't show, and the guys closed the place down. Of course, they want to try again tonight."

"What now?"

"I was going to ask how you thought we should set up surveillance on the cigar shop since you've already done recon."

Frankie placed her cup slowly back on the nightstand. "Wait. Am I still asleep?" She gave Evan her most innocent grin. "Did you just ask for my opinion on an op?"

Evan waggled a finger at her. "Do not do that. Don't make fun. I'm trying to trust you and practice delegating. Besides, you've developed every lead we have so far, so you deserve to have a say in how we proceed."

Her heart fluttered at the unexpected compliment. "Thank you, Marshal Spears, that's certainly high praise. And thanks for the opportunity. I do have some ideas. The cigar shop is in a very popular pedestrian mall, so it won't be hard for the guys to blend in. But I'd like to do my homeless person thing closer to the store and serve as point. When I see him go inside, I'll call in the troops."

Evan didn't immediately reject the idea, and Frankie loved the way her dark eyebrow arched slightly as she thought it all through. "Did you come prepared for a UC assignment?"

"I'm always prepared."

"Is there a chance he'll recognize you from the Greensboro operation?" Evan asked.

Frankie shook her head. "Winston didn't do the streets. He had minions for that."

Evan still seemed unconvinced. "But what about…you said that kind of work drains you. Are you sure you want to put yourself in that position again?"

Frankie couldn't remember the last time anyone put her welfare over a job. Yes, she could. *Never*. Her heart beat faster, and her insides tingled. She wanted to show Evan how much it meant to her, but this was not the time or place. "I'm well rested. I'll be fine, but thanks."

"Let's leave it open for now and we'll run it by the guys." She pointed to a covered tray by the window. "Have some breakfast and get dressed. I wasn't sure what you like, so I ordered a bit of everything. Meeting in an hour."

Frankie couldn't suppress a grin. She loved it when Evan used *we* and *us* to refer to the two of them. It was a small, probably unintentional thing, but she felt included and important. For the first time, Evan made her feel a valued part of the team. And in private, Frankie felt things she'd never experienced with anyone else—a depth of emotion she couldn't explain and the desire to stop pretending and settle down. How did Evan do that?

Frankie scarfed down two slices of bacon and a piece of toast before taking a quick shower. When she came out of the bathroom in a towel, Evan was sitting by the window sipping coffee and staring out into the drizzly morning.

Without turning, she said, "It's going to be wet. Maybe we should reconsider."

"No, I'm good." She dropped the towel and reached for the costume she'd need to transform into Sing Song again.

"Will you please stop doing that." Evan waved her hand toward Frankie's naked reflection in the mirror. "It's hard enough to concentrate without you flaunting all that in front of me daily."

The comment made Frankie feel hot and wet and achy. "I would say I'm sorry, but you'd know I was lying. I'm trying my best to seduce you, but you seem immune."

"Seriously? After that kiss yesterday, you think I'm immune?" Evan continued to stare out the window.

When Evan didn't move from her chair, Frankie went to her, kneeled in front of her, and eased her legs gently apart so she could scoot in closer. "I'll stop flaunting all this if you'll kiss me again. I know I promised to behave, but you do things to me. The way you look at me with those black eyes, I never know what you're thinking. And I love that cute thing you do with your left eyebrow when I say or do something you don't understand. And when you touch me…oh my God. I'm helpless."

Evan's breath hitched and she placed her coffee cup on the windowsill. "Are you actually negotiating for a kiss?"

"Why, yes, I believe I am." She leaned in and her breasts brushed against Evan's pressed shirt. "How can you resist a needy, naked woman on her knees?" She licked her lips.

"God help me, it's not easy, especially when you're trying so hard." Evan trailed her finger along Frankie's jaw and down her neck. "You're so gorgeous. I love this little freckle right here, just below your ear." She entwined her fingers with Frankie's. "And how you play with your ring when you're upset or nervous, as if I needed a clue. Your eyes reflect every emotion." She leaned closer, and Frankie felt her hot breath whisper across her lips. "And you're absolutely no help in the resistance department." Evan placed her hands gently on Frankie's shoulders and eased her back.

Frankie lost herself in Evan's touch, her hands leaving imprints on her body and in her mind as if it might be the last time. "I can't help myself. You're giving me that hungry look but saying no." One simple kiss had shattered her. How would it feel to make love with Evan? She surged against her again. "Please, kiss me."

Evan stood abruptly, her breathing erratic, face flushed, and her eyes heavy with desire. "I can't."

"You want this as much as I do."

"That's not the problem. We have a job to finish. Don't we?"

Frankie stood slowly and took Evan's hand. "I sort of apologize for crossing the line." She inhaled the sandalwood fragrance at Evan's wrist and kissed her palm. "And you're right. First we find and kill Judith Earl."

Evan laughed, the humor a welcome relief for her pent up frustrations. "Not exactly the plan, but close enough. I love that you can make me laugh and forget to be so serious."

She studied Evan's face—the steadiness of her gaze, arch of her brow, her pupils, the faint lines around her mouth and eyes—searching for any flicker of deception. "You like something besides my petite package and luscious lips?"

"Fishing for compliments, Strong?" Evan tsked playfully before her expression turned serious. "I actually find several things about you endearing, and they're all wrapped in an eclectic package I'm still sorting through…at a very difficult time. I'm sorry for the back-and-forth, but our timing couldn't be worse."

Frankie placed a hand over her heart, the sincerity of Evan's words registering. "I understand." She swallowed hard and decided to be just as candid. "Evan, I feel different with you. You make me want—"

Heavy pounding on the door interrupted her. "We're heading downstairs. Hurry up, slackers," Todd said before giving the door another series of raps.

"On our way," Evan called back.

Frankie released a long sigh. Was she grateful for the reprieve or disappointed about the sudden loss of intimacy between them? Was it a sign she shouldn't share everything with Evan?

Evan cupped Frankie's chin and kissed her cheek. "Guess we should get going. Maybe we can talk later?"

"Yeah, sure." Frankie retreated to the bathroom and came out dressed for her next role, but her heart wasn't into being someone else today. She wanted to stay here and tell Evan all the reasons being with her felt so frightening and yet so right.

"Wow," Evan said. "You'll blend right in with the homeless. Well done." She gave Frankie another careful once-over. "Impressive, but try not to overdo it. Okay?"

"Roger, boss." Frankie pulled on the fatigue jacket that covered her Hello Kitty sweatshirt and opened the door. "I'll take the stairs and meet you in the parking lot. The manager might think you're hauling homeless people off the streets for the night." She grinned and blew Evan an air kiss. "Later."

❖

Evan pressed one hand against the door when it closed behind Frankie and the other across her stomach to calm her queasiness. She'd looked into Frankie's eyes and seen her own truth—she'd always be drawn to a woman in need—but could she allow herself to be vulnerable with one again?

Getting involved with someone associated with another case was potentially career suicide, but Frankie was so compelling, so genuine beneath the chameleon façade. Everything about her pulled Evan in—her innocent looks, the mischievous glint in her eyes, her musky smell, and the delicious taste of her.

The consequences of her actions were clear. She'd faced them before, but this time, they could be worse. Was a relationship worth her reputation and career? "Finish this case and find out who she is and why you're so enamored with her, Spears." She grabbed her phone and coat and opened the door.

When she got to the parking lot, the guys were in a circle near the van laughing, and Frankie was in the middle. Her coat was missing, and Todd, Hank, and Aaron were wiping their hands up and down her body.

"What's going on?" The bite in her voice cued Evan that she'd overreacted. The image of anyone else touching Frankie irritated her too much. Everyone stopped and turned.

"They said I was too clean to be homeless." Frankie met Evan's gaze and her brows knitted together in a what-are-you-doing expression.

Evan cleared her throat and pushed the image of Frankie being manhandled, her nude body earlier, and the feelings it elicited from her mind. "Well, they have a point. I can't believe you travel with that costume."

"And many more." She waved her hands down her dirt- and grease-spotted outfit. "Am I ready for prime time, guys?"

"You'll do," Todd said as he slid the handicapped ramp in behind Aaron. Hank and Frankie followed them in, and Evan got behind the wheel.

She kept her mind on the operation instead of the smoldering looks Frankie was giving her in the rearview mirror. "I talked with

Comer this morning. No activity around Winston's container, and nothing new off the computer. Our targets are being careful, except for their pleasures. Comer and his team will spell us periodically through the day if we run long. Frankie, I'm afraid you're stuck for the duration."

"Hey, boss, it's okay. I can do this every day." Frankie's Sing Song ditty got a chuckle from the guys, but she didn't sound as cocky as usual, and Evan gave her a questioning look. "Seriously, I'm good to go. I think Winston will make a move first thing in the morning or just before closing when there are fewer customers. Shop's open from ten to six." She crumpled her empty coffee cup and shook it in her hand. "A few coins and I'm set. Somebody drop a sandwich and some water by later."

"What's your cover?" Evan asked Hank.

He pulled a suit jacket from a hook behind him. "Business dude, shopping, lunching, surfing the net, getting worked up for the strip club tonight."

Todd mussed his reddish hair and flipped up the collar of his Polo shirt. "I'll be my charming self, scoping women, and that last thing Hank said."

"Test your coms. Aaron and I will monitor from close by. Good luck and be careful." She stopped two blocks from Martin Place, and Hank and Todd got out and walked in opposite directions. She found a back street away from the crowd, and Frankie opened the sliding door. "Be careful, Frankie, and don't—"

"Don't leave my position without telling you. Got it."

Evan wanted to say so much more but couldn't. Frankie was on her own. She could do her job, but could Evan bear to watch while people ignored, insulted, and degraded her and while the effort of staying in character drained her emotionally and physically?

"You okay, boss?" Aaron asked from the back.

Sometimes he was just too damn intuitive. "I'm fine. Let's find a spot to set up." She circled the block and pulled into a commercial space that gave them an unobstructed view of Frankie's position near the cigar shop. She drew the privacy curtain behind the front seats and crawled into the back with Aaron.

"We're live," he said, pointing to the monitor. He took off his glasses and wiped them with his shirttail while glancing at her awkwardly.

"What's on your mind, Mr. Potter?" Aaron really liked his nickname, so she used it to make him more comfortable.

"I was whizzing through my wizarding world this morning looking for…" He gripped the wheels of his chair.

"For Judith?" She forced the name from her lips with a bit less venom than usual. If they caught her in the same net with Winston and Tyndall, Evan would feel a little better, but Aaron still couldn't walk. She'd never forgive Jude for that.

Aaron nodded. "I got a facial recognition match on a fake passport leaving Hong Kong. She arrived in Sydney yesterday."

The news was like a physical blow. Evan choked down a rush of emotions and memories, a few pleasurable but mostly painful. Jude was close, and Evan couldn't wait to narrow the gap and snap the handcuffs on her. She'd wasted too much time and energy on Judith Earl. "You did good, Potter. Thank you."

"Do you think she'll be with the other two?"

"I'd bet on it. Her arrival is probably why Ty wasn't at the club last night. Reunion." Aaron nodded. "In other news, how about checking a cell while we wait." She handed him the number Frankie had gotten from the shopkeeper.

"Heads up." Frankie's voice crackled through the system. "Can't make out this guy's face, but he's dressed like an old Cuban cigar poster. Straw fedora. Approaching from the north. I think it's too obvious to be Winston, but check it out."

"Eyes on," Hank said. "Moving in for a closer look."

Evan trained the binoculars on Frankie's easily recognizable spiked blond hair and panned to the left. Her hand shook as adrenaline took over, and she grabbed the binoculars with both hands. She locked on the suspect and willed him to look up. He pulled a cigarette from his inside pocket and lit it. "Stand down, guys. This isn't our man. He's too young."

"Copy," Frankie replied.

Evan lowered the binoculars, and as the surge of energy evaporated, she settled back in her chair. How had Frankie managed those explosive highs and lows over and over, possibly several times a day or even an hour when she worked undercover? Did she have a coping mechanism? Did it work long term or ever burn out? Evan's admiration for Frankie's abilities doubled. She was so much more than a jokester or a chameleon.

"We've got another possible walking down from the Reserve Bank," Frankie said.

"I've got this one." Todd moved into position.

For the next eight hours, the team worked the street with Frankie calling the plays, but Winston didn't show. "Okay, guys, let's wrap it up," Evan said. "Frankie, we'll pick you up at this morning's drop-off location."

"Received."

She sounded flat and emotionless, and Evan couldn't get to her quickly enough. When Frankie opened the side door and crawled in, she looked pale, her shoulders hunched forward, and her eyes lacked focus. The day had taken its toll, and Evan wanted desperately to hold her.

"To the strip club, please, James," Todd joked from the back.

"Really, guys?" Evan asked. "You're seriously up for that after pounding the pavement all day on a stakeout?"

"Duh," Todd said. "Why do you think we've been humping it so hard all day? Pun intended. The club is our reward, boss, and it's not far. What do you say?"

As she drove, she glanced at her team in the rearview mirror. "We have to find Tyndall and that's our only lead. So, sure, why not?"

"The boss has a heart," Todd said.

"Ooh-rah," Hank added.

Evan looked at her second in command. "Can you manage our rowdy team?" Her guys stared at her in disbelief. "What?"

"You don't really put anyone else in charge," Hank said. "You sure?"

Was that true? Had she been such a tyrant? Had her insistence on preparation, planning, and being in command kept her from delegating and helping her team grow? And had her rigidity kept her from bonding with the team as well? She didn't want to be that supervisor or that person. "Give me room to change." This time when she looked in the mirror, she caught Frankie's gaze and her stomach clenched at the look of admiration in her eyes.

"You in?" Aaron asked Frankie.

"No way. I can't play. I'm totally fried today," mumbled Frankie, still in Sing Song role.

Was she still playing the part or was she stuck some place in her mind unable to let go?

"So, who gets monitoring duty?" Aaron asked, probably seeing himself once again isolated in the back of the van while the others had fun.

Evan shrugged. "I'll drop you off, have some of Comer's guys join you, and you can duke it out. I don't care, as long as it's done properly. Your call, Hank." Everyone still stared. "And stop gawking."

After letting the guys out, Evan made the call to Comer and broke the speed limit getting back to the hotel. Frankie hadn't moved up front or even spoken since the club, and Evan kept checking in the rearview mirror to make sure she was okay. When they got to the hotel, Evan slid the van's side door open and held out her hand. "Let's get you inside."

Frankie stumbled out and grabbed for her. "My legs are like jelly so don't let go. I'll try not to grope you in public though."

Evan remembered Frankie's earlier concern about her disguise, so she took off her long coat, wrapped it around Frankie's shoulders, and encircled her waist. She wobbled and her eyes were glassy like a drugged or disoriented person. She seemed fragile. "I've got you. And we're taking the elevator."

"Thanks."

The elevator ride with strangers staring at Frankie disgustedly stretched too long, and Evan got her first taste of what this day, and every day Frankie had spent as Sing Song, must've cost her. When the door finally opened, she ushered Frankie into their room.

Frankie looked around the small accommodation and seemed to come to her senses again. "Long time since we left here this morning."

Evan released a deep sigh. "Thank God. I thought you were gone."

"I was." Frankie shucked Evan's coat, stripped the sweatshirt over her head, and tugged at the tights but toppled sideways onto the bed. "I need a shower."

"You should probably rest first. I'm not sure you're stable enough to shower."

Frankie reached for her hands with a look of desperation. "I have to get rid of *her*. I can't stay in her skin one more minute. *Please*, Evan. Help me."

Evan couldn't resist her plea. She was frantic, and Evan could be strong enough for both of them. "What do you need?"

"Would you help me shower so I don't fall and break my neck?"

Was she *that* strong? Evan swallowed hard.

CHAPTER ELEVEN

A ll right." Kneeling by the bed in front of her, Evan took a deep breath and peeled the tights down Frankie's legs. She glanced at Frankie's pale body, small breasts, protruding ribs, and hollow stomach. *She really needs to gain weight, maybe work on building muscle. A trainer could tailor a program to address core and strength issues. What?* She was babbling to herself to distract from Frankie's body, the fact they'd already kissed, how soft her skin felt, or how much she'd enjoy seeing Frankie nude under different circumstances. But right now, she needed help. "Take my hand." She helped Frankie stand, slid her arm around her waist, and guided her into the bathroom and onto the toilet.

"Get undressed," Frankie said.

Evan shook her head. "I don't think that's necessary." Being naked with her in the shower would be *so* good and *so* bad at the same time. Just standing there thinking about it gave her hot flashes. "I'll help you in the tub and stand out here just in case."

"I need you with me. Once the hot water hits my skin and I start to relax, I'll be a goner. Please, Evan? I'm totally harmless right now."

There was the urgency in Frankie's tone she'd heard earlier, and Evan wavered, but it wasn't right. "Why don't I run a bath so we don't have to worry about you falling?"

"In a few minutes, I'll be dead weight, and you won't be able to lift me. This isn't a trick, Evan. I really need help."

"In case you hadn't noticed, you're not that heavy, Frankie, and I'm stronger than I look." She turned on the tap, adjusted the temperature, and held out her hand. "Hold on to me and get in. I'll be right here. I won't even close the curtain, in case you need me."

Frankie reluctantly took her hand and stepped over the side of the tub. "Now what?"

"Stand still while I hose you down." Evan used the handheld to wet Frankie's body and tried not to think about how gorgeous and helpless she looked.

Frankie leaned under the spray and placed both hands against the tile wall for support. "Would you wash my back please?"

The skin of Frankie's back was so pale it was almost translucent, and Evan followed the gentle lines of her body to her round ass. If Frankie hadn't sounded like she was about to pass out, Evan would've thought she was teasing her or playing the innocent seductress. She tamped down her hormones, secured the sprayer and squirted shower gel into her hands, and rubbed them together to warm the lotion.

Her hands trembled as she lowered them onto Frankie's shoulders and rubbed down her back. Frankie's skin was so soft, so pliable, and felt so good, that Evan's arms tingled from the contact. She reminded herself this was about taking care of Frankie, and another kind of warmth swept through her. She'd never been so needed by anyone before, never been willing to get this close. Evan focused on the repetitive motion of washing back and forth, up and down, not the silky skin under her hands or the way it made her feel.

When Frankie turned to face her, arms spread, Evan shook her head. "Oh no. You can't expect me to…"

"Too much?"

"I'm only human." She pointed to the edge of the tub. "Sit here. That'll support you." She stepped back against the sink, still close enough to be of help if Frankie needed her and waited until she finished. "Want me to rinse you off now?"

"Please." She stood and turned until Evan finished rinsing the suds away. "Okay, that's good. I think I can get out on my own."

She reached for Frankie's hand. "Hold on until both feet are on the floor."

"Aye aye, ma'am."

Evan held onto Frankie's hand until she was safely out of the tub and settled on the toilet again. She pulled a towel from the closet and wrapped it around her shoulders. "Will you be all right while I take a quick shower?"

"Sure. And thanks, Evan." She kissed Evan on the cheek and the heat of her body made Evan step back.

"I'll be out in a sec." When the door closed behind Frankie, Evan turned the tap on cold, undressed, and stood under the spray, letting her body cool and her thoughts return to less pleasurable images. Frankie made her feel so many things, so many complicated things that she had no idea how to deal with.

She finished showering and wrapped a towel around her before returning to the other room. Frankie sat on the side of the bed staring at the floor. She looked so defeated and vulnerable that Evan's heart ached. "Are you okay?"

"Yeah, but I'm too tired to get in bed."

"Let me help you." Evan removed the bath towel, and eased her under the covers, tucking them in around her. "Sleep well." She held her own towel and leaned over to kiss Frankie's forehead before backing away.

Frankie reached for her. "Lie with me until I fall asleep?"

"You need to rest."

"No choice, but I don't want to be alone right now." Frankie's eyes were wide, as if she feared some invisible demon would claim her before sleep.

Evan wasn't afraid of being physically close to Frankie. They'd already touched and kissed, but that was mostly biology. The intimacy of this moment terrified her. Frankie had trusted herself completely to Evan's care. This situation was fraught with potential—for more wanting, more pleasure, and eventually more pain that Evan wasn't ready for.

"Please, Evan? I want to explain why—"

"You don't have to explain anything." She stared down at Frankie's face, pale with exhaustion and glowing with cherubic innocence. "Just a second." Evan dug a pair of boxers and a T-shirt out of her bag, pulled them on, and crawled under the covers beside her. Frankie didn't have to explain what happened to her tonight, but Evan wanted to know everything about her, especially what caused the vulnerability she saw in Frankie's eyes when she was tired or heard in her voice when she talked briefly about her parents yesterday. Where did all the hurt and pain come from? Was it the job, the constant pretense, or did it go deeper? She wanted it all, but not tonight. "Sleep, Frankie. Just sleep."

Frankie rolled to her side and pulled one of Evan's arms across her body. "Thank you." A few seconds later, she completely relaxed and her breathing leveled.

Evan's suppressed feelings now rushed back in force. She released her responsibility as guardian, scooted closer, and absorbed the heat and softness of Frankie's body and inhaled her freshly washed scent. She relived the sensation of touching Frankie's body as she washed her—the smoothness of her skin, the weight of her breasts and the texture of her puckered nipples pressing into her palms, her jutting hip bones that dipped to the thin patch of soft hair between her legs. She pushed her pelvis against Frankie's butt and her skin prickled with desire. She ached and wanted, but she couldn't have. She inched slowly away.

When Frankie opened her eyes again, it was still dark outside and she wasn't alone in bed. She turned slowly, trying not to disturb Evan, but she was already awake, sitting up in black boxers and a T-shirt staring down at her. "Why are you awake? You should be resting."

"I can't sleep. Are you all right?" Evan brushed her hand across Frankie's forehead and through her hair. "Sorry if I woke you."

"You didn't." She glanced at the flashing digital clock on the bedside table. "I've been out for almost six hours. That's really good, especially when I don't usually sleep with anyone. I mean I don't spend the night. Wait, that didn't sound right."

"No need to explain. I'm familiar with casual."

Frankie had a feeling sex with Evan would never be casual, even if it only happened once. She pulled a couple of the fluffy feather pillows behind her and leaned against the headboard beside Evan. "Hold me?" What was happening to her? She didn't spend the night, and she didn't ask to be held, but she didn't feel the things she'd been feeling lately either.

Evan didn't hesitate. "Of course."

They were quiet with each other, not an awkward silence but one born of mutual comfort. Evan had taken care of her last night, bathed her, put her to bed, and watched over her while she slept. And she'd never slept so peacefully. She trusted Evan with her body, but could she share her story, her past, and her secrets? She flinched from a twinge of guilt.

"You okay?" Evan asked.

"Just a chill." She hugged the plush duvet tighter and ignored the little voice in her head urging her to talk to Evan. They'd only kissed, which was nowhere close to share-your-entire-life territory, but she didn't want to be the person she used to be, hiding from her feelings and using other people's as a weapon. She wanted a new life, a real relationship.

"Can I ask a question?"

Frankie pushed her warring thoughts aside, nestled her head on Evan's shoulder, and wrapped her arm around Evan's waist. She breathed in her spicy outdoorsy scent, committing it to memory. "Anything."

"Why was yesterday so taxing for you? After all the undercover assignments you've done, I'd think you'd be used to role-playing."

"It's not just role-playing for me. I become someone else, get inside their skin, think, act, and talk like they would. When I put on the disguise, I *am* that person. Besides, undercover assignments aren't twenty-four-seven. I take breaks, make excuses to run errands, anything to reconnect and remind myself what's real. Yesterday was eight consecutive hours of being in character, and it wiped me out. I was good at UC work. That's why my bosses kept sending me back under."

"*Were* good at it?"

"Since the last one, I'm not so sure. The shooting and everything." The closer she got to the everything part, the more afraid Frankie became. Maybe she'd just tell Evan a little at a time and see how she reacted.

"That's what you meant when you said you excel at being anyone but yourself?"

"Partly." She pulled Evan closer, whether for courage or to delay she wasn't sure. "I wish you'd felt comfortable enough to sleep."

"Too much on my mind." Evan reached for the lamp, but Frankie stopped her. "You're stalling, Frankie. Tell me."

"Couldn't we leave the light off and do something entirely different? This feels sort of awesome, and I'm not really in the mood to unpack all that after yesterday." Sort of awesome was an understatement. She felt safe, comfortable, and cared for like she hadn't her entire life.

Evan leaned sideways and looked into Frankie's eyes. "Why do I get the feeling you're blowing me off? If whatever we've started is going anywhere, we have to be honest. I can't accept anything less, not again."

The pain in Evan's voice reminded Frankie how much she'd suffered lately. Evan had been honest with her about Judith. And she was right. It was probably better to be open, just not about everything. She could take a first step. "Okay."

"Can I please turn on the light now? I need to see your face," Evan said.

Frankie nodded, scrubbed her hands through her hair, and decided to start with the lesser of her sins. "Okay, here goes. In the interest of full disclosure, I spied on you before I started with the task force."

"You what?" Evan cocked her head to one side and her eyebrow arched. "Not at all what I expected, but do continue. I'm intrigued."

"I wasn't sure I was ready for another assignment so soon after the shooting, so I checked you out. I needed a sense of who you were, if I thought we could work together without too much friction."

"Obviously, you decided we could."

Frankie shrugged. "Surveillance isn't an exact science, and it was just a few hours." Evan looked like she was trying not to smile, so Frankie continued. "I observed from a distance, nothing too intrusive. All I saw was a statuesque woman in a long black coat who looked like she could take on the world…and banging. I heard a lot of banging at your place."

"Were you in disguise?"

Frankie nodded.

"As Sing Song," Evan said. "Those tights and pink Hello Kitty sweatshirt."

"Yeah."

"You seemed so familiar the first time I saw you in the office, but I couldn't figure out why because you changed almost daily. You hung around the Daytime Resource Center and downtown a lot on your last case. I saw you a couple of times when I was out for lunch."

Frankie nodded, a little embarrassed that Evan's first memory of her was as her street persona, but she probably hadn't made a much better impression her first day at work. She'd purposely dressed in funky clothes to make a point as a nonconformist. Now she wanted Evan to see her in another light—as someone she could be interested in, possibly love.

Evan planted a light kiss on her forehead. "So, why the constant changes?"

Evan's touch made Frankie warm again, and she chewed her lip as a distraction. "Old habits and a childhood of playing dress up." It was partially true.

"You mentioned your parents the other night, just before you passed out in the van. What did you mean when you said they weren't very nice?"

"Oh no, not the parents conversation. Anything but that." She wasn't ready to go there, not completely, so she pressed her hand over Evan's heart. "I'm enjoying this way too much to bring my parents into bed with us. Please?"

"When you put it like that." Evan stroked Frankie's cheek. "For the record, I prefer your natural look. And in the interest of full disclosure, I like this voyeuristic tendency of yours." Evan gave her a scorching look that made Frankie's insides ache.

Frankie flung the covers off, twisted sideways, and straddled Evan's legs, anxious to touch her again and to lighten the heaviness of the conversation. "Damn, woman, if you don't stop looking at me like that, I won't be responsible for my actions."

Evan placed her hand in the center of Frankie's naked chest and stared at her. "I want you so much, but this can't happen. Guess we'll both have to suffer for the time being."

"We'll see." She lowered toward Evan's mouth but stopped just before their lips met. She traced Evan's bottom lip with her tongue. "I want you to ache like I do."

"I already do." Evan moaned. "I have no control with you." Her breath hitched. "Mercy."

"I'm trying to be merciful." Frankie was exactly where she wanted to be, doing precisely what she wanted to do…and prayed it would never end. "I want you naked." She reached for the hem of Evan's T-shirt and started to pull it up just as Evan's phone rang. "Noooo."

"Thank God." Evan flipped her over and rolled out of bed before Frankie could stop her.

"You have *got* to be kidding. You're leaving me like this?"

"Sorry. I'm right there with you." Evan grinned and picked up her phone. "Hank?" Her expression changed from sexy and teasing to serious in a second. "Anyone else with him? We'll meet you there in twenty minutes."

"What's going on?" Frankie rummaged through her bag for clean clothes.

"The guys have spotted Tyndall in the strip club. We leave in five." She started pulling on clothes but turned back to Frankie. "And this…" She pointed to the bed.

Frankie felt like a stone settled in her gut. They hadn't made love, but the time they'd spent together was intimate in a way she'd never forget. She wasn't sure she could take being shut out by Evan again. "Never happened?"

"Is to be continued." Evan winked, and Frankie's hopes soared again.

CHAPTER TWELVE

Frankie lightly rested her hand on Evan's thigh as she drove, unwilling to relinquish the connection they'd shared in the room. She was having difficulty understanding the intensity of her feelings. She'd always been a hit-and-run type because of frequent relocation and undercover work, but now, when Evan wasn't around, she felt fragmented, unbalanced, and lonely.

Evan glanced sideways at her. "You could've passed on this after yesterday."

"I wanted to be here. Sleep helped, and so did you. Thanks." What was it about Evan that affected her so? Hopefully, she'd have a lot of time to figure that out later. When Evan focused on the road again, Frankie asked, "Did Hank say if anyone else was with Tyndall?"

"He's alone and apparently having the time of his life."

"Good."

"Why is that good?"

"Because I want him to remember how great he felt tonight, how high he was, how sweet the liquor tasted, the perfect breasts on a stripper, how tight her ass was, the smell of sex in the air, how hard he got looking at her, and his last orgasm with a woman in the room for a very long time. I hope he recalls every minute of tonight over and over while he rots in prison."

Evan chuckled. "You're ruthless, Francesca Strong. Remind me not to piss you off."

"Remember that the next time I try to kiss you." Frankie stroked Evan's leg as she parked near the club, and they walked toward the front of the Dollhouse Strip Club. "It's a shame we don't have some free time. I'd love to explore Sydney with you. There's so much to see."

"I'd like that. Maybe another trip?" Evan squeezed her hand, shifted into work mode, and keyed her mike. "Hank, we're at the front door. Where are you?" She motioned forward, and they flashed their badges at security to get inside.

Frankie blinked against the rapidly flashing strobes, trying to figure out which way to go, but was backed against a wall by an impatient man elbowing past. When her eyes adjusted, she scanned the space. The narrow entrance opened into a large, dimly lit room and a bar that covered the entire back wall highlighted with blue lights. She leaned close and yelled in Evan's ear to be heard over the thunderous music. "Classy." Evan gave her a skeptical look. "No, really. This would be a Rolls Royce in car lingo."

"Been to a lot of strip bars, have you?"

"Monthly in the skinhead gun-smuggling operation. And they insisted on sitting on sniffers' row, right up front." The memory of too much baby powder and cheap perfume made her stomach churn. She'd walked a fine line with those guys. If they'd found out she was a lesbian, she wouldn't have lasted long.

This place was upscale based on the patrons' clothes and quality of women, but typical in other ways. It was packed with men of all ages, a few accompanied by women, the music was set to ear-splitting level, the flashing lights could rival any rock show, and it reeked of booze and desperation. The entire women-entertaining-men-with-their-bodies-for-money vibe gave Frankie the creeps.

She stopped and stared at the show in progress on the central raised dais. An attractive brunette clad in only a G-string gyrated around a shiny gold pole like it was a lover, straddling, humping, and ending with an upside-down split and a fistful of cash. How had this woman gotten here? Would she ever find a way out of the business? Did she want one?

"Focus, Frankie." Evan pointed to the left of the stage. "They're back this way."

Frankie kept staring and bumped into Evan. "How do you know?" The well-dressed men occupying the seating banquettes bordering the stage were apparently having the same problem concentrating. They handed out wads of money to the dancer and to gorgeous lingerie-clad waitresses who circled them like vultures to fresh kill.

"Because I'm looking for the team, not at a stripper."

Frankie liked the tinge of jealousy in Evan's voice. It reminded her of their intimacy earlier and the promise of returning to it later. She hurried to catch up. The hallway they headed toward mirrored three others branching off the main room, and Todd stood at the entrance.

He grinned at her. "Enjoying the show, Frankie? Wait until you get back here."

She didn't burst his bubble by telling him this place made her more nauseous than excited, especially as they got closer to the private rooms in the back. She choked down the urge to gag at the smell of sex, liquor, and cigars. "Where's our guy?"

"Having a private lap dance," Todd said before pointing to a doorway where the other guys waited. "He's been in there about ten minutes."

"Let's ruin his night," Hank said and motioned for the guys to fan out on either side of the entrance. He did a silent countdown on his fingers and flung the door open.

The room was tight with dark paint and a single dim light in the corner. It reeked of stale sex and Frankie's stomach lurched. A naked woman with a mop of poorly dyed red hair was bending over in front of Tyndall swirling to gaudy music. He had his pants around his ankles and was playing with his penis.

"What the fuck?" Tyndall backed toward a cushioned chair while reaching for his trousers and fell over.

"Whoa," Todd said. "Nobody wants to see that thing. Put it away."

The dancer picked up her skimpy clothes and ran.

"Who are you and what the hell are you doing here?" Tyndall asked, rolling sideways to shield his privates and pull up his pants.

Todd and one of Comer's men searched him to make sure he wasn't carrying a weapon and stepped back.

Comer moved closer. "We're all kinds of bad news for you, mate. No relief for your stiffy, and you're under arrest." He pointed to the others. "Interpol, US Marshals, DEA, and New South Wales Police. Let's go."

❖

Evan drove quietly, trying to form a strategy for questioning the man she'd much rather throw in jail and never see again. At least she wouldn't have to deal with Jude at the same time. Evan thought she'd stick close to her meal ticket, but the guys hadn't seen her at the club. So, where was she?

Frankie slid her hand across the back of Evan's seat and squeezed her shoulders. "Want to talk through how to approach this guy?"

She shook her head. Frankie's touch sent her thoughts and feelings in an entirely different direction. Their night had been intimate, sexy, and dangerous. Hank's call had been a blessing, because she probably would've made love to Frankie without the interruption. She'd been open, sharing things Evan knew nothing about, and that was a major turn-on. But adding sex to the mixture would only complicate their situation.

"Are you okay?"

"Yeah," Evan said, her tone more clipped than she intended.

"Not buying it, but if you don't want to talk, that's okay. I'm glad Tyndall didn't fight when we arrested him. It could've turned into a freak show in that place."

"Yeah, it could've," Evan said distractedly.

"But no sign of Winston or Judith."

"No." The word sounded harsh and dismissive. Frankie didn't deserve her testiness, but discussing Jude with the woman she was heading down a similar path with annoyed Evan at the moment. "Sorry I snapped at you."

"I get it. You want to catch her and you never want to see her again. Sort of like you want to be with me, but you don't," Frankie said.

"It's not like that at all."

"Isn't it? I see the parallel, and I don't blame you for being conflicted, but I'm not her."

Evan stopped the car in front of the Kings Cross Police Station and took Frankie's hands. "Judith Earl is a lying, cheating, manipulative woman who doesn't know the meaning of honesty. You're nothing like her and you proved that tonight. I really appreciate you telling me about spying on me." She looked around the parking lot before leaning over and kissing Frankie quickly on the lips. "And I was serious about the voyeur thing. It's kind of hot. To be explored further. Now, let's go question our fugitive."

When they entered the station, Comer met them in the squad room. "Tyndall is eating a sandwich with some of the guys and yucking it up. We haven't cautioned him or asked him anything relevant yet. Thought you'd want to choose your interviewer."

"Thanks for that," Evan said. She walked toward Tyndall, and he slapped his hand on the desk.

"Well, I'll be damned. It's US Marshal Evan Spears. Can't stay away from me?" He motioned toward her and raised his voice so everyone could hear. "Is the lover of my lover my enemy or just another puppet?"

Adrenaline flooded Evan's system, and she imagined herself moving toward Tyndall in disjointed clips. If she could punch him just once, she might feel better, but she wasn't a violent person. The thoughts flashed through her mind. From the corner of her eye, she saw her own fist moving back and then forward toward Tyndall's smug looking face. "I will—"

"Evan, step back."

Frankie's voice registered first and then the pressure of her hand on Evan's chest pushing her away from Tyndall. Her guys formed a barrier between the two of them.

"Oh, I see what's going on." Tyndall laughed and pointed at Frankie. "You've already replaced my beloved with another toy. Jude will be heartbroken."

Evan surged toward him again, but Frankie pushed both hands into her chest, walked her backward, and whispered, "He's baiting you. Don't give him a get out of jail free card."

She spun around and retreated to the hallway, pressed her hands against the wall, and pulled for breath. What the hell just happened? She never lost her cool, especially with suspects, and never in front of her team. It's not like she was in love with Judith. Were her feelings for Frankie clouding her judgment about everything? Or was her ego so badly bruised that she needed to lash out?

"You're all right, Evan. Just breathe and let it go."

Frankie's voice was calm and the steady pressure of her hand on Evan's lower back soothing. Frankie was supposed to be the volatile one, not her. Frankie ducked under her arms and stood in front of her against the wall. Her head barely came up to Evan's chin, and she chuckled. "So, the guys sent you to calm the beast?"

"Something like that." Frankie smiled, and the world felt almost normal again. "Who do you want to conduct the interview?" She started to object. "You and I will observe."

Evan straightened and squared her shoulders. Seeing her wild woman so tame put everything back in perspective. "Thank you. Let's go." She reentered the room and gave Hank a nod. "Why don't we all get some coffee and a sandwich and let him cool his heels in interrogation for a while? Then will you and Todd do the honors?"

"Gladly, boss." Hank grabbed one of Tyndall's arms and Todd the other and they escorted him down the hall.

Frankie did a snack run down the street and brought back sandwiches and drinks that they ate in the observation room next door while watching Tyndall squirm. When they finished eating, Evan checked her watch. "He's about to pop. When you're ready, guys."

While they waited for Hank and Todd to set up the recording and videoing equipment, Evan turned to Aaron. "Any other signs of... Judith?"

"No, but I ran the cell number you gave me for Winston. You were right. It's a burner. We know where he bought it, but he paid cash. We're tracking the number, but he doesn't use it often enough to get a location."

"I guess Sing Song will be staking out the cigar shop again tomorrow," Frankie said.

Evan flinched at the comment. The assignment yesterday had taken too much out of Frankie, and now that Evan understood why, she couldn't watch it happen again. "No. We'll do a routine stakeout. Besides, the shop owner is going to call when Winston picks up the order, right?"

"Yeah...but."

"No buts. You can't do that again. We'll lock down the mall at both ends. He won't get past us."

Aaron nodded. "You were pretty awesome out there, but it wiped you out." He pointed at the two-way mirror. "We're ready to start."

After the introductions and advising of rights for the tape, Hank cleared his throat, but before he could pose the first question, Tyndall asked, "How did you find us? Winston's escape plan was a fucking stroke of genius. Let me guess. That little faggot, Grif, squealed like a pig when you caught him."

"This isn't your first rodeo, Ty. You know the drill. The first one to talk gets the deal."

"I thought he'd keep his mouth shut. He was paid well and he'd have plenty of partners in prison." He laughed, but no one joined in.

"You're one to talk, lover boy, caught with your dick in your hand, jerking off in a strip club. Did your girlfriend dump you already?"

Tyndall's face turned red then almost purple. "Your boss spoiled her. Turns out she's more muff diver than knob polisher."

Aaron gave Evan an enthusiastic fist bump. "Hope Judith knows what a great favor you did her. One woman saved from that pathetic excuse for a man."

Evan could've hugged Aaron for his compassion and humor, instead she blushed and glanced at Frankie. Maybe she didn't need to hear all this. If Tyndall's opening salvo was any indication, he wasn't going to play nice. "Do you want to go back to the room and rest before we start the stakeout?" she asked Frankie. "Aaron, you can go too. No sense in all of us staying up."

Frankie and Aaron exchanged a glance and both said at the same time, "No way."

"Okay, okay. We'll all be exhausted. Not a good plan." She turned back to the interview room, feeling a twinge of sympathy that Judith had spent time with this vile man, but the empathetic moment quickly passed. Jude chose Grady Tyndall, his money, and his fugitive life. If anyone deserved her pity, it was the next unsuspecting woman who crossed Judith's path.

"I guess you better get used to Grif's style of sex," Hank said to Tyndall. "He might let you quarterback occasionally, but sooner or later you'll have to receive. And those big, macho dudes in prison, I'm pretty sure you'll be receiving a lot...unless you want to help us."

"Thought you said Grif already got the deal."

"Yeah, but you might get some consideration, if you cooperate."

Evan tensed. She didn't like making deals with criminals, but it was often the cost of doing business. Griffin's deal was particularly tough to swallow because she associated him with Aaron's injury. Tyndall had slept with her girlfriend, who then betrayed her, and that pissed Evan off on so many levels, but this wasn't about her. As sick as it made her to offer Tyndall even one ounce of leniency, they had to catch Winston, and eventually, Judith.

"How much time are we talking?" Tyndall asked.

"Depends on how much information you're offering and how good it is."

Ty leaned back on the legs of his chair and scratched his chin. "What if I told you where Jude and Winston are?"

Frankie watched Evan grab the back of a chair in the observation room and grip it until her knuckles blanched. Tyndall knew where the other two fugitives were and was willing to make a deal, but would Evan go for it? She remembered the battle for Griffin's arrangement.

Evan keyed the mike and spoke to Hank. "Let's talk. Now."

Hank left Todd in the interview room and joined them a few seconds later. "Yeah, boss?"

"What do you think? Is he blowing smoke up our asses?"

"I think he knows, and he definitely doesn't want to spend the rest of his life without women. Trust me on that."

Evan stared at Tyndall. "Has he made any phone calls since the arrest?"

Hank shook his head. "Club security makes clients leave their mobiles at the door when they come in. They don't want guys photographing or videoing the women. We collected his on the way out, and he didn't call anyone from here."

"Evan," Frankie said, "excuse me, but if I were Winston, I'd have a failsafe in case one of them got caught, some way the other would know without a phone call. Maybe a time limit before they meet again or preset check-in times. Something."

"Good point. Ask him, Hank. If they have something like that and Tyndall doesn't tell us, any deal is off. Make sure he understands."

Hank turned to leave, but Evan added, "One more thing. His deal is only good if he gives us both of them."

"Works for me," Hank said. "You here until we're done?"

"You and Todd know what to do. Aaron, Frankie, and I and a couple of Comer's men are going back to the cigar shop. Basic stakeout. Hopefully, we'll catch Winston without Tyndall's help and won't have to give him a damn thing. We'll meet up later to debrief."

Hank held the door while Aaron, Evan, and Frankie exited. When they got outside, Frankie lowered the van ramp for Aaron, slid it back in after him, and then stopped Evan before they got inside. "You feeling all right?"

"Yeah, why?"

"That's the second time in two days you've turned the reins over to Hank. Just checking for fever or other symptoms of sickness or memory loss."

"Get in the van, smart-ass."

Frankie grinned. "Just FYI, redneck foreplay doesn't work for me."

On the drive back to the shop, Frankie asked, "How do you feel about another deal?"

Evan glanced at Aaron in the rearview mirror. "I feel the same way you guys probably do. Every one of our fugitives was in that room when Winston ordered Dennis Lowell to kill Franklin Weber, and they all participated in and benefited from the drug operation. I think they should get the maximum time in prison."

"They'll all do time," Aaron said, always the optimist.

"Yeah, just not enough if we keep making deals," Evan grumbled.

Three of Comer's men followed them back downtown in their vehicle, and a few minutes later the team divided to cover Martin Place. Two of the men covered the north end, and Evan and another guy took the south. Frankie and Aaron were positioned as point directly across from the cigar shop. Aaron had his laptop out, and to the untrained eye they appeared to be working or studying.

The day dragged on, and Winston didn't show. Frankie checked out four customers going into the shop around closing time, and a few minutes later, her cell rang. "Hello."

"I'm the owner of the cigar shop. Your father's order was just picked up but not by him."

She scanned the street for anyone who stood out. "Describe the person who picked it up, please." The owner hesitated. "Sir, this is a police matter. What did they look like?"

"Young Caucasian boy. I had to ask for ID because he looked like a teenager, still has spots. He's taller than you, dark hair, wearing jeans, a T-shirt, and a red splash jacket. He was carrying a backpack. It would be pretty heavy with all the cigars."

Frankie checked in both directions and saw the suspect walking casually toward the south end of the street. "Thank you, sir. You've been very helpful." She hung up and radioed the description to the other guys. "He's walking toward Evan's position. Do you see him?"

"Negative. Not yet."

"I'll follow until you get eyes on him." Frankie ran toward the suspect, he glanced back at her, and then ducked behind a building. He'd ditched the distinctive red jacket, but the backpack had a bright orange wolf emblem. "I'm at the end of Martin Place, turning east. I don't see a street name."

"Check the sides of the buildings," Aaron said over the com.

She glanced around but saw nothing identifiable to give as a landmark to the rest of the team. "I've got nothing, but still heading east…on George Street." Damn it, she couldn't lose this guy. Whether he got back to Winston or not, he'd know the police were closing in, if Tyndall's disappearance hadn't already alerted him. She stopped at the edge of the building before barreling ahead and peeked around the corner. The boy stood beside a dumpster in a narrow alley as if he was waiting for her. "Stop."

He raised his hands. "Duh, lady, I am stopped. Why are you chasing me?"

"Frankie. Come in, Frankie. What's your location?" Evan's voice sounded in her ear, but she couldn't answer while dealing with this guy. Evan would be pissed about that.

"Keep your hands where I can see them and turn around." As he turned, she pulled the backpack off his shoulders and tossed it behind her. "Put your hands against the dumpster. I'm going to pat you down for weapons."

"You're not even a real police officer. You're foreign."

"Just do as I say."

"I don't think so." He lowered his hands, turned, and started toward her. "I bet you don't even have a gun. Do you?"

Frankie felt the sudden flood of adrenaline and everything around her became more pronounced—the sharp stench of rotting food from the dumpster, the cool wind whipping around the corner of the building, the electronic buzz of overhead electrical lines, a sign above the back door of a shop, and the widened pupils of the boy's eyes as he moved toward her.

She stepped back and bumped into someone else. *Two of them.* She started to turn, but the man behind her caught her in a choke hold and squeezed. No one knew where she was. The suspect hissed in her ear, and the heat of his breath brushed against the side of Frankie's neck. She was alone. *Think, Frankie, think.* "DEA." She gasped as his grip tightened. "I'm…DEA."

"Be still, sweetie, and I might not hurt you."

A woman's voice. Frankie feigned passing out and went slack in the woman's arms. When she tried to readjust her grip, Frankie kicked backward into her knee, and she stumbled, losing her hold. Frankie spun away and pulled for breath, glancing at the woman's face. "Jude?"

"Good guess, new girl." Judith regained her balance and moved slowly forward. "Winston will be very disappointed that you interrupted his cigar delivery."

"We've done more than that."

Judith scoffed. "We'll see. You don't look like Evan's type, too skinny, no tits, and a piss poor fighter. But you are working together, which seems to be her criteria these days."

"Jealous much?" Frankie scanned the area for anything to use as a weapon, constantly moving so they couldn't back her in a corner. Then she remembered the sign above the doorway. She keyed the mike. "I'm in an alley behind an insurance company."

Her best hope now was to keep both suspects in sight, engaged, and at arm's length until the team found her. "Evan has mentioned you, in passing, nothing too complimentary though. Guess you didn't make much of an impression."

Judith swung at her, and Frankie dodged the blow.

"Has she given you her limp, 'I can't get involved' speech?" Judith asked, taking another wild punch.

Frankie easily ducked under her arm. "Not really. She's good to go."

Judith's eyes narrowed and grew dark. "Fuck you."

"No, thanks. I'm taken."

At a nod from Judith, the boy circled Frankie to the left, and Judith circled right. She picked up the backpack and lunged toward Frankie as the boy shoved her from behind. Frankie stumbled forward, and Judith swung the heavy bag with both hands and struck her across the left side of the head.

"Oh, God!" Frankie's vision blurred and then faded. She tried to key her mike again, but she was falling. She hit the concrete. *Evan, I'm sorry.*

CHAPTER THIRTEEN

"Frankie, can you hear me?" Evan nestled Frankie's head in her lap, trying to revive her. She was pale, her skin cool to the touch. The left side of her face was starting to bruise, and a cut at the hairline trickled blood. "Frankie?"

Evan scanned the area, growing more anxious. "Where the hell is the ambulance? Call them again, Aaron." The team had formed a ring around them to keep bystanders away, and Evan was trying not to let the guys see her fear. She leaned closer and whispered so the others couldn't hear. "I will kill whoever did this to you. I swear it."

"No...no killing." Frankie's eyes fluttered and then shut again. "The light. Hurts."

"Frankie, oh, thank God. How do you feel?"

"You're...upside down...or I am."

"Well, you are in the land Down Under," one of the Aussies said. "All right, mate?"

"My head hurts like a son of a bitch." She tried to get up.

"Stay put," Evan said. "An ambulance is on the way."

"Don't need one. I have to tell you—"

"Whatever you have to say can wait." Evan rubbed Frankie's forehead to soothe her so she'd lie still. "Stop thrashing about, please."

"It can't wait. Judith was here. She got away. Winston will know." Frankie tried to get up again, but Evan held firm. "Did you hear? I gave my location."

"You did good, Frankie. Just relax. You've had a blow to the head. Are you certain about Judith?"

Frankie grabbed the front of Evan's shirt and pulled her down so they were eye to eye. "The kid was a decoy. Judith was here, watching. She choked me and hit me with the backpack."

Evan clenched her jaw until it ached. She'd definitely make Judith Earl hurt with her bare hands and enjoy every minute of it for what she'd done to Frankie. She didn't trust herself to respond to Frankie's information.

"I'll lock down this area and call in a sniffer dog," one of the Aussie agents said. "We can't let her get back to Winston or he'll be in the wind again."

"Thank you," Evan managed through clenched teeth. "But I'm skeptical a dog will pick up her scent with all this afternoon foot traffic."

"It's worth a try, ma'am." She nodded, and the agent got busy on his cell.

The ambulance arrived, and when Evan relinquished Frankie to the paramedics, she stepped away. She needed a few minutes to compose herself. This had hit entirely too close to home, too much like Aaron's accident and also painfully different. It had taken the team several minutes to locate Frankie. Several minutes of torturous waiting, wondering, and fearing the worst. Frankie could've been seriously injured or killed before they found her.

Evan looked at her shaking hands. The adrenaline was wearing off leaving her weak. Frankie had left Aaron and chased the suspect alone. Evan tried not to blame her, because she'd radioed in. And she was right, the street markings sucked, but she should've waited for backup. When Frankie was around, things got out of control, including Evan. She'd panicked just a little, and she couldn't blame that on Frankie.

"She'll be okay, boss," Aaron said.

He wheeled his chair quieter than some people walked, which was disconcerting when he just showed up at her side. "Yeah."

"She did the right thing chasing him, and she called in her location. It's not her fault I couldn't provide proper backup." He looked down at his legs. "Guess I shouldn't be in the field."

"Stop it, Aaron. You've proven on this trip just how valuable you and your chariot are in the field. Suspects don't give you a second glance, and with modern technology, you can do your job from anywhere. You'll always be a valuable part of this team. Don't forget it."

He gave her a weak grin. "If Judith hit Frankie, she's in full-on panic mode."

"And I won't hesitate to go full-on badass US Marshal on her either. Nobody is going to hurt one of my team and get away with it."

She took another deep breath and felt her anxiety receding. Maybe she wanted to be upset with Frankie to avoid facing the real problem—getting emotionally attached to a work associate. Less than eight hours ago, she'd been in bed with Frankie, ready to have sex with her. Evan forced her attention back to the case. She'd have plenty of time for self-recrimination later, but right now they needed to catch two more fugitives. "Let's check on her."

Frankie was shaking hands with the paramedics when Evan joined them. "Thanks, guys."

"What's going on?"

"I'm good to go." Frankie pointed to her head. "Steri-Strips for the cut, bright light to the eyes to check my vision, and paracetamol for the headache. Right, guys?" She looked to the ambulance personnel for help, but they just shook their heads.

"She signed a waiver. We can't force her to go to hospital."

"No," Evan said, "but I can force her off active duty."

One of the paramedics nodded. "She really should rest, and someone needs to wake her every few hours to make sure she's okay."

Frankie grabbed Evan's hand and held on. "Please, Evan, don't bench me. I need to be here. I have to help catch her."

Evan should send her away, make her rest, but instead she nodded toward the van. "You and Aaron in the back. He can coordinate from there and keep an eye on you at the same time. But you are not, under any circumstances, to leave that vehicle. Do you understand?"

"How can I help if I—"

"Do you understand, Agent Strong?" Evan had too much on her mind to worry about Frankie passing out or being injured further. And if Frankie wasn't close, Evan could concentrate on her job.

"Yes, ma'am."

Frankie started toward the van but stopped. "Wait. The boy. We can track him. He might lead us to Judith."

The Aussie agent overheard and headed toward them with the dog handler in tow. "You got a starting point?"

"The boy was wearing a red splash jacket, but he chucked it somewhere on Martin Place near George Street when he saw me chasing him. It might still be there."

The dog handler and a couple of other agents headed in that direction.

"Good job, Frankie," Evan said. "Now, in the van." She accompanied Frankie to the vehicle, opened it, and motioned her inside with Aaron.

"Boss, I've got a problem," Aaron said. "I can't pick up the other agents' signals from in here. The buildings are interfering, and I don't have my booster equipment. I need to work outside and be able to move around."

"Whatever works." Evan helped him out, and Aaron clicked a few keys on the computer before nodding to her. Frankie started to follow him, but Evan shook her head. "In the van." She placed her hand on Frankie's back as she climbed in again and then took a seat in the doorway next to her. "I'm glad you're—" Her cell rang, a blocked number. "Evan Spears."

"Hello, darling, how are you?"

Evan stifled a gasp. Jude's voice triggered a sick feeling in her stomach, and she cringed. "Hello, Judith." She motioned for Aaron to trace the call.

"That's a very touching scene I'm watching right now. You just can't keep your hands off the help, can you? Do you realize she's supposed to work for you, not service you?"

"When I get my hands on—"

"We tried that, remember? Not a good fit."

How had she ever thought Judith was charming or even attractive? In hindsight, she should've seen through the ruse sooner. Evan strained to hear anything in the background to help locate Judith but heard only traffic. "You're going to pay for everything, especially today." She checked her watch. Three minutes for a trace, but she didn't want to speak to Judith for a second.

"You have to catch me first." There was a pause on the line and a deep sigh before Judith asked, "Tell me, Evan, do you have Ty?"

Evan forced a long laugh to take up time and then made Jude wait longer for her answer. "What's the matter, Jude, lost your boyfriend already? Or did he get tired of having sex with a woman who was fantasizing about other women?"

"Shut the fuck up, Evan."

She checked her watch again. Two more minutes. "If he dumps you in Australia, you'll actually have to work, which is illegal because you're not a citizen. Hell, you're not even a legal visitor. Fake passports don't count, but you never cared about legalities anyway, did you? Without your sugar daddy, you won't be living the high life you hoped for."

"Fuck you."

"Tried that. Not a good fit." She parroted Judith's words hoping to make her angry and keep her talking.

"You're one cold bitch, Evan," Judith said.

"Maybe you could get a job in a strip club. Your body isn't half bad, but men like Ty prefer younger women with high breasts and firm asses."

"And bosses prefer supervising agents who don't sleep with members of their team. Maybe I'll give Michael English a call. We might both be looking for jobs in a strip club, though you're a little too muscular and butch for most men."

"I'll arrest you first. It's just a matter of time." Aaron gave her a thumbs-up indicating he had a lock on her signal. She muted her cell. "Have dispatch send units to that address. Good work, Aaron." If she could distract Judith until the officers arrived, they could take her by surprise. "Why did you involve that kid in your pickup, Jude?"

"He needed a hundred for a fix, so I made it easy for him."

"And now I have to charge him for assault on my agent."

Judith clicked her tongue several times. "Seriously, Evan, your little girlfriend wasn't hurt badly. She'll be ready for you by tonight. All she has to do is lie there like a good pillow queen. If I recall, you like to do all the work."

Judith's crude comments and worthless dribble were wearing on Evan's nerves. She glanced at Aaron and raised her palms for an update. He held up a couple of fingers. Two more minutes until the officers arrived. "Just turn yourself in, Jude, so we can all go home."

"You mean so you can go home and screw your new girlfriend while I rot in prison. I'll pass. Aren't you enjoying the chase? You always liked it when I made you work for it."

Evan gritted her teeth and bit back an unkind response. How had she ever found this woman attractive and sexy? "Being a fugitive isn't easy, especially with no money, contacts, or resources of your own."

"Awww, are you worried about me? How sweet."

Aaron raised his arm to get Evan's attention and gave her the okay signal. The officers were on scene.

"I'm offering you a chance to come in the easy way, Jude. If you make us hunt you down, it could get ugly."

"No, thanks. I'm good taking my chances."

"Don't say I didn't warn you. The next knock on your door will be the Australian police coming to arrest you."

"Good luck with that, darling. I have to go now."

The line was still open, and Evan heard background noises, but nothing else from Judith. The seconds crawled while she waited for an update. She started to hang up but heard the distinctive sound of a door being forced open and agents issuing commands.

"Hello?" an Aussie voice said. "She's gone, Agent Spears. Her mobile was being forwarded to another number."

"Damn it." Evan dropped her cell in her lap and shook her head at Frankie. Judith had manipulated her again and it set Evan's insides roiling. Being personally duped by her was humiliating enough, but a second professional embarrassment struck deeper. It gouged at her self-image as an effective US Marshal. Maybe she wasn't the right person for this case. *Damn you, Judith Earl, and the day I met you.*

She stepped out of the vehicle and struggled not to scream as a wave of anger ripped through her. Jude would not win. Evan blew out a long breath and circled her finger in the air for the team to assemble. "Any luck with the dog?"

The handler shook his head. "Too much traffic. Sorry."

"Okay, we're done for today." She thanked the Aussies for their help and rejoined Aaron and Frankie in the van. "We'll stop by the station to debrief with Hank and Todd and head back to the hotel."

The drive back was a solemn one. Evan steamed over Judith's escape, Frankie rubbed her temples and grimaced, and Aaron tapped nonstop on his laptop. When they pulled up to the police station, Hank and Todd were standing outside with Comer. "What's up, guys?"

"Judith got away," Hank stated, scratching his fresh buzz cut.

"Do you really think you need to tell me that?" Evan snapped. She didn't need salt rubbed in the wound. She needed options and answers. "Sorry, Hank. You didn't deserve that."

He shrugged. "No damage done. We've had a pretty shitty day too." He nodded toward Frankie. "Though not as bad as you from the looks of it."

Comer led them back inside to a conference room, and Evan dropped into a chair while the others gathered round. "Update."

"Ty has been talking all day but not saying anything useful. The failsafe was a good question, but it's a moot point now with Judith on the loose. Winston knows we're here."

And Evan thought the day couldn't get worse. "I guess Ty really doesn't want a deal."

"Oh, he wants it," Todd said. "He's getting pretty desperate, but the big boss didn't trust him with all the details."

"Did he know where Winston and Judith are staying like he said?" Frankie asked.

"Yeah," Comer said. "It was a unit in the warehouse district, one of his properties. I sent some guys to check it out. The place was deserted. They'd been there recently. Food containers, liquor bottles, condoms, and cigar wrappers were everywhere, but nothing helpful."

"Are some of your guys still there?" Frankie asked.

"Just wrapping up. Why?"

"If there's a trash bin or shredder, have them bag the contents and bring it in."

"Care to enlighten us?" Todd asked, a grin raising one corner of his reddish moustache.

"I lived on the streets for months. You'd be surprised what people leave in the trash. It might be nothing, but it might give us a clue. It's worth a look, and more than we have now."

Aaron chuckled. "I know what you'll be doing tonight."

"Anything else?" Evan looked around the room, and Aaron raised his hand.

"I checked Tyndall's cell. He had a few calls back and forth to the number we have for Winston, all very short, and several longer ones to the number we now know belongs to Judith Earl. All are burners. Nothing traceable. They're all worthless at this point. I'm sure they've both gotten new ones already."

Evan nodded and addressed Comer. "If there's nothing else, mind if we break for the night? We don't have any hot leads, my guys could use some sleep, and one is concussed."

"I'm with you," he said. "I'll have the guys drop the trash off at your hotel room along with a disposable blanket."

She nodded her thanks. "And now that we've lost the element of surprise, let's get Winston's and Earl's photos and info on every news channel, radio station, and social media site in Australia, if we can. I want to make it impossible for them to show their faces."

"Damn right we can," Comer said.

"What about Tyndall, Hank?" Evan asked.

"Let him cool his heels overnight and go at him hard again in the morning."

"Agreed. Thanks for your hard work today, everybody. I appreciate it." Evan rose, followed the guys to the van, and a few minutes later, they were back at the hotel.

Frankie had been unusually quiet and reserved since her attack, and Evan worried she might be suffering side effects. A head injury on top of yesterday's eight-hour surveillance couldn't be good. She should've insisted she go to the hospital. "Are you all right?"

"Headache is back, but not bad."

"Maybe I should take you to the hospital for a quick checkup to be sure."

Frankie closed the room door behind them. "I'm fine, really. Stop worrying." She reached for Evan, but she sidestepped. "I know you're disappointed, but is something else wrong?"

Nothing Evan could, or was willing to name, maybe a combination of today's events—almost submitting to Frankie, starting work before dawn, charging at Tyndall, missing Winston, Frankie's assault and Evan's emotional meltdown, and the final straw of talking to Judith and being outsmarted by her one more time. Everything had spiraled out of her grasp, and the more she tried to contain it, the slipperier it became. "I'm fine." What else could she say? Telling any of this to Frankie would be admitting professional and personal failure, again. Having her see it unfold in real time was bad enough.

"I'm not buying it, but I'm starving, and you should always pamper a concussed woman. How about room service pizza while we wait for the trash to be delivered?"

"Fine, and take something for your headache. I need to call the boss. I'll be back soon." Before Frankie could respond, she hurried out and found a computer room off the lobby to make the call. She ensured the scrambler was activated and dialed.

"Good morning, Evan, or should I say evening where you are?"

"Yes, good evening, sir. I'm sure you're anxious for a sitrep."

"Straight to the point as usual."

Evan was anxious to finish and make the call she so desperately needed to restore her equilibrium. After recounting the port, cigar shop, and strip club events, she ended with today's activities. "We've exhausted a couple of leads and developed a few more that we'll pick up tomorrow." Michael's silence was not a good sign. He was probably flipping his blond hair off his forehead, trying to figure out how to deliver the bad news. "What's up, sir?"

"The director wants the team back within the week."

Another obstacle stacked on the others from today. Evan had never given up on a search and wouldn't walk away from this one even without the director's blessing. This one was personal to her and the team. "Is that the end of the business week or do we have the weekend as well?"

"Does it matter?"

"It does when you're on the ground chasing a fugitive. I'll take every day I can get."

Michael cleared his throat. "I'll be lenient because of the circumstances of this case, but that still only gives you four more days max. Wrap it up, Evan, and come home. There are more fugitives worthy of your team's efforts. The Aussies can take over from here."

"Yes, sir." She hung up feeling even more defeated. Now there was a timeline on the manhunt. Just what she needed, more pressure.

Evan slid her cell in her back pocket and found the hotel bar, ordered a straight whisky, and took it back to the small computer room. She locked the door and turned off the light before taking a long pull of her drink. And then another. As the heat settled in her stomach and eased the tension across her shoulders, she placed her next call.

"Hell—oooo."

"Eli? I know it's ear—ly." Her voice cracked, but hearing her big brother was exactly what she needed.

"It's okay, sis. What's up?"

She let out a long breath and choked back a sob. "Just talk to me." They'd developed a routine in high school when she came out to her parents, and they refused to talk about it. Eli babbled until she was comfortable enough to say what was bothering her. And right now, she needed their familiarity and intimacy to salve the wounds of the day.

"Work is about to drive me absolutely crazy, which means business is good," he said. "And I've been by your place for the last three nights stripping old paneling. I'm almost ready to start installing all those outlets you want. By the time you get home, we can start the fun stuff like polishing and staining the concrete floors."

His kindness and consideration brought tears to her eyes. "Thanks, but why three nights? Where's your girlfriend?"

"On a trip. You know the glamorous life of a flight attendant."

She chuckled. "Yeah, exotic locales she never gets to see, living out of a suitcase, and sleep deprivation. Very glamorous."

"Now you sound like her." They laughed together, and then Eli waited. He knew she didn't do much small talk. "So, what's going on, Evan?"

"I needed to hear your voice, to reconnect with what's important. It's been a hell of a day." She told him everything that had gone wrong, except almost having sex with Frankie. When she finished, she took another gulp of her drink and finally relaxed.

"And the new girl, Frankie, and your sledgehammer?"

At the reference to Frankie, her body tingled. "We've had some challenges, but I've been trying to take your advice and not be so heavy-handed."

"I'm proud of you, sis. And what else? Your voice changed, got softer."

"Nothing."

"Evan Spears, you're talking to your big brother."

Evan sighed like she'd been holding her breath, a tell Eli wouldn't miss. "Fine. We might've kissed." Just saying it aloud made her ache again.

"Might've?"

"Okay. We kissed. And almost had sex, but got a call out."

Eli was quiet for a few seconds. "Did you—"

"Did I think it was a good idea? Of course not. Did I try to stop? Yes." In hindsight her efforts were weak at best, token at worst. She wanted Frankie.

"I was going to ask if you liked it, but the trying to stop part answered that."

"Seriously, Eli, you're not helping."

"If you're waiting for me to talk you out of following your heart, I'll go back to sleep and save you a huge phone charge. Evan, you like Frankie."

"The way I liked Jude?"

"Not like Jude. When you told me about Frankie's assault, I heard the concern in your voice, and it wasn't just because she's on your team. You can't hide that kind of feeling."

"Are you sure you're not gay?" His sensitivity always amazed her, and his advice often included encouraging her to get in touch with buried emotions. And he was usually right, even when she couldn't see the truth clearly. Frankie represented what was missing in Evan's life—spontaneity, excitement, and fearlessness—but underneath, she was also a minefield of volatility, loneliness, and fragility, and Evan had no idea what caused her distress.

Eli remained silent after dropping his bombshell, letting her grapple with her emotions and come to her own conclusions. The wound that colored her judgment reared its head. "But I'm just not sure. I get too attached, too involved, and I can't work like that. And Frankie is so unpredictable, which I like sometimes, but it's also… jeez…I don't know."

"Cut her some slack, Evan. She's been making decisions for herself for years and is apparently pretty good at it. Trust her instincts, her results, and watch how she treats the people around her. That will tell you all you need to know about the kind of person she is. And don't be so hard on yourself. It'll work out."

"Maybe, when we get back home I'll think about it." If they could just get through this operation, she'd have time to prepare, plan, and get to know Frankie. Then their relationship would be clean, purely personal, not muddied by work or responsibility.

"Then she'll be on another assignment. Don't wait too long, Evan."

"When did you get so smart, big brother?"

"Five years before you were born. Can I go back to sleep now?"

"Yeah, I'm sorry for waking you, but thank you."

"Any time, sis, any time. Love you."

He hung up, and Evan leaned forward on the table, resting her head on her arms. She needed to check on Frankie in a few minutes. The whisky eased her body, and Eli's words soothed her conflicted mind, at least for the moment. She closed her eyes, and an image of Frankie, nude in bed, warmed and lulled her to sleep.

Chapter Fourteen

Frankie rolled over on the bed to a crinkling sound and the foul taste of pepperoni pizza in her mouth. Strips of shredded paper stuck to her arms and face. She brushed them off and sat up, glancing at Evan's undisturbed side of the bed. She'd stayed awake until after two hoping Evan would return so they could talk and possibly resume their interrupted activities of the morning. Had she gone out on another lead or was she avoiding Frankie?

She sat up slowly to prevent a return of the blistering headache from last night and choked down a wave of nausea. Why did she feel so fragile? Then she remembered—Judith and her well-placed head shot. Frankie stood, stripped off yesterday's clothes, and stepped over the disposable blanket and trash that occupied nearly all the floor space. On her way to the shower, she stopped near the small table and stared at the haphazardly taped shreds of paper and what they revealed. She had to tell Evan.

After showering, she took the elevator downstairs. No sign of Evan in the restaurant, at the bar, or in the business center. She was about to give up when she noticed several computer rooms down a side hall. Three of them were occupied, but the fourth was dark, blinds closed, and the door was locked. She flagged down a member of staff and asked her to open it.

Evan was slumped over the table, head on her arms, asleep, her cell and an empty rocks glass nearby. Without her dark eyes constantly searching Frankie for some hidden meaning, Evan was gorgeous—her mouth relaxed, lips plump and kissable, her face the perfect picture of calm. Her steady, peaceful breathing was a call Frankie wanted to curl up beside her and answer. She checked the wall clock. The kissing and curling would have to wait.

She sniffed the glass. Whisky, not her usual beer. Had Evan been trying to escape her or the memory of all the dead ends yesterday? Maybe Michael English hadn't been happy with her report. Hopefully, Frankie's news would cheer her up.

"Evan." She whispered, unsure how easily or violently Evan might awake. "Evan."

"Huh?" Evan rolled her head to the side. "Go away."

"Evan, it's Frankie. You need to wake up. We have work to do. I have a lead."

Evan jerked upright in the chair. "Oh, damn." She grabbed her lower back and stretched side to side. "Who thought this was a good idea?" She looked around the room. "I slept *here*?"

Frankie nodded.

"I was supposed to check on you through the night. I'm so sorry, Frankie. I was just resting my eyes for a few minutes. Are you okay?"

Frankie grinned, very happy that Evan was concerned about her. "I'm perfectly healthy, clean, and totally ready to go."

"Okay, good." She waved her hand encouragingly. "The lead?"

"You should probably shower before we meet the guys."

Evan glanced at her rumpled clothes and patted down her unruly hair. "Good idea." On the elevator ride, she asked, "Are you going to tell me?"

"First, shower. I'll clean up our room, make some coffee, and then we'll talk." Evan started to object, but Frankie shook her head. "No. Just this once I give the orders."

While Evan showered, Frankie piled all the leftover shredded paper on top of the trash and rolled it up in the silver disposable blanket. She placed the salvaged pieces neatly across Evan's bed and paced. When Evan came out of the bathroom finger-combing her wet hair, her cheeks pink, and smelling like sandalwood, Frankie stopped and stared. She wanted her so much her mouth dried and she felt lightheaded.

"Don't look at me like that. We've got to be somewhere in five minutes."

"Always on the clock, Spears." She moved closer to Evan for the question that couldn't wait another second. "Were you avoiding me last night?"

"No," Evan said.

Frankie checked her expression for any tells. She was being honest. Frankie released a long sigh of relief. Everything else could wait until they had more time alone.

"I made a couple of phone calls and fell asleep. I'm sorry if you worried."

"I was just afraid I'd disappointed you. And I don't want to do that again." She was surprised just how much she meant it. Planned or not, ready or not, Evan touched Frankie deeply and sparked those dangerous emotions her parents had warned her about. She stood on her tiptoes and lightly kissed Evan and felt her respond briefly before stepping back.

"You didn't disappoint me, but we don't have time for this right now. What's the lead?"

Did no time right now mean there would be time for them at some point? Frankie's body tingled from the kiss and Evan's reassurance that she hadn't totally screwed up again.

"Frankie?"

"Oh, yes." She pointed to the bed where she'd placed her work. "I dumped Winston's shredder and reassembled the contents."

Evan gave her an incredulous stare. "I admire your out of the box thinking." She studied the pages. "You put this shredded paper back together like a jigsaw puzzle?"

Frankie nodded. "The interesting bits, that's why it looks like the dog ate part of it."

"And what did you come up with?"

"Birth certificates, doctored birth certificates. I think Winston used these documents to obtain false passports. I spent most of the night taping the pieces together and then a few hours looking up the names. All of these people are dead."

Evan held up her hand. "I'm sure you have more, but let's share it with the team." Frankie gathered the pages and started for the door, but Evan touched her arm and stopped her. "You've done really good work on this. You should probably have been resting, but thank you. I hope it helps, because we're running out of leads and time."

"What's happened, Evan?"

"I'll tell everyone at breakfast." Evan hugged her briefly before opening the door.

When they reached the restaurant, the guys were gathered at the same round table in the corner that was now covered with plates piled full of breakfast food. "Well, look what the cat dragged up," Todd said.

"Morning," Frankie replied and snatched a piece of bacon from his fingers on the way to the steaming buffet trays.

"You feeling okay?" Aaron asked, peering over the top of his round glasses.

Frankie nodded. She loved his sensitivity. He brought balance to Evan's rigidity, Hank's diplomacy, and Todd's flippancy. She filled her plate and returned to the space Aaron had created for her at the table.

"Boss," Hank said. "Any news from the real world?"

"I talked to Michael last night. We have at most four more days to find Winston and Earl before we're called back to the States." All the guys spoke at once, voicing their objections until Evan motioned for quiet. "I know you're upset. I feel the same way. We've always caught our man, but the director wants us home working on other cases. He feels the Aussies can track Winston as easily, perhaps better, than we can."

"They're all right," Aaron said, "but they're not the A-Team." The guys agreed and exchanged high fives.

"So, I'm open for suggestions about how to find our fugitives fast." Evan nodded toward Frankie. "Our dumpster diving liaison might've come up with something."

Frankie swallowed a mouthful of eggs, told them what she'd discovered, and passed the pages around so they could take a look. "Do any of these names ring a bell?"

Hank shook his head. "Tyndall hasn't mentioned any of them. I'm beginning to think he's been jerking us around." He glanced at Evan. "Sorry, but he babbled on about nothing all day yesterday while time passed and Winston got the message that he wasn't coming back."

Todd handed the pages to Evan, and she looked them over again. "I've got an idea. It might be a long shot. There are six different names here. If memory serves, there are only six airlines that fly internationally out of Sydney." She glanced across the table at Aaron.

"I'm with you, boss. I'll run a reservation check for each airline under those names. Maybe Jemma can get one of her customs friends to help with access. I'd hate to hack six foreign airline companies on the same day. Might raise red flags."

"Jemma, huh?" Todd twirled his moustache and grinned.

Everybody stopped eating and stared at Aaron. Frankie felt sorry for him as his face turned pink and then red. He'd obviously made a connection with the attractive brunette, and Frankie was happy for him. "That's a great idea, Aaron, and I think we should set a trap for Tyndall to see if he's messing with us."

Aaron gave her an appreciative nod and pulled out his laptop.

"What do you have in mind?" Evan asked.

Frankie laid the six pages on the table in front of Hank and Todd. "When you guys question him this morning, ask about other names Winston might be using. If he isn't forthcoming, place the birth certificates in front of him one at a time as you say each name. Give him a chance to look closely before laying down the next one."

"O—kay," Todd said. "What's the punch line?"

Everybody was looking at her, and Frankie grinned. "I'm going to watch him."

"And how will that help?" Hank asked.

"I can tell which one strikes a nerve. It's sort of like a shell game. He knows the truth, and his body will betray him. Trust me. I already have my guess, but I'd like confirmation."

"What are you, some kind of human lie detector?" Todd joked and punched her arm.

"You might say that. We're grasping at straws, so I'm willing to take my turn."

Evan finished her coffee and toast and pushed the plate aside. "Unless we get a hit on the passports or birth certificates, we've got nothing, and that's not okay with me." She hesitated, "And none of this helps us catch Judith Earl. I don't have to tell you how badly I want her caught. I'll check with Comer when we get to the station and see if he's had any actionable intel from the media blasts. Let's get going."

Frankie's step was a little lighter as she followed the guys toward the van. None of them pooh-poohed her idea, and Evan said she'd done a good job. Maybe being part of a team wasn't so bad after all, but having a mad crush on the boss was challenging. Would Evan ever be interested in someone with a past as colorful as hers, but then she didn't know about it. Frankie had chickened out before telling her.

When they arrived at the Kings Cross Station, everybody bailed out. Comer had called for Tyndall to be brought from the detention facility, but he hadn't arrived yet. The interview room was set up, and Hank and Todd were waiting. Aaron and the Aussie customs tech that Jemma sent over went into a closed-door session to check the airlines. Evan and Comer huddled in a corner of the large squad area, and Frankie took her place in the observation room again. She could see Evan's irritation rising with each wasted second and didn't want to add to her stress.

After two hours, Comer called to check on Tyndall. The excuse was they were finishing breakfast and the staff was too busy to bring him over. After noon with no Tyndall, Comer called again, his words a little more colorful. This time he was assured Tyndall was on his way. Half an hour later, he arrived.

Tyndall shuffled in wearing baggy drawstring pants hanging off his hips and a blue T-shirt several sizes too small. He had a fresh black eye and goose egg on his cheek and didn't waste any time mouthing off about it. "They served me scrambled eggs, bacon, and an ass-whipping for breakfast. I don't know what kind of joint you're running here, but I'm filing a complaint and then I'll sue for damages and mental anguish."

"Oh, boo-hoo," Todd said. "Talk to the New South Wales Police Force. You're not in America anymore, and I'm pretty sure these folks don't care how much you complain or sue. And just FYI, you ended up here because you ran. We can help you get out, if that interests you at all. You didn't seem to care yesterday. What about now, stud?"

Tyndall's cocky grin vanished. "What do you mean? I was cooperating."

"Like hell you were," Hank said. "You were stalling to give your pal Winston a chance to escape. Well, I don't see him rushing to help you. It's always the poor schmuck who pays for the rich guy's mistakes. Maybe you should start looking out for yourself."

Tyndall seemed to be considering his options or either just stalling for more time. Frankie couldn't figure out why, but he definitely fell in the more brawn than brains category. The afternoon was quickly disappearing, and they were no closer to finding Winston and Judith.

"We're tired of playing games, Ty. You have exactly two minutes to tell us something we don't know, or we're out of here and you're back in the cage with your boxing kangaroo friends. We know Winston had fake passports in several other names. What are they?"

Tyndall looked like he'd been slapped and wiped his face on the sleeve of his T-shirt. "What? Like aliases?"

Frankie pumped her fist in the air. They had him on the ropes. He knew, but would he share the information with them?

"I don't know. He didn't tell me everything, but you're right. There were aliases. I just don't know what they were. Honest."

Frankie keyed the mike that fed Hank's earpiece. "He's full of crap, and we're wasting time. Show him what we've got."

"I'm going to help you out. Look and listen closely and then answer truthfully, Ty."

"I swear, I don't know."

Hank shook his head. "I hope you're a better drug dealer than you are a liar."

One by one, Todd placed the pieced together birth certificates on the table in front of Tyndall, calling each name aloud as he did so. When they got to the fourth name, Tyndall's bottom lip twitched and he glanced up and to the left. Bingo. It was the same name Frankie had chosen earlier. She loved it when a hunch paid off. "Okay, Hank. I've got what I need."

"Last chance, Ty."

"Sorry, guys, these names don't ring any bells."

"I think you're going to like it in prison, Ty," Todd said. "Maybe they can put you and Grif in the same cell so you can get reacquainted." Hank and Todd rose without another word, left the room, and joined her next door.

A few seconds later, Evan, Comer, and Aaron came in. "Anything?" Evan asked.

"Winston is using a passport in the name of Alfred Lerner," Frankie said proudly.

"How the hell do you know that?" Todd scratched his head and eyeballed her.

Frankie shrugged. "Lucky?"

Aaron placed his laptop on the table so everyone could see. "I don't think it's luck at all. Winston has booked a flight with an airline under every name on our list, except that one."

"What?" Frankie's heart thumped double time. "I was so sure—"

"Because he used that name to book a private jet to Jakarta tomorrow evening."

"Yes!" Frankie fist-bumped Aaron. "My man. Well done."

Evan watched the exchange before posing the question Frankie had been expecting. "So, care to enlighten us how you knew he'd use that name?"

"Alfred Lerner was rich, an avid Montecristo No. 2 cigar aficionado, and he's dead." Evan's gaze settled on Frankie, and she felt the awe and admiration spread through her. "Simple if you know your opponent. One of the first things you told me."

Evan finally broke eye contact and tapped on her phone for several seconds. "And he chose Jakarta because they don't have an extradition agreement with the United States."

"And he'll be a multi-billionaire with the rupiah exchange rate," Aaron added. "Any tips on Judith Earl?"

Comer waved a handful of note cards in the air. "Several look promising because of some similar information. The callers we've verified as legit, not loony or after the reward money, say she was in a lesbian bar called Ching-a-lings last night having a great time."

"What an effing cliché," Evan said. "But Judith was never very original."

"She spent handfuls of cash and left with the bartender when the club closed. Probably went to her house, since Earl doesn't have one and her face is plastered all over social media."

"Well, guess the boss and I are going dancing, drinking, and fugitive hunting in an Aussie club on the government's dime."

When nobody responded with a smart-ass comment, Frankie looked up. The guys were staring at her, and Evan was doing a fish mouth imitation. "So, is that a no to the club, boss? I can definitely go by myself and just hang in the shadows if you're uncomfortable providing close cover." Evan blushed. "I mean I don't really need backup. Right?" She glanced around the room at her teammates. "Will somebody please pull me out of this enormous hole before I dig any deeper?"

Todd sat back and crossed his arms over his chest. "No way. I'm really enjoying this. I haven't seen Evan so flustered since that first day when you used her desk as a serving tray for biscuits and powdered donuts."

"Thanks, pal," Frankie said.

Todd grinned. "Just keeping it real."

"I think it's a good idea," Aaron said, and Evan glared at him. "What?"

Hank nodded in agreement but was too diplomatic to say anything.

"The other option is we can just stake out the club," Frankie said. She enjoyed watching Evan squirm because for once she wasn't the one on the hot seat. "But Judith might not be there at all. The only way to be sure is to go inside." Frankie purposely rolled her chair closer to Evan. "You could wait by the back door, and I'll just flush her into your arms."

Evan stood, her face now bright red. "If you've all had enough fun at my expense, we've got things to do." She tried to sound annoyed, but the hint of a grin at the corners of her mouth said she wasn't really too upset. "Fine, we'll stake out the club. Never let it be said that Evan Spears isn't a team player." Without waiting for anyone to make another comment, she turned to Aaron. "Find out where Winston's charter flight is leaving from."

"What about us, boss?" Hank asked. "We've wasted most of the day on Tyndall. He isn't going to give us anything."

"Send him back to lockup, and then research the bartender. Find out everything. If she has a record, where she lives, if she's working tonight, and you and Todd stake out her place. Judith might be lying low there since she's running out of friends."

Frankie cleared her throat, unsure if she wanted to draw attention to herself. "And me?"

"Check out the club. Find out if it's a specialty place, if we need a membership, opening time, that sort of thing."

"We're really going?"

"Of course, we're going. It's a viable lead."

Frankie waited until Evan turned around and then shrugged at the other guys and mouthed *okay*. They all laughed.

"What's so funny?" Evan asked. "Get moving. Daylight's burning, and we're on a deadline." When Hank and Todd rose from the table, Evan added, "If Judith is still at the bartender's home, take her down if you can. I'd prefer that, because she'll recognize me and Frankie. If that doesn't work, let them return to the club, provide cover for us, and we'll make the arrest there. We have coms but might not be able to hear you inside. Do the legwork and meet back at the hotel at twenty hundred hours for a briefing."

"And if the bartender isn't working tonight?" Todd asked.

"The gods will be smiling on me," Evan mumbled under her breath just loud enough for Frankie to hear. "Then we need to find out if Judith is still at her place. Get creative. One way or the other, I want Judith Earl in custody before morning. Am I clear?"

Frankie had never been more certain how much Evan disliked Judith. She'd hurt Evan, humiliated her, and dumped her in a cruel, public way. After the assault yesterday, Frankie felt some of Evan's loathing for Judith was because of her. And it pleased her quite a lot.

CHAPTER FIFTEEN

Evan hated wasting valuable hunting hours on stakeouts or research. The only blessing at the moment was that Frankie was in another room checking on the club, while she was securing transportation for the team and three prisoners as soon as the arrests were made. After the club discussion, which she was pretty sure clued the team in to the attraction between her and Frankie, she needed some space to think and plan the evening's activities, but her thoughts kept returning to Frankie.

She and Frankie hadn't been alone since this morning, and the day seemed to lack some of its vibrancy as a result. Evan missed the connection to Frankie's energy and the occasional glances they shared when no one else was looking. Though she remained cautious, her attraction to and desire for Frankie was growing every day. She was proving to be a valuable asset to the team, and she'd mostly adhered to the rules. When she didn't, Evan felt more alive, challenged, and engaged than she had in years.

"Ah-hum, boss." Hank cleared his throat from the doorway of the conference room.

"Yeah?" She turned from the computer, and her team and several of Comer's men stood outside. She glanced at the wall clock, surprised that it was almost eight at night. "Yes, let's get started." Frankie gave her a questioning look as she settled across from her, and Evan nodded that she was okay. "What do we have?"

"The bartender." Hank looked down at a computer printout. "Katie Kwon, Australian born, twenty-nine, no criminal history. She works the club at night and goes to university during the day studying law. Her residence is listed in Manly."

Comer nodded. "We checked it out. She lives near Manly Hospital in a very small unit over a chip shop owned by her parents. No history on them either. They all seem to be model citizens, working, paying taxes, and chasing the dream."

"Looks like she just got mixed up with the wrong woman," Todd added, and then shook his head as if realizing what he'd said. "Sorry, boss."

Another reason Evan would never forgive herself for Judith. No one who knew what had happened between them would ever look at her the same again. In their eyes she was to be pitied. "Let's stay focused. Is Ms. Kwon scheduled to work tonight?"

"She's supposed to be there at nine and work until closing at one," Hank said. "When we break, Todd and I will head to her place and join Comer's men on stakeout. We'll make the arrest when they leave, if we can."

"Sounds good." Evan looked at Aaron. "Winston?"

"He booked a private jet from Bankstown Airport tomorrow night at ten."

Evan chilled at the thought of another arrest at an airport. "Any indication of him using the Lerner alias elsewhere? Credit cards, hotel bookings, restaurants, cell phones, anything?"

Aaron shook his head. He knew exactly what she was thinking. "Sorry."

"And where is Bankstown Airport in relation to us?" Evan asked.

"About thirty minutes by car," Comer answered. "It's a general aviation hub, pretty busy for its size. Several fixed-wing and helicopter flying schools are located there along with charter operators, aircraft maintenance businesses, and private aircraft. It could be a nightmare of activity during the day, but at ten at night, we shouldn't have crowd issues. There's only a small terminal, if you can call it that. Should be easy to spot Winston when he shows up."

She preferred a more easily containable location but she couldn't control everything, like the woman sitting across from her. "At least it's not Sydney Airport, right? We'll make it work."

"I'll put a man at the airport posing as security. When Winston shows up, we'll move in."

"Agreed," Evan said. "You all have your assignments for tonight. Frankie and I already have a taxi waiting to take us to the club. The next twenty-four hours are going to be busy. Stay safe. Keep in touch."

When the cab stopped on a nondescript stretch of street, Evan thought they might've been taken to the wrong place. The neighborhood wasn't one she would've walked alone at night, and there was no sign of a bar or business of any kind nearby. "Are you sure this is right?"

The driver pointed to a leather-clad woman standing in front of an open door. "She'll direct you to the club. That's forty dollars."

Evan slid the company credit card through the reader and signed before following Frankie outside. *Heaven help me through this night.* Frankie was wearing a red skirt that barely covered her ass, a snug white tank top that highlighted the fact she wasn't wearing a bra, and knee boots. Just looking at her sent Evan's mind in every direction except work. Why did she look so damn good in everything, and why did Evan always notice? "You're killing me, Strong," Evan mumbled.

Frankie obviously heard what she said and grinned over her shoulder. "Just getting into character." She added an extra sway to her walk, and Evan moaned.

"Evening, ladies," the greeter said. "Twenty dollars cover charge. Up the stairs."

Evan dished out the cash and took Frankie's hand. "Are you ready for this?"

"So ready." Frankie looked down at their joined hands. "That's nice. Trying to make sure I don't go missing or get assaulted again... or do you just like me maybe a little?"

"Possibly all of the above," Evan replied honestly. "Hard to say just now with you in that outfit. It's distracting, as if you needed help."

"Thanks, I think." She planted a quick kiss on Evan's cheek.

Evan pulled her closer as they navigated the narrow staircase lined on both sides with a combination of faded and vibrantly colored show posters. Evan's pulse beat faster. She hadn't been inside a lesbian club since she was a teenager with her first girlfriend. The stair treads were smooth and lighter in the center from years of wear, and she imagined the scores of women who'd come here looking for the same thing she had as a younger woman. She hoped they'd had better luck.

The club itself was only three times the width of the stairway with a few tables to one side. The exposed brick walls gave it an industrial vibe, while the music was old-school soul. She'd danced to these tunes, felt the thrill of first love, and the excitement of an evening filled with the promise of a sure thing. She glanced at Frankie and reminded herself that she wasn't an impressionable teenager anymore, and Frankie was a long way from a sure thing.

"Now this is my kind of place," Frankie said. "Cozy with good dance music."

Just before they stepped into the noise of the crowd, Hank's voice sounded in Evan's ear. "The bartender just left her place, but Judith isn't with her. Advise."

Frankie heard and motioned Evan closer. "We can talk to her when she gets here."

Evan took a few seconds to consider the suggestion before relaying the instructions. "Have you been able to verify that Judith is there?"

"Affirmative. They went out to dinner earlier, but the team wasn't able to get close enough to make the arrest."

"Stay on the house. If she leaves, take her. I'll advise further soon."

Frankie pulled Evan with her toward the bar. "We need to blend. Try to smile. What would you like to drink?"

"Nothing. I'm good."

"Consider it part of your cover." Frankie slid her arm around Evan's waist and waved at the bartender with her other hand. "One vodka tonic and one house whisky on the rocks."

"How did you know I like whisky?"

"I'm observant, especially where you're concerned."

"Why does that worry me?" Evan tried to relax and blend, but Frankie's arm around her and the heat from her body was distracting. She felt like a nerd at the homecoming dance, except she had a date but didn't know what to do with her. Frankie, on the other hand, seemed as comfortable here as she did everywhere else. How had she become so adept at mingling with her surroundings and being at ease no matter the situation?

Frankie handed her the drink and guided her through the standing-room-only crowd to a high-top table. "Stop clocking the room every second like a cop and look at me adoringly."

Evan almost choked on her drink. "Adoringly, huh?"

"What shall we do to pass the time?" Frankie stroked her hand down the front of her body seductively and paused at the hem of her very short skirt.

Evan's mouth dried. She hadn't planned for this woman, for these feelings, in fact she'd fought them, but the pull between them was strong and urgent making her body burn and pulse. "You...I..." Words failed as Frankie pressed against Evan and tilted her head up. Frankie didn't have to ask for anything. Evan couldn't stop.

She slowly set her drink on the table, encircled Frankie with both arms, and pulled their bodies closer. She gazed into Frankie's blue eyes. "What have you done to me?" Without waiting for a response, Evan licked her lips and claimed Frankie's. Heat and sensation exploded through her making her weak and wet.

Frankie moaned. She pulled Evan's arm from around her waist and guided her hand between her legs and up to her crotch.

"Oh, my." Evan groaned when she felt Frankie's wetness. "I can't believe you."

"I want you, Evan. I have since the first moment I saw you on the street near your place in that long black Dracula coat with your dark, piercing eyes. You were so mysterious and sexy as hell."

Evan wanted her too, but not here, not now. "There's nothing I'd like more. Believe me. But not like this."

"Evan, it's okay. I want to be with you. I have so much to tell you. You make me feel...I don't know, different. I really like you...a lot. I think I'm in—"

"Don't." She kissed Frankie again, wanting to lose herself in the soothing stroke of her hands and the depth of her kisses but also wanting to stop the words she was so afraid to hear. Dare she wish for more? "You're so beautiful."

"Touch me, Evan. Please?"

Emotions and desire warred with her better judgment. Frankie meant more to her than a quickie surrounded by strangers in a bar during a takedown. She kissed Frankie's forehead, withdrew slowly, and picked up her drink. "You deserve better than this."

Frankie flinched and stepped back. Her eyes dulled and the corners of her mouth tightened. "Did I say something wrong?"

It was so hard for Evan to stifle her feelings that she couldn't speak, so she shook her head, unable to make eye contact.

"I'm sorry for putting you in this position, Evan. It won't happen again."

The words sounded final. Was that what she wanted—to push Frankie away so she wouldn't have to face reality? Now wasn't the time to think about it. Evan downed her drink and glanced toward the stairway as an attractive Asian woman entered and walked to the bar. "This could be our bartender."

Frankie smoothed her skirt, gave Evan a last hurt look, and said, "I'll find out." She followed the woman through the crowd, and Evan ached with each step she took.

A few minutes later, Frankie waved her toward the back of the club, and Evan joined her and the woman at the ladies' room. "This is Katie Kwon."

Evan held the door open, waited until the room cleared, and then threw the lock that looked like it wouldn't hold up against a strong wind. The space was barely large enough for two people, so she nudged Katie against the door. "We're US Marshals looking for a fugitive." Her voice was harsh and no-nonsense. They were getting close to finding Judith, and she didn't have time to play nice.

Katie's alabaster skin turned pasty white. "I haven't done anything wrong. I've never been in trouble." Her bottom lip quivered. "I've never even been to America."

Frankie glared at Evan and shook her head like she'd done something wrong. "What?"

Frankie slipped in beside Katie and placed her hand on her shoulder. "Marshal Spears isn't accusing you of anything."

Katie visibly relaxed, and it bothered Evan that Frankie seemed as comfortable touching Katie as she had her minutes ago. *Focus.*

"We just need to ask you a few questions," Frankie continued. "You met an American woman here last night and took her home with you."

"How do you know that?" Katie's eyes were wide with fear.

"It would be easier if you assumed we know everything and just cooperate. We don't want to arrest you for harboring a fugitive and ruin your future as a solicitor. We only want Judith." Frankie clasped Katie's hand and made eye contact. Evan looked away.

"Okay."

Evan couldn't stay silent any longer. "Where is she right now?"

"At my flat."

"Is she alone?"

"Yes."

"What are your plans for later?" Evan asked. She wanted Judith's arrest over so she could move on to something more important—like arresting Winston…and eventually Frankie. The things she'd said to her felt wrong. She had a feeling if she didn't clarify what she wanted soon it would be too late.

"She's spending the night again. We planned a trip on the Parramatta Ferry tomorrow since I'm off."

"Call her and tell her you're coming home early because the club is dead," Frankie said.

"But I'll lose money."

Evan scoffed. "You'll lose a lot more if you're arrested for aiding a fugitive. Call her and be very careful not to tip her off. If I hear anything unusual in your tone, you're going to jail."

Katie fished her phone out of her back pocket and made the call. "She's excited."

"I'm sure," Evan said sarcastically. She and Frankie accompanied Katie outside, and once on the sidewalk, Evan keyed her mike. "Hank, we've got the bartender. We'll meet you at her place. Comer, can you pick us up?"

"Be there in ten."

As they waited on the sidewalk for their ride, Frankie cupped Katie's elbow and asked quietly, "You understand that you're not under arrest, right? And that you're assisting us voluntarily?"

Katie nodded and offered her a smile. "Thank you for being so kind."

Evan pointed at Katie. "Stay put." And then pulled Frankie to the side. "What are you doing? She's not your friend."

The corners of Frankie's mouth quirked into a grin and her eyes flashed warmth. "Are you jealous? I'm being civil. More flies with honey, remember that saying? I'm not sure who you're upset with right now, me, or yourself, but maybe we can talk about it later."

She'd been afraid of what Frankie would say...and how *she* would react to an expression of love, but apparently Frankie had seen through her fear. God, she was all over the place with her, but maybe there was still hope, in spite of her. "It's...I'm..."

"You're what, Evan? Say it. Say *something*." Frankie stared at her, pleading for an encouraging word. She touched Evan's arm. "It's okay. Let's just get through this case so I can get back to my nomadic lifestyle, and you can return to your warehouse. Apparently, that's what you want."

Evan flinched at the implied finality of Frankie's voice. When they met, all Evan wanted was to do her job and go back home, but now she wanted something else entirely.

CHAPTER SIXTEEN

E van stared out the front window of the van while Frankie squirmed on the seat next to her pulling on a pair of skinny jeans, and shucking off her short skirt. Evan couldn't stop thinking about the feel of her hand sliding up Frankie's thigh earlier, the slick heat of her center, and the urgent longing it sparked in her. She'd been emotionally frayed the past few hours—aroused, angry, aroused again, and now verging on overload. "How much longer?" She needed to be out of this vehicle, away from Frankie, and doing something productive.

"First leg of the journey." Comer stopped in front of the blue, yellow, and gray Kings Cross Police Station. "We're on foot and public transit from here. Vehicle accident on the A8 has traffic backed up for hours. My guys will pick us up at Manly Wharf."

"We're walking?" Evan couldn't keep the sting out of her voice, because every second wasted put Judith farther from her grasp.

"Six minutes to Kings Cross Station, fifteen-minute train ride to Circular Quay, and then thirty-minutes by ferry to Manly," Comer said. "And believe me, this is the fastest way tonight."

Evan followed the other three down the street to the train station, watching Frankie chatting amicably with Katie as if they were on a date. What was so different about Frankie? Why was everything about her either annoying or arousing? She was frustrating, argumentative, exciting, entertaining, sexy—that was it exactly. She stirred emotions and made Evan feel again. Dangerous territory with her history of failed relationships. And she liked control. Evan stepped onto the train and grabbed a handrail for support, but nothing could steady her riotous emotions and the sense that something inside her was shifting.

After a quick train ride, Comer herded them onto the Manly ferry at Circular Quay as it prepared to leave. If not for the distinctive Sydney Harbour Bridge on the left, Opera House on the right, and the occasional mate or g'day from Comer's men, she could've easily forgotten they were in Australia. She glanced across the harbor at a huge clown face between two towers. Luna Park, the sign read, probably a fun place with friends on holiday. The ferry backed out toward the bridge and past the Opera House before heading into deeper water.

The evening air was cool, and after asking Comer to keep an eye on Katie, Evan stepped onto the bow into the bracing wind. She kept her gaze forward toward their destination because one glance in Frankie's direction would send her mind on another tangent. She couldn't afford to lose focus now. The chugging of the engine and lapping waves calmed her as she prepared for battle. She'd waited too long to bring these people to justice, and the end was in sight.

Thirty minutes later, the ferry docked at Manly, and one of Comer's men picked them up outside. "Anything going on?" he asked.

"Quiet. We've got men in position. The unit is on a corner, upstairs over a chip shop with an estate agent's office in front. Stairs lead up to the residence in the rear. Unless she jumps out a window, we'll have her."

"Is there another way out?" Evan asked Katie, who shook her head. "Good, let's do this. I don't want any mistakes. Frankie, wait in the car with Katie. I'll guard the door, and Comer's men will make the arrest to keep it nice and legal."

When Frankie didn't object to being sidelined, Evan knew she was preoccupied. Maybe she just wanted to make it through this assignment, get back home, and forget she'd ever met Evan.

She followed the guys to the rear of the building and upstairs to the landing. Two agents waited on either side of the door while Comer slowly eased the key Katie had provided into the lock. Evan heard the mechanism disengage and worried that Jude had as well. She motioned for him to slow down. One final click, and he nodded to his men and flung the door open.

The agents fanned out in the room, and Judith jumped from the sofa. A bottle of beer flew from her hand, spewed through the air, and crashed to the floor. She ran toward the door, realized she was surrounded, and then glanced at the window. The stunned look on her face was the most satisfying sight Evan had seen recently.

"New South Wales Police. Show your hands. Interpol." Agents' shouts mingled with Judith's demands to know what was going on.

Evan waited outside on the landing holding the storm door open. She heard a loud crash, and Judith was taken to the floor by two agents. In a matter of seconds, she was cuffed, on her feet, and heading toward the door. Evan waited until Judith was crossing the threshold, reconsidered only momentarily, and let go of the storm door. When she saw the blood streaming from Judith's nose, Evan felt a surge of freedom and vindication.

Judith howled in pain, and the agents behind her looked in the opposite direction. "Watch where you're going, lady," Comer said. "Those doors are unforgiving."

Judith dabbed her bloody nose with her sleeve. "Damn you, Evan. You did that on purpose. You broke my fucking nose."

"I have no idea what you're talking about," Evan replied as she led the team down. "Careful on these stairs. Wouldn't want you to fall and hurt yourself."

Frankie was helping Katie out of the van as Comer shoved Judith in. "You dimed me out, Katie," Judith said. "Why?"

Katie slapped her face. "Seriously? You're a fugitive. You put my whole life in jeopardy. One night with you would never be worth that. Good riddance."

"Anybody else want to beat up a handcuffed woman?" Judith grumbled. She glanced at Frankie. "What about you? I probably owe you a shot."

Frankie shook her head and grinned. "I'm good."

Hank, Todd, and Aaron joined the group gathered around the van. "What happened to her face?" Todd asked.

"She ran into a storm door," Comer said. "Evan, you want us to handle the interview?"

Evan looked at the exhausted expressions on her team members' faces and decided for everyone. "If you don't mind, that would be great. She doesn't have anything significant, and my guys could use a rest before we go after Winston tomorrow night. Just make sure she doesn't make any phone calls before we have him in custody."

"No worries," Comer said.

"And one more thing," Evan said. "She doesn't get a deal."

"Roger that. We'll drop you off at your hotel on the way back to the station. If all goes well tomorrow night, you could be on your way home the following day."

"Fingers crossed," Evan mumbled. Part of her wanted that desperately; another part wanted the case to continue so she'd have an excuse to spend more time with Frankie, but she had a feeling she'd torpedoed those chances tonight.

❖

Frankie brushed past Evan when she opened the hotel room door. "If you don't mind, I'd like to shower first." The last couple of days had been exhausting and she just needed to sleep.

"Sure."

Frankie grabbed her backpack and disappeared into the bathroom. She'd tried to tell Evan how she felt about her at the club, but Evan made it clear she didn't want to hear it and pushed her away. What was left to say? They hadn't done anything that couldn't be forgotten eventually. A few kisses, a bit of touching. No promises or lifetime commitments. She should be happy they hadn't gotten more involved, so why wasn't she?

She turned on the shower and stood under the hot spray, the water beating the knots and tension out of her shoulders and back. She'd survived by avoiding emotional involvements and moving on to the next job, but it felt wrong to pretend Evan didn't matter.

She rubbed the water from her body with the rough towel as if doing so would wipe away her pain. Evan wasn't really interested, beyond possibly a fling after the case was over, so nothing she could do would change the situation. Frankie wrapped the towel around her and stepped into the room. "All yours."

"Frankie—"

"Don't worry, I'm not going to drop my towel again. You're safe."

Evan's gaze paused at the exposed skin above Frankie's breasts before making eye contact. "I wanted to apologize for earlier. I was a little tense about…being in a club, with you, about everything really. I got carried away with the atmosphere and memories, but we were getting too close to Judith to be preoccupied."

"No harm done." Frankie moved to the bed and pulled her covers back, slid in, and tugged the towel off, dropping it on the floor. "Good night, Evan." She waited for Evan to answer, but the next thing she heard was water running in the shower.

She'd come close to telling Evan she loved her tonight. She was grateful she hadn't. Evan's rejection hurt badly enough without exposing the depth of her feelings—her need for the passion Evan hid just below the surface, her strength, and yes, even her annoying control.

Lessons of the past flashed through Frankie's mind, but she swept them aside. She wanted a different life, so she'd tried a different path, but Evan's meaning was clear. Beneath her mixed messages and occasional slipups, she wanted their relationship to remain professional. Judith had burned her, and Frankie was paying. She pulled the cover under her neck, rolled onto her side away from Evan's side, and prayed for sleep.

She must've dozed off and started dreaming because she imagined Evan snuggling behind her and draping her arm over Frankie's body. "Mmmm." She pulled Evan's hand up between her breasts. The contact felt so real. "I love you."

"What did you say?" Evan's voice was too clear to be a dream.

She bolted upright, bringing the covers with her. Evan was staring at her, the stunned look in her eyes reflected in the muted light from the street. She'd said it out loud. "If it'll make you feel better, I'll tell you I was dreaming."

"But you weren't?"

She caressed the side of Evan's face and tried to look into her soul through those dark eyes. Her subconscious had outed her, might as well own it. "No, I wasn't. I love you, Evan. I wish I could tell you when and how that happened, but I can't. God knows you didn't make it easy. You've been trying to get rid of me from day one. First you interrogate me, then chew me out for interviewing Griffin and again for leaving my post to talk to the ship crewman, and *then* you were furious when Judith clocked me in the head. To top it off, I have no idea what was going on tonight at the club. If Winston's arrest goes well tomorrow, you'll never have to see me again once we get back home. But stupidly, none of that changes the fact that I do lo—"

"Please stop talking." Evan brushed her fingers across Frankie's shoulder, sending goose bumps over her skin. "You absolutely do my head in, Francesca Strong. In fact, you're my greatest fear."

"Why?" Frankie was getting whiplash from Evan's constant push-and-pull, but maybe she was finally coming to the cause.

"I've made some of the same mistakes with you that I did with Judith. And I can't blame you for that."

Frankie's mouth dropped open and she tried to comprehend what Evan was saying. "What do you mean? I haven't lied to you, and you're *not* my boss."

Evan twisted a corner of the sheet in her hands. "That's not the point. It's about boundaries, a principle I tried to maintain…and failed with Jude, and I've crossed the line again with you. Every time I kiss you or touch you, I'm in danger of completely losing that battle with myself." Evan finally looked at her. "Does this make any sense at all?"

"I had no idea. I thought the problem was trust. I'm sorry I've been so demanding…and tempting."

"Don't." She took Frankie's hands. "None of this is your fault. I probably haven't explained it very well. I'm sure part of my problem is trust, but maybe I wasn't sure what the real issue was until I said it aloud. I think I've been afraid of getting hurt again and using boundaries as an excuse. But you made me look at things differently, see possibilities I hadn't considered."

"What kind of possibilities?"

Evan grinned and kissed Frankie's ear until she stretched and exposed her throat. "How a little humor can go a long way toward relieving stress, lifting the mood of an operation, and passing the time. And other stuff."

"Glad to help." Frankie started to move away because being teased by Evan and not really touching her after baring her soul was painful.

"Please don't pull away."

Evan's request was a fist squeezing Frankie's heart and stealing her breath. "What do you want from me?" Evan trailed her finger up Frankie's arm and stopped at her shoulder, the touch registering in Frankie's core. She backed against Evan and nestled into her body. "Tell me."

"I'm not sure I know exactly, but for right now, I want to be with you. If that's okay. I understand if you don't want to. I haven't made things easy for you."

"Do you think that's a good idea under the circumstances…and after what you've just said?" She would've said yes to Evan under any circumstances. Her body already had, but she needed Evan to be sure.

Evan smiled and hugged her closer. "No, but I'd still like to test my theory, because you see, I think you're worth the risk."

The heat in Evan's eyes called to Frankie, pulled her in despite her reservations. Evan hadn't said she loved her back, but Frankie couldn't change how she felt and wouldn't if she could. "What risk?"

"Any risk." Evan lowered her onto the bed and eased her leg across Frankie's body, her hand stroking the tender flesh above Frankie's breast. "Thank you for this, Frankie."

"For…what?" She struggled for breath with Evan's hands on her.

Evan kissed the swell of her breast lightly and licked with her tongue. "Giving yourself to me when I've put you through so much. You're so beautiful."

Frankie tried to laugh but only managed a croak. "I'm too skinny. My tits are too small, and I have no hips."

Evan laughed. "Well, you could use a few extra pounds, but that's nothing more ice cream and French fries won't cure. Everything else is perfect…for my taste." She nipped the side of Frankie's face and trailed kisses down her neck. "I love the curve of your neck. How soft your skin is right here." She licked a spot under Frankie's ear. "And that freckle drives me crazy."

"Tease." Frankie's body burned, her thighs already wet. She'd been touched before but never felt it so intensely, never wanted it so badly. She cupped Evan's hand and brought it to her stomach. "Feel that?"

"You're trembling."

"I want you," Frankie moaned. Evan traced light circles on Frankie's stomach, and her muscles clenched. When Evan brushed higher and teased her nipples, Frankie cried out. "Evan, please." She rolled sideways and urged Evan's leg between her thighs.

Evan kissed her way up Frankie's body, stopping to nip at her skin and then ease the sting with her tongue. "You taste amazing." By the time she reached her lips, Frankie was squirming. "I'm going to take my time with you, possibly all night."

"Need you, Evan." She squeezed Evan's ass, positioned her on top, and rolled her pelvis. "Now." Frankie fisted Evan's hair and brought their lips together again. "Your mouth is magic…oh my God." She traced Evan's lips with her tongue and felt herself get wetter. "Hold me like this and move against me."

"I'll do anything for you." Evan gripped Frankie's hips and rocked with her. "Is this how you like it?"

"Just like that." She wanted all of Evan, in every way, but right now she needed to hold her as close as possible, kiss her, and feel their bodies move in sync as she came. She met Evan's pace as their easy rocking turned to urgent thrusts. "Yes, Evan, faster."

Evan kissed her deeply and then hovered over her, her moans matching Frankie's. "Look at me, Frankie."

When she looked up, Evan's eyes glistened with tears, and Frankie saw love. But would Evan ever be able to accept it, accept her? "So gorgeous. I'm coming. Ohhhh, yes." She clung to Evan with one hand and grabbed the headboard with the other, needing the stability. She felt she might fly apart as she trembled and shuddered until the last wave of release passed. A few seconds later, Evan stiffened and cried out as she climaxed.

"Wow. That was fast, for both of us," Evan said. "I intended to take it slow."

"It was exactly what I needed." Frankie snuggled into the crook of Evan's arm, placed her head on Evan's chest, and listened to the powerful pounding of her heart. How could something so basic give her so much pleasure and make her feel so connected?

She'd finally made love, not just had sex, and it was exquisite, but her heart was breaking. She admitted to herself and Evan that she was in love and gotten no reply. Evan confessed she was afraid of getting hurt, struggling with boundaries, and that Frankie was worth the risk, but no mention of love. So many feelings right now, but not satisfaction, because this one night with Evan would never be enough.

"Thank you," Evan said, gathering Frankie in her arms tighter.

Frankie put on a brave face. She couldn't force love, only give it. "No need for thanks. I love you, Evan."

"Mmm." Evan kissed her way down and then up Frankie's body again, stopping occasionally to lavish extra attention on certain areas, before planting a final kiss on her lips. "You're amazing." She started to roll away, but Frankie held her in place.

"Where are you going?"

"To catch my breath?"

Frankie shook her head. "No." She rolled them over so she was on top. "I want to steal your breath entirely while I explore every inch of your magnificent body."

Evan woke shortly after noon with Frankie's head on her chest and her leg thrown across Evan's lower body. The smell of sex still hung in the air, heady and arousing. Evan bit back a groan. Parts of her that were sore—and she'd thought numb—throbbed and moistened again when the memories from last night flooded her. Frankie was everything she wanted in a lover—sexy, sensitive, playful, responsive, and adept at reciprocating. She smiled at Frankie's mumbled question before they drifted off to sleep.

"Did you really slam the door in Judith's face and break her nose?"

Evan grinned. "On advice of counsel, I invoke my right against self-incrimination."

"You did. I love you so hard right now. I just wish I'd seen it."

"I'm not usually a violent person, but damn it felt good, and the look on her face was worth any discipline that might follow."

"Everybody should get what they want at least once in their lives." Frankie's words faded into a soft snore.

"Once will never be enough with you, Francesca Strong," Evan whispered in the dark.

Thinking about it made Evan want her again right now. But she should let Frankie sleep. This could be their last day in Australia. She snuggled closer to Frankie, unwilling to part with her just yet. Once they left the room, Evan had no idea how the day would unfold or where she and Frankie might be tonight, and she wasn't eager to find out.

Frankie was in love with her, and if she was honest, she felt the same way. So, why hadn't she told Frankie last night? She'd done the hard part—admitted her fears—all that was left was saying the words. The feeling had been growing since the first day Frankie barged into her squad room and turned it into chaos. She'd never felt more complete, more excited, optimistic, and loved. She'd tried to run from it, blaming Judith and then work, but failed. Could she trust her feelings? She'd been betrayed by them before. Maybe she didn't trust that Frankie's feelings were real. If last night's marathon hadn't convinced her, what would it take to remove the doubt?

Evan leaned close to Frankie's ear. She wanted to taste and feel the words before releasing them into the world. "I love you too." Her heart rate doubled. Her body tingled and heated, and she wanted to laugh and sing out loud. She was most certainly in love with Frankie.

CHAPTER SEVENTEEN

"Stop thinking. Those squeaky wheels are keeping me awake," Frankie murmured and nuzzled closer to Evan's side. "I want you all to myself for as long as possible." Her body ached from all their lovemaking, but she'd gladly go again.

"You're spoiling me," Evan said.

"Good, so why do I detect a but in there somewhere?"

"Because you're very clever, and because we have to get up at some point, shower, eat, and have a briefing before the operation tonight. Life goes on."

Frankie sat up straighter but stayed close. "Can we have a couple of minutes more? I'd like to tell you something." She'd been selfish, making love with Evan all night while keeping her last secret. If she hoped to have a future, Evan had to know everything. Frankie couldn't hold back any longer.

"Can't it wait? You've already dropped the L-bomb. I need to process."

Frankie shook her head. "If you need time to process the fact that I love you, you're going to want to include this in the mix."

"That bad?" Evan's eyes widened, and Frankie saw a flash of panic.

She turned sideways, took Evan's hands in hers, and kissed them gently. "Please remember that I love you and I've never said those words to another woman."

"O—kay, you're starting to freak me out a little."

"It's about my parents." Frankie took a deep breath. If she hoped to get through this, she had to say it quickly and not bury the lede. "My parents were scammers, very successful con artists." She checked Evan's expression for disapproval, and seeing none, continued. "They taught me the trade, and it was my life until I turned eighteen. We worked all over the world, changed our MOs, perfected our craft, and lived off other people's misfortunes."

Evan pulled the cover tighter around her. This was a bad idea. She'd been duped by someone she trusted, and Frankie was admitting to conning people for a living. "Do you want me to go on?"

Evan nodded.

"Just before I quit the business, I worked a con on a guy we targeted in a Monaco casino. He was a high-roller, throwing lots of cash at the tables every night, in restaurants and bars, and bedding top-of-the-line prostitutes." Frankie swallowed hard, the memory a bitter one full of shame and regret. "I worked the hooker angle, got to know him, secured his account details, and wiped him out." She paused, giving Evan time to comment or put an end to her misery, but she stared straight ahead and said nothing.

"Before the Winston case, I saw that man on the streets of New York, homeless." The image returned, and Frankie felt the familiar disgust and shame again. "He'd lost his high-paying insurance job, his wife, kids, and his home because of what I did." Guilt churned like razors eating away at her insides. "I'll never...forget the haunted look in his eyes, the hopelessness." She wiped tears from her face and glanced at Evan.

"I don't know what to say."

"Probably best not to say anything until you've had time to think. It's a lot to digest. I wanted to be honest with you. Do you understand now why I don't want to be me sometimes? Why it's easier to pretend?"

Evan didn't respond, her expression unreadable.

"But I can't be that person any more, Evan. I don't want to be, not even for my job. My parents called it grifter's plague, a hardening of the line between sham and reality, and the death of a con artist's career." Evan stared off in the distance, a vacant look on her face, and Frankie had a very bad feeling she was losing her. "And the other reason I'm telling you this is to help you see your situation in a different light. You blame yourself for something that happened because you cared about someone. I destroyed lives for money."

Evan flinched and finally looked at her, anger sparked in her eyes, and her skin flushed. "How can you draw any correlation between those very different scenarios?"

"I'm just trying to make the point, very badly apparently, that you *can* forgive yourself for something you had no control over," Frankie said.

"Have you, forgiven yourself?" Evan sounded incredulous. "Is that even possible? You had control of your life and made those choices. You're a criminal who should be behind bars."

Frankie cringed at the venom in Evan's tone. "No, I haven't forgiven myself by any means. It's not an excuse, but I was a child. I still have nightmares about what I've done, long periods when I can't eat or sleep properly." She reached for Evan, but she jerked away. Her rejection ripped through Frankie, exposing old wounds and creating deeper ones. "And..." she choked down her tears, determined to finish. "...ever since I saw the results of what I'd done, for over a year now, I've been trying to find my parents. That's the other case I've been working on part-time. I'm making amends—"

"Really? And how is that working for the family whose life you destroyed? For the kids? What about the devastation you caused but never saw?" Evan got out of bed and paced the small room, clenching and unclenching her hands as she moved.

"I want you to trust me, Evan, so I had to tell you everything."

"You're unbelievable. I should've listened to what's left of my instincts. Judith Earl is an amateur compared to you. Your parents would be proud, because you played me like a pro. I have no idea who you are and I will *never* trust you." Evan went into the bathroom and slammed the door behind her. When she came out a few minutes later, she was dressed and just as angry. "Be at the Kings Cross Police Station at nine if you want to be part of Winston's arrest."

"Evan, wait."

Evan held up her hand. "Don't. I need to think. I can't hear any more right now."

Frankie's hope that Evan could look beyond the behavior of a juvenile still under the control of her parents and see the woman she'd become vanished. Relationships required sharing, and sharing led to misunderstanding and pain. No one could understand her past and love her in spite of it. Evan had proven that.

❖

Evan left the hotel and waved down the first available cab. "Manly Beach."

"The ferry from Circular Quay would be a lot cheaper."

"I don't want the damn ferry," she snapped. "Sorry, I'd enjoy the ride." She rolled down the windows and let the chilling breeze in. Maybe it would knock some sense into her or freeze her numb. Either way, she wanted Frankie Strong out of her head. She'd tried to scrub the feel of Frankie's hands and mouth from her body while she showered, but the sensations persisted now more painful than pleasurable. What was wrong with her? Why did she keep falling for lying women who only disappointed and hurt her? What a fool.

The wind whipping in through the windows belted and burned her cheeks. When she reached up to brush her hair out of her eyes, she was surprised that her cheeks were wet. No. She would not cry over Frankie. They'd had a brief and unfortunate fling during a stressful time while on an assignment away from home, nothing more. She wasn't in love with her at all. Repeating the words over and over didn't convince her any more than it stopped the flow of tears. When the driver finally pulled over on the street in front of a stretch of beautiful sandy beach, she was a wreck.

"You okay, miss?"

"I'll be fine, eventually." She counted out the exorbitant fare and added a hefty tip for her rudeness. As she walked toward the beach, she glanced at her watch. Plenty of time before the briefing to purge her mind and refocus her thoughts on work before she had to face Frankie again. Just thinking about her made Evan's chest ache.

She pulled the hood of her sweatshirt up, tucked her chin against the wind, and followed a line of people walking a path toward an outcropping of rocks. The ocean was a contrast of tranquility near the beach and a surfer's paradise nearer the rock face. Wetsuit-clad swimmers bobbed up and down in the surf while boarders vied for the next rideable wave. Evan stopped at the overlook and watched the skilled and unskilled alike succumb to the force of nature, like she'd surrendered to Whirlwind Frankie.

Evan started walking again, mumbling to herself. "You will not obsess over this woman another minute. She's a con artist, a liar, a cheat. And she waited until you fell for her to tell you the truth. The classic con. Draw in your prey. Gain her trust. Take what you want. Leave."

She was a besotted woman who'd lost her struggle for professionalism by ignoring her boundaries again and expecting a different outcome—the definition of insanity. She walked on, scolding herself in time to her footsteps. *You. Do. Not. Love. Her.* But with every repetition, an image of Frankie flashed through her mind, challenging her to forget.

After twenty minutes of fighting gusts off the water, Evan turned around at Shelly Beach and started back. Her phone buzzed in her pocket and she glanced at the caller ID. Hank. She considered not answering, but the case had to take priority. "Yes?"

"Thought you needed to know that Frankie is gone."

Evan stopped abruptly, causing people to bump into her. She grabbed the rock retaining wall for support. "W…what do you mean gone?"

"We stopped by your room to see if you wanted to grab something to eat before the op, and she was packing. Said we didn't need her to arrest one old man and she'd gotten a lead in another case she was working. What other case?"

Frankie's gone? She couldn't move. Her clothes whipped around her, but she felt only a gnawing sensation eating its way through her, purging her of feeling. Numb. That was probably good.

"Evan, what case?"

She stared at the phone in her hand. "Nothing to do with us. I'll see you at the briefing."

Evan hung up, and the wind pushed her, first one direction and then the other, urging her toward nothing. Frankie was gone. By the time she returned to the hotel, she felt exhausted and defeated. She'd made a mistake, one of many in her lifetime, but none rattled her the way this one did. Why hadn't she given Frankie a chance? She'd been a child, under the influence of her parents. How did she feel about those times now, and how was she atoning for her mistakes? Instead of listening, Evan had dragged out her sledgehammer, crushed Frankie, and walked away, too afraid of her own feelings to stay and fight for what she wanted.

When she opened the door of her room, loneliness attacked like a splash of cold water. Her knees trembled, and she slumped against the wall for support. What had she done? She glanced around for any sign of Frankie. Nothing, no indication that she'd changed her mind and returned, not even a note. Everything was gone.

The rest of the afternoon and early evening passed in a blur—calls to Michael to update him on the pending arrest; Eli to vent and get a pep talk; and the embassy to confirm flight arrangements for tomorrow. Other than Eli's gentle scolding and suggestion to talk to Frankie ASAP, Evan barely registered anything else.

When Frankie didn't answer her cell after several attempts, Evan joined the rest of the team for the briefing. She was content to let Comer take charge and make assignments, which earned her a few curious looks. She passed out floor plans of the rectangular manufactured building that served as the Bankstown terminal and glanced down at hers.

"Where's Frankie?" Aaron asked.

"Another case," Evan said. Her tone made it clear she wanted no more questions about Frankie. She wasn't sure she could hold it together if she didn't change the subject. "How much time do we have, Comer?"

"We better get moving now," Comer said. "Bankstown Airport is a thirty-minute drive. One of my men is already in place inside the terminal. The good news so far is there aren't many passengers waiting for flights. Winston shouldn't be hard to spot."

Evan was barely listening. Piedmont Triad International was a small airport too, and that op had gone wrong in a really horrible way. She started sweating and couldn't blame it entirely on the heavy vest. Worst-case scenarios flipped through her mind, and she glanced at Aaron.

"Don't worry," he whispered. "I'll be safe in the van. Monitoring."

She gave him a weak smile. "If I could just get everybody else to stay with you."

Comer parked away from the terminal, and the guys spread out to their assigned posts. Evan followed Comer and Hank inside and scanned the small waiting area. One entrance and one exit. Perfect. Easy to cover. A few passengers—a family of four, including two children between the ages of three and five, a woman in a full burka, two businessmen, and a couple of nuns but no sign of Winston. She caught Comer's gaze and shook her head before taking a seat far enough away from the other passengers not to endanger them if something happened.

She placed her backpack beside her on the floor and picked up an airline magazine. Where had Frankie gone? They needed to talk. Regardless of Frankie's past, Evan still cared about her, loved her actually. Having Frankie disappear and then talking with Eli helped clarify that once and for all. Maybe her initial response to Frankie's news had been a knee-jerk reaction, a self-preservation tactic against being deceived again. The fact remained. She was in love with Frankie. Her heart fluttered and a jolt of adrenaline raced through her. Yeah. She was in love, but was it too late? Frankie must've thought so or she wouldn't have left without a word.

A movement across the room caught Evan's attention, and she looked over the edge of the magazine. A man wearing a business suit, heavy overcoat, and a hat pulled low on his forehead came out of the men's room. Matthew Winston. He walked toward the passenger area, and Evan eased forward in her chair and planted her feet, ready to jump when he got closer. Winston scanned the terminal as he walked, checking the exits, eyeballing anyone who moved.

"Be ready, guys," Aaron's voice came through Evan's earpiece. "From the camera angle, it looked like he tucked something shiny into his right coat pocket as he came out of the men's room. Could be a weapon."

Winston was almost to the row of seats when one of the young children broke free of his father's grasp and ran toward him. Evan flinched and her gaze met Winston's. He made her. Glancing toward the exit behind him, he decided to go for the closer one, barreled over the child, and charged straight at Evan.

She rushed forward to stop Winston as he reached into his coat pocket. A flash of metal. A knife. She reached for her weapon but didn't have time to draw. He'd bolted too fast, and she was too close. *This is going to hurt.* A flurry of black fabric. A groan of pain, followed by a thud as Winston and the burka-clad passenger fell to the floor.

No, no, no, no, no. Not another disastrous operation. Evan keyed her mike. "Aaron, we need medical. A civilian has been injured." Blood oozed through black material and pooled at Evan's feet while Comer and Hank handcuffed Winston.

She rolled the woman over, pulling at the bulky fabric, searching for the wound to stop the bleeding. The blue eyes that stared up at her were unmistakable. "Frankie?" Panic seized her. *Please. No.*

CHAPTER EIGHTEEN

Frankie woke in a dimly lit room that smelled of bleach and medicine. She tried to sit up, but a sharp ache in her left side forced her back onto the hospital bed. Then she remembered the arrest, the knife, and Evan. She had to get up, to fight the nausea and pain. Frankie shoved the covers off, grunted, and pulled at the gown until she could see the injury, and was relieved it looked smaller than it felt.

"Six staples. You probably shouldn't rip that bandage off just yet, Superwoman," Evan said as she moved closer to the bed from a dark corner of the room. "I'm so glad you're awake."

Frankie couldn't stop grinning even though she hurt like hell. "And I'm glad you're okay, not hurt. I was worried. But what are you doing here?"

"My DEA liaison was injured in the line of duty. Where else would I be?" She cupped Frankie's hand. "How are you feeling?"

"Like I tangled with a sharp object and lost. If memory serves, the case is closed and I'm a free woman again." Frankie tried to swing her legs off the side of the bed, but Evan blocked her and tucked the covers back around her.

"Wherever you think you're going, it can wait until you're more healed and less drugged. I'm not letting you leave again without a fight."

"But I—"

"I'm pretty sure I was the only clear-headed one in the room when the doctor left your care instructions. One day of complete bed rest and then light activity until the staples come out. No heavy lifting for a week. You were lucky the knife didn't go deeper." She pulled a chair closer to the bed and took Frankie's hand again. "Since you're awake, I want to tell you something." She brought Frankie's hand to her lips and kissed her palm. "I owe you an apology for not listening…about your past."

"No, you don't."

"I do and I'm glad I get to deliver it in person. I thought you were gone."

Frankie grinned. "So did I, but I couldn't leave without seeing the case through after all. And it turns out, you needed me. You could've been hurt, and I'd never forgive myself if anything happened to you." Her throat tightened. Evan was okay. Maybe the next part wouldn't be quite so hard.

"Frankie, I'm so sorry I didn't give you a chance to explain. I should—"

"No, Evan." This was going to be more difficult than she thought. She wanted to look at Evan's face, her expressive eyes, but couldn't risk it. She had to get through this, and it would be hard enough without breaking down.

"You were right about me, Evan. The truth is I'm not really that different from what I used to be. I still con people for a living. I still leave chaos and disruption wherever I go. And I can never love you the way you deserve. You helped me understand." Evan had been right about all their differences and challenges. Maybe that was why she couldn't love her.

Evan gripped her hand harder. "Frankie, please don't say that. I was shocked and hurt when I said those things. I've had time to think. Let's talk about it when you're not drugged."

Frankie swallowed and blinked back tears. Thank God there wasn't much light in the room and Evan couldn't see how this was ripping her apart, how much she loved her. The anguish on Evan's face was enough torment for a lifetime. "There's nothing else to say, Evan. I'm not right for you. Never was, and you've known all along." She slid her hand from Evan's grasp. "If you don't mind, I'm really tired. Must be the painkillers."

"I don't want to leave like this. It feels too final, and I'm not going to accept that."

"Please, Evan."

"As long as you agree to continue this discussion when you feel better." Evan leaned over and kissed her lightly on the lips. "I'll see you in the morning."

"Good-bye, Evan." Frankie offered a weak smile and closed her eyes. She'd hurt Evan, but without love on both sides, there was no hope.

Frankie waited until she was sure Evan wasn't coming back before she climbed gingerly out of bed, dressed, and hoisted her backpack onto her shoulder. When the nurses' station outside her room was unattended, she made her way to the emergency stairs and the exit. She had unfinished business.

Frankie stood outside the Disney store in terminal one of the Hong Kong International Airport scanning every person who passed for the faces she hadn't seen in over fifteen years. Ted Curtis had finally gotten the information she needed, and she'd snuck out of the hospital as soon as Evan left her side. Sixteen hours later, her nightmare was finally drawing to a close.

She perused the crowd again. Would she even recognize her parents? What was the first thing she'd say? Would they be happy to see her? She hoped not. After years of guilt over scamming people for a living, and the last one feeling guilty for what she was about to do, she was ready for it to be over. She fiddled with her ring. Where were they? Maybe they weren't coming. She felt a momentary rush of relief followed by anger and disappointment.

Frankie paced in front of the brightly decorated store, waiting and watching. She'd chosen this location because her early childhood had been much like one continuous visit to Disneyland—games, toys, and disguises—followed by an adolescence of deception masked as play. It seemed appropriate that it should end here.

"Francesca, is that you, darling?"

She recognized the barely distinguishable French cadence of her mother's voice and steeled herself before turning. "Mother." Frankie nodded and then glanced at the slightly stooped man beside her.

"Father." They'd both aged noticeably—grayer hair, wrinkles around the eyes and forehead, and smiles not as quick or genuine. Was she doing the right thing? A wave of guilt blindsided her. After all these years, now was not the time to second-guess her decision. "I wasn't sure you'd come."

"Of course, we came. It's the first time we've heard from you in years," her mother said, moving closer.

Frankie stepped back, recognizing the ploy—smile, make eye contact, and establish a physical link. She wasn't falling for that again.

"Don't be difficult," her father said. He tugged at the lapels of his expensive suit and attempted to stand taller, but the years had taken a toll on his body. "We're trying."

"You always do," she snapped, disliking the angry tone of her voice but unable to control it. "This isn't a family reunion."

"What then?" Her father seemed to suddenly understand, looked around, and grabbed her mother's arm. The protective instinct tugged at Frankie's heart but vanished when she realized he'd never shown her one ounce of care or concern. "What have you done, child?"

"What's going on?" her mother asked, eyes wide with fear.

Then Frankie saw everything clearly on her parents' faces—the lives they'd destroyed, the damage they'd caused, and the guilt. They knew what they'd done and felt the shame of it. She breathed her first truly free breath and answered, "Time to pay for your crimes."

Frankie nodded to Comer who stood just inside the storefront. Within seconds, several officers of the airport security unit surrounded Frankie and her parents and escorted them to a secure room on the main floor.

"How could you?" Her mother's eyes turned dark, just the way Frankie remembered when she'd failed to follow through on a con. "We're your parents."

Frankie shook her head. "Don't bother playing the biology card now. I never felt safe or loved with you. I don't even know who you are. You were my trainers, my handlers, and my captors, but never my parents."

Comer moved to her side. "You all right, mate?"

"Never better. Check their bags for fake passports, stolen identities, and money."

Comer placed their carry-ons and personal items on the table and searched them. "Six passports each and roughly a million Hong Kong dollars. Pretty good petty cash for scam artists. We've pulled their luggage and confiscated their phones. I'm guessing the rest of the money is managed electronically."

Frankie stared at her parents, trying to hold on to one pleasant memory of her childhood, but each one disintegrated into a scam and a devastated victim. She wanted to feel compassion, but found only sorrow that they'd spend their final years separated behind bars and that she'd never been anything to them but a moneymaker.

"I guess my work here is done." She'd closed the door on her past. She didn't think her parents would serve hard time, maybe a cushy federal facility, but if she had anything to do with it, they'd make restitution for the rest of their lives and live under continuous monitoring. She nodded to the Hong Kong police, and motioned for Comer to follow her outside. "Thanks for your help."

"No worries," Comer said. "But you might let Evan know you're okay, mate. She was pretty concerned when you just snuck out of the hospital, and they had to fly back to America without you. I'm sure she'd like to see you." He held up his hands. "Totally none of my business. Just a suggestion."

"I'm catching a flight back to the States now." Frankie made her way to the departure gate and boarded just before the doors closed. Was Comer right? She'd broken things off with Evan abruptly and then left, thinking it best. She'd seen the hurt on Evan's face, the hope in her eyes. Would Evan really want to see her again?

She had to try. With the weight of her past and the specter of her parents finally lifted, Frankie was free to live her life without fear or restraint. What remained was her love for Evan and the certainty that she had to see her again. No more secrets. The sixteen-hour flight was going to be torture.

CHAPTER NINETEEN

Three weeks later

The heavy pounding on her garage door drowned out Evan's hammering on the studs for the downstairs bath. "Damn it. What now?" She dropped the mallet and stalked toward the door, ready to take her frustration out on whoever dared to disturb her at midnight. She flung the door open. "*What?*"

"Hey," Frankie said, scuffing her boot on the welcome mat.

Evan gripped the door and started to slam it shut, equally relieved and cautious at Frankie's return. Could she live with the constant turmoil and uncertainty that surrounded Frankie? If Evan let her back in, would she continue to pull these disappearing acts? Would there be a time when she wouldn't reappear? Evan wasn't ready to hang her heart on her arm yet. "I'm surprised you came back."

"Figured I owed you an apology this time."

Frankie was pale and even thinner than before, but her blue eyes were brighter. Her hair had returned to its natural blond color and was longer but still shaped in her messy style. She wore skinny jeans and a tailored blouse that fit perfectly. She seemed happy, but Evan needed to know Frankie was really okay and able to move on with her life after confronting her parents.

"Are you going to invite me in or should I say my piece out here and leave?" Her tone was more conciliatory than normal, and Evan wondered what had caused the change.

She stepped back and then closed the door after Frankie entered. Evan stopped only a few feet into the warehouse and shoved her hands into her pockets. She raised her eyes to Frankie's questioning stare. She'd let Frankie inside, now she had to really let her in. "The ship, your reconnaissance, chasing a suspect alone, the hotel, and the hospital. Every time you disappear, I'm afraid you won't come back."

"There were times I thought I wouldn't, but I can't stay away from you. I don't want to."

Evan stared at the floor. Just like the first time Frankie had pleaded for a spot on the team, her words were heartfelt, and, damn it, Evan believed her, again.

Frankie tentatively brushed her hand down Evan's arm. "I've missed you."

Evan couldn't meet her eyes. Not yet. She retreated to the comfortable. "How was Hong Kong?"

Frankie stopped beside her. "How did you know—Aaron?"

"He *is* a genius."

"Yes, he is. I was finishing some family business. I'm sorry for not explaining to you then, but—"

"But I wasn't exactly understanding about your past."

"And I get why." Frankie glanced around at the space. "Wow. You've seriously renovated. This place looks great."

Evan studied Frankie a few seconds longer, drinking in the changes in her appearance and her lightened mood. Frankie grinned when she caught her staring, and Evan cleared her throat. "Eli and I did all the work, but fitting it in around his busy construction projects and my erratic hours, wasn't easy. I thought the job might outlive us."

"It's seriously amazing, like a playpen for adults. Mind if I look around?"

"Go ahead while I get cleaned up. I've been at this all day. If you want something to drink, help yourself to the fridge or there's beer and wine in the cooler at the side of the island."

Evan used the time in the shower to calm her jumble of emotions. She was still in love with Frankie, and she'd never told her. "What's wrong with you?" She slapped the shower wall. She'd thought about Frankie every day since Australia, wondering where she was, how she was, what she was doing, and if she'd ever see her again. She never gave up hope. Evan pulled on a pair of jeans and a button-up shirt and took the stairs two at a time. *Don't overthink. Speak from your heart.*

Frankie was leaning against an exposed brick wall staring as Evan walked toward her.

"What do you think of the place?"

"Impressive. Can I see the floor plans?"

Frankie started toward a framed set of blueprints that hung on the wall, but Evan blocked her path. "Are you stalling, Strong?"

"Very possibly." Frankie eased by her and dropped onto the edge of the oversized sofa.

Evan joined her and waited for Frankie to initiate the conversation. Frankie had broken up with her, and Evan needed to know how she felt now. She forced herself to breathe normally as she prayed for the words she so badly wanted to hear.

"I didn't mean those things I said to you in the hospital. And I shouldn't have left." Frankie twisted the spinner on her thumb, a tell Evan now recognized as a nervous habit.

"Why did you say them?"

"I wasn't sure I could make you happy, Evan. I had so much baggage about my family. And our situation wasn't...clean, if that makes sense. I'm sorry if I hurt you. It almost killed me to let you go." Frankie wiped her eyes.

"And I'm sorry I didn't let you explain in Sydney."

"We were both pretty raw at that time. I'm sure the *L* word caught you off guard. And I'd never spoken about my parents before, except to my background investigator at DEA and my boss, and it freaked me out." Frankie scooted closer. "You were still struggling with what Judith did to you and your doubts about me. How could that scenario not go wrong? I should've been honest from the start. I was hoping to clear everything up first...but I fell in love with you. Can you forgive me?"

Evan took Frankie's hands in hers. "If you forgive me for being so harsh and stubborn when you told me. *And* you took a knife for me. That's lifetime payback stuff right there." She leaned over and kissed Frankie's cheek and pulled back quickly, afraid if she lingered they'd never finish the conversation. "Can you tell me about Hong Kong?"

"I had my parents arrested." The lines around Frankie's mouth tightened, and Evan squeezed her hands, encouraging her to continue. "We were never a conventional family, and they taught me to survive in the world the only way they knew. I'll always be grateful for that because it helped me in life and in my job. But I never agreed with how we lived. I saw the suffering we left behind. Still—"

Frankie choked back a sob, and Evan hugged her. "Take your time."

After a few seconds, Frankie broke their embrace and took a deep breath. "They forced me to work the cons every day, including using my body to lure men. When I turned eighteen, legal age, I left my parents and their lifestyle. For the past year, my boss and I have been chasing them off the books. Our last day in Australia, Ted notified me that they were passing through Hong Kong. It was the closest I'd ever been to them. I had to go and I couldn't ask you to wait not knowing what would happen."

"Of course you had to go." Evan rubbed Frankie's back and felt the muscles under her hands relax. "And I understand."

"I was afraid if I told you, you'd try to stop me or insist on going with me. It wasn't your fight. I had to face them alone so I could hopefully forgive myself one day for some of the things I've done. And…I wanted to come to you a free, whole person, and outside the job."

"So, you hunted your parents like any other suspects and then had them arrested?"

Frankie nodded.

"I can't imagine how difficult that must've been for you, not to mention the trauma of your childhood. I'm sorry for not acknowledging that sooner. I let my own emotions get in the way." Evan pulled her into a hug and held her while she cried. "But you did it, and I'm proud of you." She'd always sensed a deep vulnerability and hurt in Frankie and now she understood its origin. She'd been such a fool not to listen to her.

Frankie fiddled with her ring again without looking up. "So… what happens now? Would you like me to go?"

"You're kidding."

"You want me to spend the night?" Frankie looked genuinely surprised, and she couldn't resist teasing her.

"We'll start with that." Evan stood and offered her hand. "You must be exhausted after your trip. How could I possibly send you into the streets in your condition?"

Without answering, Frankie took her hand and followed her upstairs but stopped beside the bed. "I have one more thing to tell you."

"Oh yeah?" Evan reached for the hem of Frankie's blouse, but she clasped her hands.

"I feel comfortable with you, grounded somehow, and that's new for me. I felt it the first time I saw you in the office and it's grown every time I've been near you since."

Evan chuckled. "Grounded, huh? You make me sound like the footings of one of Eli's buildings."

"Way better than that. You're my home, the place I finally belong. I love you so much."

Evan hugged Frankie and pressed her cheek to the rapid pulse at her throat, basking in the vitality of it and their closeness. She inhaled the scent of her hair, traced her body with her hands, memorizing the shape and size of her. When she finally stepped back, she was weak with desire and so full of love she thought she might burst, but Frankie needed something else tonight. "Let's get you into bed so you can rest."

"And if I don't want to rest?" Frankie slowly lifted the hem of her blouse over her head, skimmed her jeans to the floor, and stood nude before Evan.

The sight of her made Evan moan. "You're not making this easy."

"I never want it to be easy for you to resist me. And especially not right now. Please? I've waited a long time for you."

Evan tugged clumsily at her own clothes, suddenly too nervous to unbutton her shirt. Fabric ripped as she stripped it over her head and flung it aside. She unzipped her jeans and kicked them away along with her briefs and moved closer. Frankie had never looked as beautiful or as vulnerable, her alabaster skin glowing in the moonlight and her slight frame quivering. "Are you cold?"

Frankie shook her head.

"Nervous?"

Frankie shook her head again.

"What?" Evan asked.

"I want you to touch me so badly it hurts."

Evan reached for Frankie's hands and slowly pulled her closer. Energy crackled between them, and the hairs on Evan's body bristled as every nerve inside her answered Frankie's call. When she wrapped her arms around Frankie and brought the length of their bodies together, her legs trembled and she slumped forward. No one had ever felt this right in her arms. She clung to Frankie, tucked her head under her chin, and ran her hands up and down Frankie's smooth skin, feeling her own body heat, burn, and grow wet with anticipation.

"You feel so good, Evan." Frankie kissed the side of her neck.

Evan bent her knees and rubbed her breasts against Frankie's and then teased her with her taut nipples. Frankie tugged her hair, and Evan's knees gave way. She fell in front of Frankie and pressed the side of her face against the soft flesh of Frankie's stomach. Evan's hand hovered over the fresh scar slashing across Frankie's ribs. "What were you thinking when you jumped in front of that knife?"

"That I'd rather die than let Winston hurt you."

Frankie's words cut free the last of Evan's reservations. "I love you, Frankie. I waited too long to say the words, but I'm absolutely certain of it."

"You are?" Frankie took Evan's face in her hands. "That's the other reason I left. I wasn't sure you did and I couldn't settle for less…not with you."

"I love you. I love you so much." Clutching Frankie's ass with both hands, Evan inhaled her arousal and felt the surreal sensation of losing control in the most erotic and spectacular way. Love really did make a difference. She'd never felt this connected or certain of her feelings.

"Touch me," Frankie moaned.

Evan sat back on her feet and caressed Frankie's waist and stomach with her hands, edging her thumbs along the join of her thighs. Frankie bucked, and Evan blew softly on her center.

"Please, Evan." Frankie gazed down at her through hooded eyes.

Evan wrapped one arm around Frankie's hips to steady her, licked her two middle fingers, and slowly eased inside Frankie. Her warm wetness created an immediate tightness in Evan's core. "So good." Frankie's muscles tensed and she came up on her tiptoes as Evan slid her fingers in and out. Evan watched Frankie's eyes flutter and her mouth gasp for air as their pace increased. "You're so beautiful."

"Ohhh." Frankie pumped up and down to meet Evan's thrusts. "Not much longer."

"It's okay, babe." Evan leaned forward and placed a kiss on Frankie's clit and felt her spasms begin. "That's it. Let go." Frankie's legs quivered, and Evan felt her clenching and releasing around her fingers. In that moment, all Evan's fears and doubts vanished. Frankie was hers.

"Can't...stand up." With a long breath, Frankie collapsed forward across Evan's shoulders. "That was a—maz—ing." She kissed the top of Evan's head. "I don't think I can move right now."

"You don't have to." Evan got to her knees and slowly stood with Frankie across her shoulders. At the edge of the bed, she stooped and laid her gently across the covers. "Rest." She started to back away, but Frankie caught her hand.

"Not yet. Come here."

Evan settled slightly to the side of Frankie and straddled her leg. "Maybe for just a second." She rubbed her center against the firm muscle of Frankie's thigh and moaned. "Maybe less."

"Let me." Frankie eased her hand between them and cupped Evan's sex.

One stroke of Frankie's finger, and Evan was gone. Light exploded behind her eyelids. She stiffened, released, and clung to Frankie, surging forward to meet her hand until every tremor drained from her. When she could breathe evenly again, she said, "You're magic."

"Thank you. I like to think I'm pretty handy." Frankie yawned and snuggled into the curve of Evan's arm.

"When did you sleep last?"

"Not sure. It feels like three weeks. Every time I closed my eyes I saw you and knew I had to get back to you...but...things to settle... in Hong Kong." Frankie yawned again. "But two days ago for sure. I came...came straight from the...airport."

Evan leaned back so she could look at her. "Are you serious?"

"I couldn't wait to see you, to find out if we have a future... beyond great sex. Do we?"

Evan kissed her deeply before answering. "You DEA agents are so hard to train, but you have potential. I'm certainly willing."

"Great answer, Marshal Spears."

"Get some rest. We've been summoned to the office at ten in the morning. And I was asked specifically to make sure you came, if I saw you."

"Summoned?" Frankie asked.

"Aaron."

"I'd do anything for that guy," Frankie said. "Except get out of bed with you on Saturday morning."

"I got the impression it was important. Go with me?" Evan kissed her again, and felt Frankie melt against her. She couldn't remember a time that she'd felt more loved or more certain of her love. This felt right.

"I'd do anything for you." Frankie rolled over in Evan's arms and in a few seconds was sleeping soundly.

"I know you would, my love, and the feeling is mutual."

CHAPTER TWENTY

Evan woke Frankie early the next morning so they could make love before facing the world again. She couldn't get enough of her—the way she looked, felt, tasted, and the responsiveness of her body. But after two rounds, she forced herself to stop and sat up.

She tickled between Frankie's breasts, enjoying the moan it elicited. "You need to shower and change clothes before our meeting. Are you checked into a hotel somewhere?"

"Still at the Marriott Downtown."

"Go change clothes. And check out of that hotel...unless you prefer to sleep alone surrounded by strangers."

"Never again." Frankie kissed Evan deeply and tried to pull her back down.

"Good answer. See you at the office." Evan jumped up and headed toward the shower, adding over her shoulder, "And never forget I love you."

"Ditto," Frankie called on her way out.

Evan showered and dressed slowly, savoring the memory of Frankie's mouth and hands on her skin, their whispered and shouted moans, and the loving words they'd exchanged. Frankie loved her, and Evan had every intention of showing her just how much that feeling was reciprocated as soon as they got back home.

On the way to the office, she made two stops and arrived just after the others. She spread the biscuits and donuts across her desk and left napkins on the corner. "Enjoy."

The guys stared at her for several seconds before anyone spoke.

"You feeling all right, boss?" Todd asked, scratching his red-stubbled chin.

"Perfect, thank you."

Hank gave her one of his military evaluation stares, dropped his briefcase, and headed for the treats. "Well, I don't know what brought about this change, but I like it." Frankie charged through the door a few seconds later, and Hank glanced back and forth between her and Evan. "And maybe I do."

Evan felt her cheeks burn. "Just eat and be grateful."

"Roger that," Aaron said, his eyes sparkling behind his dark Potter glasses.

"Glad to see you in one piece, Frankie," Todd said.

"Thanks." Frankie picked up a donut and waved it at the spread. "This is certainly a change." She grinned at Evan before biting off a chunk and moaning. "I'm starving."

"That was some dumb shit you pulled in Sydney, but it was also brave as fuck." Todd said. "Why didn't you tell us you were going undercover?"

Frankie shrugged. "Didn't know I was until the last minute."

"Good call." Todd slapped her on the back. "Except for the knife injury. You okay?"

"Yeah, just a flesh wound."

Evan flinched at the image of Frankie flying through the air, putting herself between her and a knife. She forced her attention back to last night and the amazing woman across from her. She was safe now. They were both safe and together, for the time being. "So, Mr. Potter, you called this meeting. What's up?"

Aaron wiped his hands on a napkin and brushed the biscuit crumbs from the front of his shirt. "I wanted to tell you guys something, actually, show you." He reached down and pulled up the footrests of his wheelchair. Gripping the arms, he straightened both legs. "Ta-da."

Evan felt her mouth drop open and her heart swell with joy. "You...you moved."

"Yep. The doctor said if I continue vigorous physical therapy, I can probably walk again." He grinned and spread his arms. "The next time we have a case at a strip club, I'll be standing tall with the rest of you ugly mugs."

"Then I'll make sure that happens," Evan said.

Frankie dropped to her knees beside Aaron's wheelchair and hugged him. "You're a rock star, dude, with or without the chariot. Remember that."

"Damn straight." Todd gave him a fist bump, and Hank shook his hand.

Evan stood back, watching, disbelieving, and slowly accepting. She finally made her way to Aaron and offered her hand, but he pulled her into a hug instead. "I'm so happy for you, Aaron. This is the best possible outcome for the case, for you…for all of us."

Winston, Tyndall, and Judith were in jail awaiting trial, Aaron would walk again, and she and Frankie were in love. How could it be any better?

Frankie cleared her throat. "Attention, please. What I have to say doesn't come close to your news, Aaron, but if I may." She raised her coffee cup. "To the best fugitive task force in the business. Thank you for letting me work with you. I learned a lot. And…" Frankie caught Evan's gaze and gave her a big smile. "And my boss informed me this morning that Colby Vincent asked that I be transferred to her team."

Evan's initial excitement and hope for an assignment close to home were followed by concern. "A new assignment." Was Frankie leaving again?

Frankie nodded.

"Undercover work?"

Frankie waggled her hand side to side. "Colby mentioned something about training new agents, but no more undercover assignments, unless I want."

"So…you'll move again?" Evan knew the guys were all staring, but she didn't care.

"Oh, go on, kiss her," Todd said. The other guys hooted and whistled.

She almost did exactly that, but pulled Frankie into the hallway instead. Some things weren't meant for public viewing. "What does this mean, Frankie?"

"I accepted on the condition that it was a permanent assignment, no more relocations. I want, no I need, to be here. You're my home."

"I love you, Frankie."

About the Author

A thirty-year veteran of a midsized police department, VK Powell was a police officer by necessity and a writer by desire. Her career spanned numerous positions including beat officer, homicide detective, vice/narcotics lieutenant, captain, and assistant chief of police. Now retired, she devotes her time to writing, traveling, and volunteering.

VK can be reached on Facebook at @vk.powell.12 and Twitter @VKPowell.

Books Available from Bold Strokes Books

Beautiful Dreamer by Melissa Brayden. With love on the line, can Devyn Winters find it in her heart to stay in the small town of Dreamer's Bay, the one place she swore she'd never remain? (978-1-63555-305-5)

Create a Life to Love by Erin Zak. When sixteen-year-old Beth shows up at her birth mother's door, three lives will change forever. (978-1-63555-425-0)

Deadeye by Meredith Doench. Stranded while hunting the serial predator Deadeye, Special Agent Luce Hansen fights for survival while her lover, forensic pathologist Harper Bennett, hunts for clues to Hansen's disappearance along the killer's trail. (978-1-63555-253-9)

Death Takes a Bow by David S. Pederson. Alan Keys takes part in a local stage production, but when the leading man is murdered, his partner Detective Heath Barrington is thrust into the limelight to find the killer. (978-1-63555-472-4)

Endangered by Michelle Larkin. Shapeshifters Officer Aspen Wolfe and Dr. Tora Madigan fight their growing attraction as they work together to destroy a secret government agency that exterminates their kind. (978-1-63555-377-2)

Incognito by VK Powell. The only thing Evan Spears is focused on is capturing a fleeing murder suspect until wild card Frankie Strong is added to her team and causes chaos on and off the job. (978-1-63555-389-5)

Insult to Injury by Gun Brooke. After losing everything, Gail Owen withdraws to her old farmhouse and finds a destitute young woman, Romi Shepherd, living in a secret room. (978-1-63555-323-9)

Just One Moment by Dena Blake. If you were given the chance to have the love of your life back, could you ignore everything that went wrong and start over again? (978-1-63555-387-1)

Scene of the Crime by MJ Williamz. Cullen Mathew finds herself caught between the woman she thinks she loves but can no longer trust and a beautiful detective she can't stop thinking about who will stop at nothing to find the truth. (978-1-63555-405-2)

Accidental Prophet by Bud Gundy. Days after his grandmother dies, Drew Morten learns his true identity and finds himself racing against time to save civilization from the apocalypse. (978-1-63555-452-6)

Daughter of No One by Sam Ledel. When their worlds are threatened, a princess and a village outcast must overcome their differences and embrace a budding attraction if they want to survive. (978-1-63555-427-4)

Fear of Falling by Georgia Beers. Singer Sophie James is ready to shake up her career, but her new manager, the gorgeous Dana Landon, has other ideas. (978-1-63555-443-4)

In Case You Forgot by Fredrick Smith and Chaz Lamar. Zaire and Kenny, two newly single, Black, queer, and socially aware men, start again—in love, career, and life—in the West Hollywood neighborhood of LA. (978-1-63555-493-9)

Playing with Fire by Lesley Davis. When Takira Lathan and Dante Groves meet at Takira's restaurant, love may find its way onto the menu. (978-1-63555-433-5)

Practice Makes Perfect by Carsen Taite. Meet law school friends Campbell, Abby, and Grace, law partners at Austin's premier boutique legal firm for young, hip entrepreneurs. Legal Affairs: one law firm, three best friends, three chances to fall in love. (978-1-63555-357-4)

The Last Seduction by Ronica Black. When you allow true love to elude you once and you desperately regret it, are you brave enough to grab it when it comes around again? (978-1-63555-211-9)

Wavering Convictions by Erin Dutton. After a traumatic event, Maggie has vowed to regain her strength and independence. So how can Ally be both the woman who makes her feel safe and a constant reminder of the person who took her security away? (978-1-63555-403-8)

A Bird of Sorrow by Shea Godfrey. As Darrius and her lover, Princess Jessa, gather their strength for the coming war, a mysterious spell will reveal the truth of an ancient love. (978-1-63555-009-2)

All the Worlds Between Us by Morgan Lee Miller. High school senior Quinn Hughes discovers that a broken friendship is actually a door propped open for an unexpected romance. (978-1-63555-457-1)

An Intimate Deception by CJ Birch. Flynn County Sheriff Elle Ashley has spent her adult life atoning for her wild youth, but when she finds her ex, Jessie, murdered two weeks before the small town's biggest social event, she comes face-to-face with her past and all her well-kept secrets. (978-1-63555-417-5)

Cash and the Sorority Girl by Ashley Bartlett. Cash Braddock doesn't want to deal with morality, drugs, or people. Unfortunately, she's going to have to. (978-1-63555-310-9)

Counting for Thunder by Phillip Irwin Cooper. A struggling actor returns to the Deep South to manage a family crisis, finds love, and ultimately his own voice as his mother is regaining hers for possibly the last time. (978-1-63555-450-2)

Falling by Kris Bryant. Falling in love isn't part of the plan, but will Shaylie Beck put her heart first and stick around, or tell the damaging truth? (978-1-63555-373-4)

Secrets in a Small Town by Nicole Stiling. Deputy Chief Mackenzie Blake has one mission: find the person harassing Savannah Castillo and her daughter before they cause real harm. (978-1-63555-436-6)

Stormy Seas by Ali Vali. The high-octane follow-up to the best-selling action-romance, *Blue Skies*. (978-1-63555-299-7)

The Road to Madison by Elle Spencer. Can two women who fell in love as girls overcome the hurt caused by the father who tore them apart? (978-1-63555-421-2)

Dangerous Curves by Larkin Rose. When love waits at the finish line, dangerous curves are a risk worth taking. (978-1-63555-353-6)

Love to the Rescue by Radclyffe. Can two people who share a past really be strangers? (978-1-62639-973-0)

Love's Portrait by Anna Larner. When museum curator Molly Goode and benefactor Georgina Wright uncover a portrait's secret, public and private truths are exposed, and their deepening love hangs in the balance. (978-1-63555-057-3)

Model Behavior by MJ Williamz. Can one woman's instability shatter a new couple's dreams of happiness? (978-1-63555-379-6)

Pretending in Paradise by M. Ullrich. When travelwisdom.com assigns PR specialist Caroline Beckett and travel blogger Emma Morgan to cover a hot new couples retreat, they're forced to fake a relationship to secure a reservation. (978-1-63555-399-4)

Recipe for Love by Aurora Rey. Hannah Little doesn't have much use for fancy chefs or fancy restaurants, but when New York City chef Drew Davis comes to town, their attraction just might be a recipe for love. (978-1-63555-367-3)

Survivor's Guilt and Other Stories by Greg Herren. Award-winning author Greg Herren's short stories are finally pulled together into a single collection, including the Macavity Award nominated title story and the first-ever Chanse MacLeod short story. (978-1-63555-413-7)

The House by Eden Darry. After a vicious assault, Sadie, Fin, and their family retreat to a house they think is the perfect place to start over, until they realize not all is as it seems. (978-1-63555-395-6)

Uninvited by Jane C. Esther. When Aerin McLeary's body becomes host for an alien intent on invading Earth, she must work with researcher Olivia Ando to uncover the truth and save humankind. (978-1-63555-282-9)

Comrade Cowgirl by Yolanda Wallace. When cattle rancher Laramie Bowman accepts a lucrative job offer far from home, will her heart end up getting lost in translation? (978-1-63555-375-8)

Double Vision by Ellie Hart. When her cell phone rings, Giselle Cutler answers it—and finds herself speaking to a dead woman. (978-1-63555-385-7)

Inheritors of Chaos by Barbara Ann Wright. As factions splinter and reunite, will anyone survive the final showdown between gods and mortals on an alien world? (978-1-63555-294-2)

Love on Lavender Lane by Karis Walsh. Accompanied by the buzz of honeybees and the scent of lavender, Paige and Kassidy must find a way to compromise on their approach to business if they want to save Lavender Lane Farm—and find a way to make room for love along the way. (978-1-63555-286-7)

Spinning Tales by Brey Willows. When the fairy tale begins to unravel and villains are on the loose, will Maggie and Kody be able to spin a new tale? (978-1-63555-314-7)

The Do-Over by Georgia Beers. Bella Hunt has made a good life for herself and put the past behind her. But when the bane of her high school existence shows up for Bella's class on conflict resolution, the last thing they expect is to fall in love. (978-1-63555-393-2)

What Happens When by Samantha Boyette. For Molly Kennan, senior year is already an epic disaster, and falling for mysterious waitress Zia is about to make life a whole lot worse. (978-1-63555-408-3)

Wooing the Farmer by Jenny Frame. When fiercely independent modern socialite Penelope Huntingdon-Stewart and traditional country farmer Sam McQuade meet, trusting their hearts is harder than it looks. (978-1-63555-381-9)